CLAREMONT

CLAREMONT

a novel by

WIEBKE VON CAROLSFELD

Prepared for the press by Kodi Scheer
Front cover image: Copyright © Lorna Kirk and National Film Board of Canada, cover image from Him/Lui, 2016, published by permission.
Quotation from Pablo Neruda is used by permission
Author photo: Guntar Kravis
Cover design: Debbie Geltner
Book design: Tika eBooks

Printed and bound in Canada.

Library and Archives Canada Cataloguing in Publication

Title: Claremont / Wiebke von Carolsfeld.
Names: von Carolsfeld, Wiebke, author.

Identifiers: Canadiana (print) 2019006692X | Canadiana (ebook) 20190067047 | ISBN 9781773900230 (paperback) | ISBN 9781773900247 (EPUB) | ISBN 9781773900254 (Kindle) | ISBN 9781773900001 (PDF)

Classification: LCC PS8643.O52 C53 2019 | DDC C813/.6—dc23

The publisher gratefully acknowledges the support of the Government of Canada through the Canada Council for the Arts, the Canada Book Fund, and Livres Canada Books, and of the Government of Quebec through the Société de développement des entreprises culturelles (SODEC).

Linda Leith Publishing
Montreal
www.lindaleith.com

Not till we are lost,
do we begin to understand ourselves.

—*Henry David Thoreau*

May 28th

Flipping over the plastic arm without tearing it off at the shoulder took skill, but Tom had transformed Brawl so many times he'd be able to do it with his eyes closed, behind his back, in his sleep. In fact, he had done it with his eyes closed and behind his back—though not in his sleep—and it had made Saanjh laugh so hard, he choked.

Sleeping was exactly what Tom was supposed to be doing right now. Mom had tucked him in hours ago after telling him her favourite bedtime story, the one about the curious friendship between the Town Mouse and the Country Mouse. Tom felt much too old for that kind of tale, but he hadn't had the heart to say so just yet. Mom seemed happy every time she recounted the story, who was he to say no? So instead, he had nestled himself into the crook of her arm, run his fingers through her thick, curly hair and savoured the singsong of her voice.

"Everything's gonna be okay," she said after the last of six kisses goodnight, only to linger the way she did when trouble was brewing. At dinner, Dad had been silent, aside from that tuneless hum that occasionally escaped his tight lips. Then he finished his bottle of wine, pushed away the plate still full of pasta, and left without bothering to give an excuse.

Brawl's quadruple-barrelled cannon slid into position just as a scream, Tom's mother's, rang out. Startled, the boy let go and the Transformer flew across his unmade bed, bouncing off the wall before coming to rest on the floor. Tom wedged his head between his hands and kneaded the cartilage of his ears as hard as he could, creating a roaring wall of sound. Just like the ocean at Old Orchard Beach.

"It'll be fun to explore the coast," Dad had promised, way back when Tom was only six years old. "More fun anyways than going to the cottage and listening to the sisters argue about what condiment they'd pick if they could only have one for the rest of their life." And Dad had a point. Mom and her two sisters, Aunt Rose and Aunt Sonya, could spend hours debating details nobody cared about until Uncle Will would shut them up with stories about eating guinea pigs in Peru. Gross. But then, after driving east for two days straight, Tom and his parents wound up in a mouldy motel, blocks back from the sea, and he had to sleep on a cot, even though he had been promised a room of his own.

"This is beyond idiotic," Mom whispered in that tiny voice that could push Dad to the edge. Slipping her new beach dress on the lone hanger, she shook her head. "We could be sitting at the lake right now, drinking G&Ts. For free."

The more she talked, the quieter Dad got. "Let's go for a swim," he finally said to Tom. "You'll love it."

Again, Dad was right. Tom loved to swim in the lake, but the ocean, that was something else. What joy to have the waves pick you up and toss you about. No point trying to hold onto solid ground, to fight for control, to stay afloat—not until the surge had run its course, letting him come back up for air. Gasping. Happy. Proud.

Back on the beach, his parents had settled under a blue-and-white striped umbrella, sipping beer from coffee mugs. Eating chips. Smiling, even.

But that was then. Now, huddled on the floor, frozen with fear, Tom waited.

And waited.

After counting to a hundred twice, he released his ears.

The house was quiet.

Mom was quiet.

And so was Dad.

Tom grabbed a small silver-coloured box, rotating each panel before splitting open Frenzy's side, working with a focus that would impress, if not surprise, Mr. Dukali, who only yesterday returned Tom's latest math test with a sigh, saying, "What's going on in that brain of yours? I know you've got one. Better start using it before it shrivels and dies."

Tom grabbed a yellow car and rapidly Bumblebee emerged, followed by Ratchet, Jazz, and of course Optimus Prime, the incredibly heroic, yet also deeply caring, leader of the Autobots. Not even halfway through transforming Megatron—who better to fight evil but evil—Tom heard a muffled cry. Followed by a heavy thud, wood splintering.

The boy slowed down his breathing. He counted his Transformers, still seventeen, recited the multiplication table twice, and drew his broken fingernail across the soft inside of his arm. Around him now was nothing but silence. Skin-tingling, puke-inducing, thought-freezing silence.

Minutes, maybe hours passed as Tom cowered in his toy-cluttered room on the second floor of a house that was surrounded by so many similar looking houses that he used to get lost when they moved into the neighbourhood. In one of her bouts of frantic activity, Mom had painted the front door purple, something Tom loved but Dad had been complaining about ever since.

Returning to breathing normally, Tom allowed himself to imagine his parents making up, cuddling, laughing the way they

3

did when nothing, not even he, mattered. But then, just as he split apart Ironhide's chassis, Tom heard his mother's howl.

The boy froze.

Moments later, his parents' bedroom door cracked open and steps approached.

Ten, nine, eight ...

Tom counted as each foot fell in front of the other, coming down the narrow hallway towards his room. The walls decorated with memories trapped behind white plastic frames. They showed Tom jumping into the lake, fishing in the bright red canoe, Saanjh's arm wrapped around his shoulder, huge smiles on both of their faces, their bodies caked in grey mud. Memories of hot summer days. Laughter. Untainted love.

Seven, six, five ...

Folding further into himself, Tom tried to will the steps away. Leave me alone. Go watch TV. Sleep until afternoon.

Four ...

Tom grabbed Optimus Prime.

Three ...

He counted, fearing that he ...

Two ...

was useless now.

One.

The footsteps came to a stop just outside his door.

Tom went numb. Please, he thought, please let this pass. Please, let night turn into day, let Mom make porridge and let us laugh at the funnies before leaving for school. Please let this night, like so many others, be forgotten. Please. Please. Please.

Outside, the boy's father let go of the knob and walked away, downstairs.

Tom waited a hundred more breaths before opening his door one millimetre at a time. He was afraid to make even the tiniest of noises, but he needn't have worried; this was a home with doors that did not creak. Emboldened by the continued silence, Tom took a tentative first step toward his parents' bedroom. A patch of light seeped out from underneath the closed door.

Once there, Tom stopped. Pearls of sweat stung his eyes. He wanted nothing more than to retreat to his room, to fall asleep, to be done with this night—but still, he opened the door. Mom might need him. Again.

Inside, once carefully folded shirts were scattered here, there and everywhere. A slipper sat on top of the rumpled bed, the sheets were covered in dark red stains. Tom nudged the door open further, his feet now moving forward of their own volition, side-stepping a shattered vase, a bright pink bra, beads from a broken necklace.

Next to one of his father's golf club, he found his mother. Her face smeared with blood, her right eye swollen shut, only the left one open. Barely.

"Tom?" she whispered as a colossal roar exploded inside the boy's brain, drowning out her voice. She closed her eye, and her head rolled to the side. An angry lump already growing on her forehead, her left foot stuck out, off to the side. Unmoving, naked, twisted. Disconnected, just like Brawl.

Then her big toe twitched, and the boy remembered what he was supposed to do next. He scrambled to find her phone, but it had been unplugged from the charger, and it took time to unearth it from underneath a pile of scattered clothes. Tom couldn't remember the number he was supposed to dial, though he knew it had a 9 and a 1. When he at long last he hit upon 911, his hands shook so hard the phone slipped and fell to the ground.

"My mom," he whispered when finally he got through. Just

then he heard a sharp bang explode below. "Please," he said. "Blood," he added, but his voice sounded hollow, and his words made no sense at all.

"My mom," he tried again, but then he heard her moan, and from her lips, instead of words, spilled blood.

"We're dying."

June

Sonya heaped three spoons of sugar into her coffee. So what if it destroyed her liver, increased her chances of diabetes, and made her temper worse? She deserved comfort, and she needed it now.

"Let me help you with the food," said Penelope, dropping off empties she'd collected in the backyard. Sonya swung around to see her best friend pick up the tray of stuffed mushrooms. Dressed in dark purple and blue, Pen looked elegant, even if she was thirty pounds overweight. But after years of accommodating her ever more outlandish diets—lemon detox, really?—Sonya was tired of being supportive. Why couldn't Pen just eat less, move more, and in the meantime, talk about something else?

"I'm fine," Sonya said and pulled the tray of mushrooms away. It had taken her forever to stuff those finicky little buggers; she wasn't going to have anybody else take credit. "In any event, it's my siblings who ought to help."

Except that Will had yet to tear himself away from the TV, and Rose was busy out front, wrecking her lungs. Smoking. At her age.

"Please," Penelope pleaded, "give me something to do."

"Fine," Sonya said and handed Penelope a bottle each of red and white wine. "But do us all a favour: Skip Rose. No need for a scene today."

Watching her friend scurry off, Sonya felt ashamed of her rancour. At least Pen was still trying to improve herself, which is so much harder than giving up.

Sonya checked the time, not even six. Too early to leave this most dreadful day behind, to drop a couple of pills, to vanish into the night. Plus, the house was still swamped with mourners and would be for hours to come. With her sister's murder splattered on page two of the *Toronto Star*, there was an endless stream of visitors, all bursting with concern and love, yet also undoubtedly relieved that this horror had not happened to them. Grateful, if only for a moment, for the families they had.

It reminded Sonya of the days after her mother passed. Then as now, hushed voices went silent every time she entered a room, hugs inevitably ended in tears, and friends like Pen were suddenly unable to look her in the eyes. At least back then, there was no Facebook. No likes for *RIP sweet angel*. Grade school mates waxing on about someone they hadn't bothered to stay in touch with, endless links on how to deal with grief.

Sonya picked a stack of soggy paper plates off the stove, popped open the garbage can, but found it already stuffed with lipstick-smeared napkins, bits of neon-coloured cupcakes, and the remnants of one of her mother's crystal wineglasses. She should never have allowed Rose to take out the good ones. Now, only three were left.

On the way out to dump the garbage, Sonya saw her neighbour Anna Stanley holding court, hair, as always, perfectly coiffed, nails matching her cleavage-spilling dress, her figure irritatingly shapely, despite having given birth three times in five years.

"The problem these days is the complete disregard for the benefits of hard work," she said with that self-important tone only people with limited smarts can muster. Then she took a needlessly languid sip of wine, luxuriating in the men's gaze, taking a lap from one end of the pool of admiration to the other.

It was Alex—Sonya's husband—who insisted on fostering neighbourly relations, something Sonya quite frankly could do without. Especially since the Stanleys were bent on showing off their perfect lives. Three kids in French immersion, a cedar sauna in the backyard, and then those annual trips to the Bahamas. Derek, only a few years older than Alex, but already VP of sales, travelled the globe in pursuit of new markets, returning home with ever more lavish souvenirs. Alex, who never went anywhere, had long given up on getting Sonya presents. "Why buy stuff," he'd say, "when you exchange everything I get you anyway?" He had a point. But still, a pashmina woven by monks in Tibet was decidedly more romantic than a gift certificate for Indigo.

"People want everything right here, right now," Anna continued, "but that's not how it works. Investments take years to grow. It's future gains that make present-day sacrifices worthwhile."

Tell that to Mona, thought Sonya, as she tried to stuff the garbage into the already overflowing bin. The image of her baby sister covered in blood, her skull fractured by her husband's golf club, holding on to life until the ambulance arrived, only to expire on the way to the hospital, made Sonya want to scream. Instead, she punched the garbage, hard, unfazed by its filthy contents spilling out onto the floor. Relishing the feeling of control, of discharging some of that anger that had been building up inside her like steam inside a sealed pot. And who could blame her? One moment, she was annoyed about missing a crucial moment of *Top Chef*, and the next, her entire world collapsed. Only last Thursday, and yet in some other life, two police officers had rung her bell. "Might we come in," one asked, as if Sonya had a choice to say no.

Now, looking at the scattered garbage all around her, she almost laughed. How appropriate. Just like her life, a pile of shit.

By the time Sonya had cleaned up her mess, Anna had moved on to the virtues of bonds. What would it take to shut that woman up? A sale at Holt's? A smack in the face? Nuclear devastation? Whatever the price, Sonya was ready to pay.

Desperate for one more moment of respite, she headed for her pantry, a closet-like room loaded with lingonberry jam from the Scandinavian diner on Bloor, preserved lemons from Morocco, tapenade from the farmer's market in Bracebridge. She had never told Alex, but Sonya had insisted on buying this house over the others because of this pantry. Perfect for storing all the canning she planned to do, once she finally got to stay home from work to watch her children grow—those kids she had been so cruelly denied.

Alex, ever the pragmatist, had resisted buying a house this large, but Sonya won that fight, of course. Prices were going nowhere but up, she argued. Might as well buy into the market while they could. Prepare the nest before they needed it. Plan ahead, rather than chase happiness from behind. How was she to know that with each day the empty rooms would become ever more incriminating? An irrefutable sign of her failure to join the natural order of things.

"How can you stand that woman?" asked Pen, intercepting Sonya's escape into the pantry. "I timed her: she's been going for eight minutes straight."

"Each to their own," said Sonya, surprised at the hypocritical words that escaped her mouth. There was something uncontrollable about her these days, something blunt and unsparing. Disturbing, especially for someone who prided herself on keeping her cool. To make up for being unkind, Sonya handed Penelope the tray of stuffed mushrooms, saying, "But no more than two per person."

Sonya escaped into her pantry, only to find Tom already there. Clad in a hoodie he'd been refusing to take off even at night, her nephew was cowering on the floor, arms crossed tightly over his skinny legs, chewing his nails. His once bright eyes were now stuck somewhere between stupor and despair. What a difference from the boy Sonya remembered, the one with the gap-toothed smile, who could do six cartwheels in a row, who had just last year jumped gleefully into the near-frozen lake.

"Oh sweetheart, what are you doing hiding in here?" Sonya asked, knowing she sounded idiotic. What did she expect the boy to be doing? Going back to cartwheels? It had been only five days since she picked Tom up from the police station out by Highway 7, all bundled up in hospital blankets, shivering despite the early summer heat. The social worker, Stacie with an I and an E, a woman with sensible shoes and grey braided hair, had sighed with relief when Sonya arrived.

"Far too few parents make provisions in case of their untimely deaths," she said with a solicitous smile that made Sonya want to puke. "Thank God, your sister had the foresight for that." Had it really been foresight, Sonya wondered, no longer listening to the words that kept flowing out of the woman's mouth.

Back when Mona had asked Sonya to become Tom's legal guardian in case of death, it had just seemed to Sonya like something any responsible parent would do. Of course, she had agreed, assuming that this commitment would entail little more than presents twice a year and the occasional trip to the zoo. Not in her wildest nightmares could she have imagined that she would end up here, in this pantry with a boy who refused to speak, to cry, or even to be touched. A boy who was now in her charge. Her instant child.

Sonya grabbed a box of apple juice and wrangled the straw from its plastic wrapper. "Here," she said. "I got this special for you."

Tom blinked and shoved his thumb even deeper into his mouth, biting down hard. His gaze fixed on an empty space somewhere behind Sonya's left ear. Sucking saliva as if that might quench his thirst—his sole reaction so far to all her offerings.

"Maybe you would like some hot chocolate?"

Slurp.

"How about a snack?"

Slurp.

"Anything at all?"

Slurp. Slurp. Slurp.

Each and every day. Each and every time.

Slurp!

Make him look up! demanded a voice that sounded like her mother's, but was her own. Just yank his hand away from his mouth and make him speak. Make him engage. Cry. Anything at all.

Sonya closed her eyes. She was the adult here. She needed to get ahold of herself. Now.

"Please know," Sonya said, when at last she could trust her voice to remain level, "that I am here for you. Whatever you want, just ask."

Tom looked up—and took the juice.

Could this be it? A tentative first step forward? Encouraged, excited even, giddy almost, Sonya leaned toward Tom for that long overdue hug. But before she could reach the little boy, he jumped up and ran off, leaving the door ajar. Her failure exposed, for all to see.

Sonya returned to the kitchen, just as Rose refilled her wine, the glass so full she had to take a sip before she could put it down. Sonya's remaining sister was clad in tight blue pants, not exactly jeans, but hardly appropriate for a wake. And what's with the bright red lipstick? But then, even at age thirty-five, Rose still delighted in doing the unexpected and somehow, irritatingly, she got away with it.

"You sure have a way with kids," Rose said, as if raising one child made her an expert.

"I take it you're aware," responded Sonya as she opened the dishwasher, "that your son and Phoebe are now officially kissing cousins."

"What's that?" asked Rose.

"I saw them out back when I brought out the garbage. Nick's hand was halfway up Phoebe's shirt, and if her moaning was any indication, I'd say she was enjoying it."

As Rose went after her errant son, Sonya's spirits lifted, if only for a moment. Her world, their world, had gone to shit, but that did not mean she'd have to let her sister get away with being a self-righteous cow.

By now Sonya's heart pumped in triple time and the only way to calm her nerves was to move. She emptied the dishwasher, collected a tray of half-empty wine glasses, and put a leek tart into the oven. Then she went to straighten the dining room, but found it already done. Even after a decade of marriage, Alex had not lost his power to surprise. Too bad that lately those surprises were rarely great.

She had been smitten by his calm self-assurance from the moment they first met at Pen's wedding to Vincenzo, a marriage that, despite its $70,000 price tag, lasted barely six months. "You look like you need a dance," Alex had said after crossing the floor, singling her out among the eight bridesmaids. And she did need a dance. Something, anything, to shake off the feeling of dread that had settled upon her ever since Pen's sudden engagement.

Should she have intervened? Pointed out that being Wife No. 4 meant likely being just one in a line? That money would not keep her warm at night when Vincenzo was out chasing fresh prey? That one day, she too would most likely be discarded? But there was no stopping Pen, who had set her mind on "marrying up," so Sonya bought the fancy dress her friend had picked, accessorizing it with even fancier shoes. Who am I to judge? she decided. It's Pen's life, not mine.

And then Alex had asked her for a dance, looking sharp in his three-piece suit. His eyes hungry, but oh so enticing. His hand warm on her bare back. So, in a ballroom overlooking Lake Ontario, decked out in hundreds of white roses and flickering candles, they danced until the band stopped playing. Then Alex drove her home, and after she asked him in, he leaned over for their first kiss.

Alex was everything the mercurial men in her own family were not. He had an uncomplicated sense of belonging, never questioning that he would spend his career within his father's plastic injection molding company. Unlike her own convoluted life, his seemed charmingly clear. Unencumbered by the past.

Three months later, Sonya moved into his apartment just north of St. Clair and then, days after Penelope's divorce was finalized, they got married. Ten long years ago now.

Pretending to be too busy to talk to the group of mourners sitting around the dining room table, Sonya approached the fireplace, now a makeshift shrine. On the mantel stood a life-size portrait of Mona. The sun danced on her freckled, lily-white skin, emphasizing her awkward but kind smile. Tears sprang to Sonya's eyes but—unwilling to elicit more unwanted attention—she pulled out an already soggy napkin and dried her cheeks. Then she focused on rearranging the mementoes mourners had felt compelled to leave behind. An origami elephant, a frayed college yearbook, photos chronicling Mona's progression from awkward child to lanky teen to bride and mother. On each end of the mantle sat the two identical urns.

At the funeral home, Sonya had been overwhelmed by choice. "Wood, stone, marble or glass?" the droopy-eyed woman had asked, years of professional mourning carved into her cheeks like badges of honour. The simpler the design, it turned out, the more expensive, but Sonya didn't care about the money. What irked her was that neither Rose nor Will had stepped up to help out—not with the urns, not with anything else. As per usual when things went wrong, her two younger siblings reverted right back to being scared little kids, waiting for Sonya to swoop in and set right what was all too wrong.

Sonya slid Russell's urn even farther over to the right. The marble felt hard, even foreboding. In her mind's eye, it kept inching to the lip of the mantle, hovering on the cusp, before finally slipping off and crashing onto the floor, scattering its hateful contents.

"You don't think it's odd?" asked Rose, coming up from behind.

"What?" snapped Sonya, hoping that her tone would be enough to send her sister away. Don't give me lip, not today.

But Rose was not to be deterred. "Having Russell here," she said, "with her. Like it was a car accident or something."

"And what do you suggest I do with him, Rose? Mail him back to Australia?"

And so, the two sisters stood across from each other, waiting to see who would back down first. Both knew there was nobody to mail Russell to. Like it or not, he had become part of their family long before fathering Tom, even if that thought was now enough to make Sonya want to throw up. After all, she was the one who had kept inviting Russell over for dinner, enjoying his carefree manner when they all had needed cheering up after their mother had suddenly passed. Russell was nine when he came to Canada and eighteen when his father's tenure teaching neurosci-

15

ence at York ended. While his parents were glad to pack up their bags to depart for warmer climes, Russell had refused to return to Brisbane, or, as he called it, "The arse end of the world." He had stayed away from Australia ever since, even when his parents got sick a few years later and died within three weeks of each other. "What's the point of returning now?" he asked. "They're dead and gone."

A man with little sentiment, something that had never struck Sonya as odd. Not until now.

"This was taken at the cottage, no?" asked Rose, picking up a photo left behind by one of the guests. It showed Mona and Russell lounging in an orange hammock with baby Tom between them. Legs intertwined, drinks in hand. "How positively idyllic."

"Please, Rose. I can't. Not today," said Sonya, pulling the photo out of her sister's hand.

Sliding off her glasses, Sonya did take a better look. How vibrant Mona seemed, despite almost complete lack of sleep, how enchanted with her baby boy, and how foolishly proud of the man at her side. Blind, just like them, to the darkness that lived behind the affable smile.

Sonya placed the photo face down and picked up Russell's urn. "You're right, Rose. He's got to go."

★

Watching her elder sister scurry off into the living room, Rose could not believe they shared fifty percent of the same DNA. One of them had to have been switched at birth. Or maybe their mother had had an affair? What else could explain how Sonya, only six years older than Rose, acted like she was born in a different century? Looking every inch the boring suburbanite she was, Sonya was clad in a slick, all black ensemble that looked brand-new and overpriced. Her hair, rolled up this morning in an uptight bun, was now straggling around her neck; her lipstick was a shade too dark; her heels an inch too high. She could be pretty, if only she didn't try quite so hard.

Rose turned to the fireplace and picked up the watercolour of pink carnations that Leslie had dropped off with a dramatic flourish before ushering Tato, their father, off to some hotel downtown. Leslie was his latest companion, an iPhone-obsessed vegetarian with a painted-on smile, twenty years his junior. Pickings must be slim for the post-menopausal set. Why else would Leslie waste the rest of her life watching Tato chew every bite forty times and go to bed at nine o'clock? He had some money, sure, but stingy as he had been when he was young, age had made him tighter yet. "I do not," he declared with a decisiveness that gave Rose the chills, "want to be dependent on any of you."

"Here," Rose heard Sonya say in the living room, her voice sounding brittle yet firm. "You take care of him."

Rose pitched Leslie's watercolour—which looked more like a Rorschach test than an accurate rendition of anything real—into the trash. Nobody would notice, and anyway, by tomorrow morning those two would be on their way back to their tchotchke-filled home in The Villages, a retirement community in Florida. After Mama's sudden death, their father immediately put as much distance as he possibly could between himself and his previous life. First, he asked Sonya to return home from Montreal. "To help out with the kids," he said, but really so he could minimize time spent in the house. Then, days after Will's graduation from high school, he sold his plumbing business and moved down south, first for the winters, but eventually refusing to return home to Toronto at all. "I like it here, what can I say? It's easy," he told them. And as a bonus, Rose wanted to add but managed not to, you get to put two thousand kilometers between you and all reminders of your dead, bipolar wife.

By the time Rose made it into the living room, Sonya was shoving Russell's urn into Will's face. Their brother's dark hair was, as usual, an unruly mess, his burgundy tie had gone missing along with his shoes, and the big toe of his left foot was poking out from a hole in his sock. Since returning from the church service, Will had been parked on Sonya's brand-new calf-leather sofa, his scrawny legs sprawled across the coffee table, beer in hand. Why Sonya had acquiesced to Tato's ridiculous request to "celebrate" Mona's life in church was beyond Rose. Mona had not shown any interest in religion when she was alive. What was the point to pretend otherwise, now that she was dead?

"Why?" asked Will, turning up the volume on the TV, as if that might scare his sister away. "Why do I have to take that?"

If Sonya acted old for her age, their brother had gone the other direction. At thirty, Will still sounded like a petulant teen. Not that her son Nick, the actual teen in Rose's house, conformed to the sitcom stereotype, even if he was too naïve, or too horny, to understand that his cousin was trouble best left alone.

"You'll have to take him, because Russell was *your* friend," Sonya said, as she plonked the urn between Will's legs. The clank on the glass was as unpleasantly sharp as her voice.

"Sonya," Rose sat down next her brother and muted the TV, "how's that even fair?"

"Don't you dare talk to me about fair. Where were you when that lady at the funeral parlour tried to upsell me? Or when the cops wouldn't let me into Mona's house to get a change of clothes for Tom? And then there's Child Protection, and all those messages on Facebook someone needs to deal with oh, and did I mention that some guy from the *Toronto Star* called, looking for a statement from the family? Why don't you call him back, Will, or are you too busy walking dogs?"

"They gave me time off," said Will. "Obviously."

"Exactly," said Sonya, "which is why it's so ridiculous that I've had to arrange everything on my own."

"It must be awesome to be as perfect as you," said Rose. "You should cash in. Write a book. *Perfect as Perfect Can Be: My Incredible Story of Perfection*."

"Well, at least I try."

"How's it our fault that you're too bossy for anybody to ever do anything right? Ever?" The last *ever* slipped out before Rose could rein herself in. Embarrassed to have fallen back into her childish default mode when dealing with her older sister, she took a sip of Will's beer, hoping her moment of puerility might pass unnoticed.

"Excuse me," said Will, eyes still glued to the now-silent screen where a geeky boy-man in a striped sweater was trying, unsuccessfully, to climb a tree. "That beer's mine."

"Well, it's not like you paid for it," Sonya said, snatching the bottle. "And you, Rose, you're smarter than having to revert to words like 'ever' or 'never' or—"

"You don't even like beer, Sonya," said Will, cutting off his sister's lecture.

"Well, today I do," she said and took a swig.

"So what's ... ," asked Rose, pointing at Russell's urn between Will's legs, "going to happen with that?"

"Will brought the murderer into our house. Let him take care of it now."

Rose opened her mouth, but opted not to speak. Sonya was right. Partially, anyway. It had been Will who had first invited Russell into their lives—but they all had wanted him to stay. His easy jokes had provided much-needed relief in the dreadful months that followed their mother's death. A distraction from their grief, and an excuse not to probe too deeply into what exactly had happened and why.

Rose was fifteen years old when their mother died. Sonya still called it her "passing," but they all knew, even then, that it was suicide. One day she was there, all action and worries and rules, and then she was gone. "There is a season for everything," the priest had said in his eulogy, and he was right. Why worry about the future, when it might never come? Two weeks later, Rose lost her virginity to a guy with a moustache whose name she could no longer recall. The following summer, she hitchhiked to Alberta with Michael, her best friend, who would die of AIDS three years later. When she found herself pregnant at age twenty, she kept the child. Eugene, the often on-again, though mostly off-again boyfriend, was adorable enough and—who knew?—this might be her only chance at procreation. Tomorrow, she might be hit by a bus, get gunned down by an angry loner, or be knocked sideways by a sadness so profound that the only way out was to pop some pills and die.

"And you're keeping Mona's ashes?" Rose asked now.

"Of course. Until we've figured out where and when to scatter them, she ought to stay with her son," said Sonya and disappeared into the kitchen, to deal with snack No. 53.

Will unmuted the TV and returned to flipping channels. The geeky boy-man was replaced by a bleached blonde talking about how much she loved the gym. Followed a car driving, a bomb exploding, a lion roaring, a man...

"Slow down, Skipper," Rose told Will. "I'm getting a headache."

"How is it possible that we share her DNA?" Will asked, instead of slowing down. "We really should get that tested. Apparently, it's only... "

"Will, please. Not today."

As kids, they had spent hours speculating about who their real father might be. Angus, the handsome butcher. Maybe Colin from next door. Or, how about Johnny Cash?

"Seriously, how can she be such a hypocrite? You remember the way she used to fawn over Russell? She's the one who kept inviting him over. She's the one who ... "

"I can't do it," whispered Rose. "Not today."

"Sorry," said Will and put down the remote. Aware, as always, on just how far he could push—and when to stop.

Ten minutes later, Rose had enough of *Alaska, The Last Frontier*. She went into the kitchen to replenish her wine and found Alex doing the dishes. The sleeves of his shirt were rolled up on his muscular arms, a beautifully worn-out leather apron tied around his trim body. Why had she never been able to keep a guy like him, someone who could hold down a job, dress nicely, and help around the house?

"Is there really no more?" she asked, after rooting around the kitchen for more wine, and coming up empty.

"If you can handle something stronger," said Alex, "I've got a stash upstairs."

Only when she stepped into his office did it occur to Rose that she had never been there before. On the far wall sat a crooked shelf that was stuffed with books that looked well-chosen but unread, dusty medals from long-distance running, a collection of wrought-iron scissors, and a dead tarantula in a glass dome. Framed photos covered the wall above a small desk: a panorama of craggy Connemara, Sonya posing with a turtle, plus one portrait each of Alex's parents, both unrelentingly stern behind their smiling faces. Under the window sat a faded blue sofa, its mismatched pillows unfluffed. This office was a world apart from the serene perfection that the rest of the house exuded, incongruous, like the room of a rebellious child. The only thing missing was a "KEEP OUT" sign at the door.

"Wow, this is nice."

"You sound surprised."

"Well, I thought you were a plastics guy, so…"

"Even plastics guys are allowed to dream," said Alex. He picked up a book entitled, *How to Write a Damn Good Novel*, and said, "See this. It's helpful, though not as much as *The Artist's Way*. That book is special."

Rose moved the PlayStation controller off the sofa and sat down, more than ever in need of a drink. Why had Sonya never mentioned Alex's literary ambitions? And how could she have missed such an important aspect of her brother-in-law's life? What else was hiding in plain sight?

"To be honest," Alex confessed as he pulled out a bottle of Laphroaig, "I haven't written a word in years, but I like to think that one day I'll be tough enough to get back to it."

"Good luck with that," Rose replied. Then, embarrassed to have sounded mean, she held out her glass: "Tell you what. Fill 'er up, and I'll let you tell me all about that great novel of yours."

An hour later, Rose stepped out of the house, feeling both giddy about having gained new insight into her brother-in-law's inner life *and* guilty about that very insight. On the front walkway, she found Tom crawling up and down, battling an army of ants trying to reach a puddle of apple juice.

Rose lit her cigarette and sat down at the far end of the stoop. Tom, his new pants already ripped at the knees, looked tiny for his nine years. His eyes were masked by his shaggy hair, his shoulders bent.

"Did you know that some ants live off the vomit of others?" Rose asked. Years of staffing the help desk at the library had made her a fountain of random facts, and talk of bodily-fluids had always done the trick with Nick. Refusing to engage, Tom continued to pile leaves upon sticks upon pebbles in an effort to thwart the ants' attempts to break through. The boy had yet to speak a word, but who could blame him? Rose, too, was at a loss for words, not that that had stopped her from speaking.

"They have one abdomen, but two stomachs. One for personal use and one to store food for the community. How cool is that?"

Tom scooted over to Sonya's bed of geraniums, searching for more ammunition. Mulch. Gravel. An abandoned mitt. All of it now rained down on the unsuspecting ants, making them scatter in every directions.

"Fine. I'll leave you to it, then," Rose said, as she flicked away her cigarette. "But never underestimate the little ones. These guys can carry fifty times their own body weight. That's like you lifting a horse and a cow at the same time."

★

Why did adults insist on talking when that only made things worse? Tom picked up Aunt Rose's abandoned cigarette, not even half-smoked, glowing still. One drag was all it would take for the nastiness to slip away, for serenity to come. Tom knew this from watching Mom race to the corner store when Dad was in one of his moods. She would rip open a pack even before getting out of the door, flicking her lighter, inhaling deeply. "Sorry, Pumpkin," she would say, once peace was restored. "Now I'm all yours."

The cigarette butt, still moist from Aunt Rose's saliva, smelled yucky, but Tom knew what had to be done. "It's important to finish what you start," his mother had said so often it became a joke between them. "It's important to finish this ice cream," he'd say. "Absolutely," she'd reply, looking as if she might melt with pride.

Tom closed his eyes and inhaled, waiting for his anger to ease, for those nasty feelings to go away, for calm to arrive. Instead, the smoke seized his lungs, toxic like the fumes when Dad had burned the plastic chairs in a fit of rage. With each cough, pain dug more deeply into the boy's chest, like a miner probing for ore. Tears blurred his vision, numbing his senses, his brain racing in ever tightening circles.

Then, everything disappeared. The coughing, the pain, the past, and even the future. Nothing existed but the right here, right now. Free of all that no longer was. At peace, like gliding through the crystalline water in the canoe. Joyful, like laughing without fear.

But then Tom's breathing levelled out, and puke pushed up his throat. The butt burnt into his fingers and reality returned along with doubt, terror, and guilt.

Tom heard a woman laugh. He opened his eyes, only to be blinded by the late afternoon sun. A pickup truck sped down the street, spoiling the fresh air with its exhaust. A dog barked. Loneliness made Tom's jaw ache. He would never see his mother again. Never snuggle in her arms, listen to her stories, feel loved. But that's what he deserved for being a coward, for playing with his stupid toys, shrinking away instead of being there for Mom when she needed him most.

The sun moved behind the yellow house, and a chill settled onto the boy, his eyes scratchy with every blink. Over on the walkway, the ants had built a new path to the apple juice lake, goading Tom with their unwillingness to give up, taunting him with their determination.

Not far from his feet, Tom noticed the still-glowing butt. The smell of burning ants was comforting in a way tears simply were not.

★

The next morning, Sonya took a deep breath and nudged open the door to her former guestroom, confronting a wall of stagnant air. She put the breakfast tray down on Tom's bedside table and opened the windows. She would have to repaint, mauve being hardly appropriate for a nine-year-old boy, but already, she had added Spiderman bedding, a shelf for Tom's hideous toys, and a desk for when he would return to school.

"Look, Tom, I've made you pancakes," she said, trying to sound more cheerful than she felt. Like a larva trapped inside its cocoon, the boy's tiny shape rose semi-rhythmically under the duvet. Mona's child who was hers now. Tears, again, sprung into Sonya's eyes. How pathetic that it had taken a tragedy to make her a mother.

After years of trying, even Doctor Blumenthal was at a loss. "Life is precious," he'd say. His smile was kind, but his tired voice betrayed the fact that he said these very words over and over and over to too many women with fleeting hopes. At first, they had blamed Alex's sperm count, then Sonya's fallopian tubes, their stress at work, her abnormal uterine lining, his tight pants, her cervical mucus, his sperm motility and then, of course, her biological clock. No matter how many Hollywood stars have babies well into their forties, regular mortals wanting a child past age thirty-five were in for a shit show.

Sonya knew, because of Imogene, Max and, worst of all, Hannah. Against all advice, she had named each of her foetuses. Naming them had each given a life, validating what Sonya had felt and lived, even if they never got to exist in the outside world.

Twice Sonya thought they had made it to twelve weeks, but then the ultrasound revealed the horrifying truth. Not that she ever saw the dead tissue floating about her uselessly inflated uterus. All she ever got to see was the sudden look of unease on the technician's face, who immediately fled to fetch the doctor. Sonya, left behind with her bare legs spread, the ultrasound wand dangling out of her vagina, needed no second opinion. The foetus, first Imogene and then Max, was dead. Her dreams of motherhood ending in a D&C and a necklace from Alex.

Then, a year and a half ago, a sudden and entirely uncharacteristic aversion to coffee, combined with overpowering fatigue and a hypersensitivity to smells made Sonya dare to imagine that she might be pregnant again. For a few, delicious weeks, hope returned. Could their time in purgatory be over? Were they, too, finally allowed to live their proper lives? Would Hannah be the one to stay? But then, at the cottage, the bleeding began. By the time she told Alex, crimson blood overflowed her pads every twenty minutes, followed by cramps that left her speechless. Scared now, not just for the life of the baby but for hers, too, Alex tore down the highway, burning red lights along the way. Still, by the time they arrived at the nearest hospital, the passenger seat was drenched in blood.

"Maybe this is just a particularly heavy period," the doctor had said, sauntering into the ER. Alex started yelling, but all Sonya could do was close her eyes and focus her anger on holding back the puke. Except, she was no longer in control. As her heart galloped, vomit pushed up her throat, and blood gushed out of her vagina in apple-size clots. The voices around her grew urgent but dim, needles broke her skin, and finally even Alex's voice faded away.

When she woke, Hannah was gone.

And now here she was, with an actual living, breathing child. Tom. A wish come true out of the worst of horrors. Sonya sat down on the bed and extended her hand, but before she could reach the little boy, Tom rolled away toward the wall, exposing a large yellow stain.

Kids his age still wet their beds? Sonya was surprised. Clearly more research was needed. Along with a set of fresh sheets.

"You want maple syrup with those pancakes? Nutella? Peanut Butter? Fruit?"

Instead of an answer, all she got was Tom's breathing.

"They won't taste as good once they're cold."

"Please," she said, waiting.

"Tom?"

"Maybe you could take him fishing," Sonya said to Alex, dumping the uneaten pancakes into the garbage. "It would do him good to get out of the house."

Alex took a bite of his toast, followed by a drawn-out sip of coffee, before glancing up from the *Weekend Star*.

"After all," Sonya said as she looked her husband straight in the eye, "he's *our* son now."

Alex coughed, showering his shirt with a spray of coffee. Without so much as a blink, Sonya handed him her napkin and re-buttered her already-buttered toast.

Sometimes Alex was too infuriating for words. Even if the legal adoption process would take months, maybe years, it was silly to pretend it wasn't happening. Mona was not coming back. An inconceivable tragedy, yes, but one that had to be faced. Yet, ever since she had brought Tom back to the house, Alex had all but disappeared. "Deadlines," he claimed, "don't go away just because they're inconvenient." So he vanished first thing in the morning and returned only after he could be certain Tom had been put to bed, avoiding the boy, as if the whole mess were somehow Tom's fault. As if his grief might be contagious. As if they had any choice but to take in Mona's kid.

"Actually, I was wondering," said Alex as he wiped imaginary crumbs off his chin, "if maybe it would make more sense for somebody else to try."

"Try what?"

"Sonya, please. It's not like we know what we're doing here. Did you see that social worker's look when you asked to keep Tom out of school?"

Sonya grabbed a knife and cracked open her egg. How dare Alex say such a thing? Doubt her ability as a mother? She was sick of condescending looks when the topic of children came up. As if not having a child of her own made her a second-class citizen, a woman outside the natural order of things. Like she hadn't watched the mistakes of others, or read her share of Oprah-endorsed fucked-up-childhoods-make-good-books. Or spent her best years raising the three siblings—granted, with mixed results.

"They say it takes a village," said Alex. His voice pleading now, eyes soft. "Maybe Rose and Will are the kind of village this kid needs."

"Oh, be serious, Alex. Will still thinks walking dogs and hauling dirty plates a few times a week qualifies as a career, and Rose is barely keeping it together as is," Sonya said, her little finger twitching out of control. "Did you know that Nick made out with Phoebe? During the wake! And they're cousins."

"Three times removed."

"Anyway, Tom belongs here, with us. It's what Mona wanted, so it's what we are going to do."

Alex flipped the page, clearly relieved to stumble upon the crossword.

Five minutes of silence passed.

Five minutes for doubt and worry to return.

"It's just …," Sonya said, looking at her husband. Pen poised in his hand, yearning to turn back the dial. To restore life to what it had been. This, at least, he had in common with Tom.

"Yes, hon?"

"I just can't imagine what it must've felt like for Tom to find his mother covered in blood, to cradle her head in his arms, to watch her... die."

The knife in Sonya's hand shook. Bits of egg yolk dripped onto the tablecloth, but she didn't care.

"Fine," said Alex. "I'll take him fishing or something. Soon."

★

Farther north, near Highway 7, Rose stood in front of Mona's house, unwilling to move forward, yet unable to turn back. "Time for you and Will to chip in," Sonya had declared at the end of the wake and handed each of them a list. "Here are your chores."

Rose took a deep breath and turned the key. It felt wrong to enter her sister's house without ringing the bell, to stand in her kitchen without being offered a snack. On the table she noticed Russell's Sudoku awaiting completion. A few twists of his pencil's wood shavings still curled up in a bowl. Picking up the puzzle, Rose was oddly satisfied to see that he had failed, even though it was only rated moderate. Next to a pile of unopened letters, she spotted a brown ceramic mug. Homemade. Residue of coffee now dried out and black. Rose let her finger trace the writing, etched unevenly into the clay. Mona had loved making things, though she lacked the patience for perfection. Simple pottery like this mug, paintings (watercolours mostly), writings (poems, or haikus, really), and a couple of origami projects (unfinished).

Sensing Mona's presence, Rose spun around—but she was alone, her sister still gone. A nightmare Rose was not allowed to leave behind. Only this morning, she had wakened from a dream in which Mona and she were running along a path through a thick, dense forest, like the one behind the cottage, but this one led to a meadow covered in a carpet of tiny yellow flowers. Rose easily outran her little sister, stopping only at the creek. The water was clear and cold and oh so enticing, but when she turned, Mona had disappeared.

Rose put down the mug. Sonya had told her to set aside whatever should be kept for Tom and take anything else she wanted. But every single item in this house was tainted. Proof that she had failed. For she had allowed her sister to drift away, made excuses when Mona refused to talk, didn't ask about the bruises, the tears.

And now Mona was dead.

Rose stepped out of the stifling house into a backyard that looked like all the others in this subdivision, nestled at the northern edge of what could still be called Toronto. The stone patio was cluttered with brand-new, fake rattan furniture. Off to the right stood a red maple no more than three years old. The flowerbeds needed weeding. In the far corner sat Mona's favourite lounge chair, the blue and white canvas stained, the wood bleached and brittle. She had kept it despite Russell's complaints. It made her feel as though she were back at the beach. "All you have to do is close your eyes," she'd say with her sly smile, "rub your ears gently with the palm of your hands, and drift off." If only she'd been right about that. If only escape were that easy.

DING.

Rose pulled out her phone: *Wanna go for a walk?*

A text. From Alex. A first.

Rose sat down. From here, her sister's nondescript two-storey house looked even more ordinary than from the front. How disheartening that Mona had sat in this very chair, content to spend her life in a place so uninspiring. So bland. So sad.

Are you serious? Rose typed, waiting until she finished her cigarette before sending off her text.

Always, Alex texted back immediately.

On the ground, Rose noticed a can filled with butts, most of them not even half-smoked. All of them had once touched Mona's lips.

Fine. Pick me up at 6 she wrote, dumping the butts into the garbage. We only have one life, she reminded herself, might as well live it.

Rose went back indoors. Avoiding the bedroom, she entered Russell's office that was furnished with prefab, pseudo modern, cheap Swedish crap interspersed with the odd hand-me-down, like the squeaky swivel chair painted yellow. Metal bookcases lined the walls, filled with boxes, each labelled in Russell's punctilious handwriting: *Taxes. Tom. Mortgage. Us.*

Rose scoured several boxes labelled *Us* before she found the marriage certificate. She remembered waiting for them outside City Hall, the spring sun reviving her winter-pale spirits. She remembered the hope they had all felt, not just for Mona and Russell, but for one another other, too. Having survived another harsh Canadian winter, they were all on the brink of a lighter, brighter future, the legacy of their mother's death finally behind them.

Aside from her, Will and Rose, just a handful of guests had attended the wedding—Mona's childhood friend, Maggie (who drank so much that she had to be put into a taxi and then to bed), a couple of Russell's colleagues—a total of no more than twenty people. "You're all I need," Russell had declared to Mona, making her beam in her peach-pink dress. It had felt so romantic.

Now, Mona's tiny signature looked pathetic next to her husband's determined scrawl. Yet another sign Rose had somehow overlooked, blinded by Russell's winning smile, mollified by her sister's reassurances.

It took three hours, but finally Rose had found all the items on Sonya's list, including the passports and the deed to the house. As per the will, everything was to go to Tom, held in trust until he turned eighteen. His legal rights were protected by the oddly

31

named Office of the Children's Lawyer, another cog in the army of well-meaning people who had appeared to offer up their unsolicited concerns. Rose grabbed the documents and closed the door to Mona's house. This was the last time she would ever be here. Soon the place would be sold. Another goodbye. Another chapter closed.

Eager to get home to her own life now, to Nick and Will, to a glass of wine, Rose quickened her step. The air felt invigorating after so many hours steeped in regret. Two girls raced by on bikes adorned with rainbow-coloured streamers, a woman hung up laundry in her backyard, the old man next door washed his car. Life went on, in spite of what had happened at No. 415. Soon, new people would move into Mona's house, fill it with their own triumphs and disappointments, and before long, her sister's death, and then her life, would be forgotten.

Rose stopped in her tracks, horrified at the idea that her little sister was already fading away into the past. Just one of so many women murdered by angry men. She turned around and ran back to the house. As she crossed the driveway, the neighbour stood up from lathering his car, curiosity dripping off him along with the soap.

"You want to come in, is that it?" Rose asked. She pulled out the keys, but try as she might, she could not make them fit. Exasperated, she turned toward the still gaping neighbour. "If you ask nicely, I'll even show you where she died."

The man turned away, pretending not to have heard. The key finally slid into the lock, and Rose raced into the kitchen to grab Mona's misshapen mug. This mug she would keep, to use and cherish in her everyday life. To never forget that her sister had died, isolated and alone, disconnected not only from life, but from her family, too.

★

A week later, Will flopped down on Mona's sofa, dwarfed by a tower of boxes destined for the Salvation Army. Now that Rose had done her bit, and Sonya had stashed away everything Tom might want one day, Will was tasked with wrapping up the rest of the house. Why couldn't his cheap-assed sisters spring for a professional? It's not as if they didn't waste money on ridiculous crap, like shoes they couldn't walk in.

He pulled out his phone, but of the five emails, four were spam and aside from yet more "sad faces" on Mona's obit, there was nothing of interest on Facebook. Then Will noticed a travel alert to Korea. *$499*, he read, *Only today, leaving tomorrow.* As a dare to himself, he updated his status: *Korea bound. Who can hook me up with a job?* Next, he texted his friends Burt and Lisa to see what was up, but after playing five rounds of Ridiculous Fishing, neither had bothered to reply.

Will took a deep breath, promised himself beers later at the Done-Right-Inn, and got up. The sofa and most of the chairs had already been tagged for pick-up. He would take the TV, Sonya the computer—but the big stuff was easy. It was the small decisions that were wearing him down. Were Russell's skates worth saving? What to do with the three wooden monkeys, a gift to Mona from Bolivia? How about her own tear-stained letters from Camp Pinewood, the Wildflowers of the World playing cards, or the raccoon skull Will had found at the cottage but that somehow wound up here?

He slid the cards into his pocket. They might come in handy, possibly even later tonight. Yes also to the letters, the eagle feathers, and any books Tom might want to read—out with *Fear of Flying*, *The Golden Notebook* and *The Greatest Hunting Stories Ever Told*. No to the boomerang, Russell's reading glasses, and three almost identical tennis rackets. If the kid wanted to follow his father's obsession with running after a ball, he would have to do that on his own.

Will turned toward the stairs, adding a stop at Burrito Boyz, three whiskies and a trip to the racetrack to his mental list of rewards. The walls of the upstairs hallway were checkered with rectangular patches of faded paint, left from what had once been Mona's gallery of family portraits. How much effort she had put into decorating this house, into accumulating things. All of it to be disposed of now, meaningless.

Will forced himself onward, one step at a time. It was only last year that he'd helped Russell refinish the floor. Back then, Russell seemed fine, ranting about the Leafs, the weather, and the stupidity of his latest boss. The contract had something to do with public relations for a developer west of the city. Or was it for the proposed high-speed rail link to Montreal? A mechanical engineer by training, but a marketing man by temperament, Russell had never been able to hold down a job for more than a year, impossible to keep track.

The brass knob to the master bedroom felt flimsy. One push and the door would swing open. One kick and the wood would splinter. Nausea rolled over Will like waves in a roiled up sea. Less than a month ago, Tom had stood here, finding his mother covered in blood, while his father was about to blow his brains out downstairs.

Taking a deep breath, Will stepped into the bedroom. General order had been restored, thanks to Steamatic, a company that specialized in cleaning up crime scenes. At least Sonya hadn't been too cheap for that. Even with his own history of questionable jobs (including a stint in a turkey factory that turned him vegetarian for a couple of years), Will could not imagine what kind of wage would make it worthwhile to rearrange a murdered woman's toiletries, never mind scrubbing her splattered blood off the walls.

Aside from the missing door, Mona's closet would have done well on Pinterest. Shirts were sorted by colour, coats by season, shoes stood neatly lined up. He had argued with Mona about her addiction to cheap clothes, how each cute outfit meant another child working instead of going to school, how fast fashion was ruining the earth. Now, Will wished he'd simply complimented his sister on her latest find and moved on.

He quickly filled six bags for the pick-up, but the silk wedding dress made him pause. Letting the still lustrous fabric slide through his fingers, he remembered how thrilled Mona had been to marry Russell, a man she had known for most of her life, her brother's best friend. Will dropped the dress into the garbage. Nobody needed to step into married life burdened by karma this bad.

Russell's closet proved harder yet, because Sonya was right: Russell had been his friend first, the friend he desperately needed after his mother died. For years, they had crisscrossed Eastern Canada travelling to swim meets, growing closer without ever losing their competitive edge. Beating Russell at the Ontario finals was still one of Will's proudest memories. What did it matter that they had come in fourth and fifth? After retiring at seventeen from the endless battle against the clock, they turned to Dungeons & Dragons, once playing for three days in a row. Then, after high school, they shouldered their backpacks to explore Nicaragua and Costa Rica, eventually travelling as far south as Cabo Polonio, a hippy enclave in Uruguay. For two months, they lived without electricity or running water, content to let one day flow into the next, to play cards and drink beer, until they ran out of money and had to move on.

Russell returned home, reconnected with Mona, and shortly thereafter they got married. They had Tom less than six months after the wedding, while Will continued to travel, teaching English to pay his way, his circle of friends ever widening, his attachment to home loosening to the point that the word *home* itself no longer made sense. Then, on the eve of his thirtieth birthday, he decided to return to Toronto. "Time to grow up," he told Veronique, a lanky girl with boundless energy he'd hooked up with in Ho Chi Minh City. "As if," she said, and walked away from their hut on Ho Coc Beach, never to be seen again.

Will and Russell had stayed in touch. Whenever Will came back to Canada, they went canoeing in Algonquin Park or hiking on the Bruce Peninsula. But then Russell started to hang out with a different set. He went fly-fishing with his golf buddies and hunting on Anticosti—though that had not ended well. "Bloody tourist trap," Russell complained, after returning without having seen, never mind shot, even one of the 160,000 white-tailed deer that roam the island. "Bloody locals upselling the joint," Russell insisted, unwilling to consider his own inexperience.

Will grabbed Russell's shirts and pitched them into a bag, followed quickly by pants, belts, underwear, socks and more than fifty ties. A pair of R. M. Williams boots, just one size too big, caused Will to hesitate. Handcrafted and smooth, they would only get better with age. But then, before slipping in his second foot, Will changed his mind. There was no way he would walk in Russell's shoes.

Will finished clearing out the bedroom and returned downstairs, but he stopped at the kitchen door. This is where Russell had pushed the gun into his mouth, maybe holding his breath, knowing that his wife lay upstairs in a puddle of blood, that his son was listening in fear. And still he pulled the trigger. A man who had been Will's friend, whom he had trusted, not just with his own life, but with his sister's, too.

Will grabbed his jacket and stumbled out of the house. Screw Sonya and Rose and everybody else. He was done packing up dead people's crap. Throw it all out, he thought, see if I care.

On the bus home, Will re-read his emails: *Only $499 to Korea.* Then came a PING and a Facebook message from Jimmy, his buddy from Auburn, Maine, who had been on the road for eight years straight: *Amazing, dude! Connie wants to check out Bali before it's completely gone to shits, so I've been looking for somebody to take over my gig teaching pre-K. How soon can you come to Busan?*

By the time Will got downtown, the only question left was how to pay for his flight. Coco, his boss at the Supper Club, didn't care that he wanted time off and quitting Happy Pooch had been a relief. No more having to walk seven dogs, who all pulled in different directions, inevitably wanting to shit at the same time.

Will returned home to Claremont, thrilled to find the house empty. The last thing he needed was Rose giving him 18,000 reasons to stay. In the fridge, he found yesterday's pad thai, but before he could heat it up, his phone dinged again with a message from his friend Burt: *Get yr arse over here, I got us some good ones.* Will smiled. Lady Luck had returned.

Will had met Burt on the beach in Borneo, and the two had bonded over their shared love of playing the odds. Before long, they hooked up to make money off dipshits too high or too lazy to count their cards. After a few delirious months of travelling up and down the coast, Burt returned to Toronto and bought an apartment in Kensington Market, where he now hosted the occasional game for dimwits he would pick up in the cheesy clubs along Richmond Street.

Arriving at Burt's not fifteen minutes later, Will was pleased with the dupes his friend had rounded up today; three buddies taking a break from their soul-crushing jobs, overachieving wives and ADHD kids, ready for some action, with money to burn. The blond one twitched every time he got a good card, and the short one with the beard couldn't keep his eyes from roaming.

Only the third had enough sense to hide his eyes behind wrap-around shades—yet even he couldn't help shaking his legs.

"Let's eat before I die of starvation," said Burt, when the three men had stumbled away, relieved of their money but enriched by a story they'd tell for years to come.

"I can't," said Will, busy counting out his share: 380 bucks. Close enough. The rest he would borrow from Rose. "I'm off to Busan."

"Why the fuck Korea?" asked Burt, who had refused to leave downtown Toronto ever since he got back from his own world travels. "That's the place where buildings keep collapsing."

"The fare's cheap."

"Did you hear about the auditorium that collapsed a few years ago, killing ten? Or that ferry? The captain who told the kids to stay in their cabins?" said Burt.

"I had no idea you love me so."

"Don't laugh, I speak from experience," Burt replied, not taking the bait. And about that, he was right. After all, he had only narrowly escaped death himself, riding a bus that had plunged into a ravine near Kuching, killing four, leaving Burt with a permanent limp.

Will bid a hasty goodbye, knowing that once Burt got started, it would be impossible to stop him from sharing his entire trove of disaster trivia. Once back on the street, though, Will dreaded returning home. Sonya would flip out about him leaving instead of cleaning out Mona's house, and she did. But Rose surprised him: "Shit just never changes," she said, somehow comforted by that thought. "Anyway, you know where to find us, once you're done running away."

★

Tom sat in Aunt Sonya's car, unmoving, as all around him kids were dropped off for school. A group of boys chased after terrified squirrels, a mother straightened out her son's shirt, girls in matching sweatpants were giggling at some joke. Tom was not interested in any of it. Tom wanted to go home. To be left alone. For the world to burst into a ball of fire.

"School, I'm afraid, is not optional," said Aunt Sonya and leaned over to unsnap Tom's seatbelt. "It's the law. So please don't make this any harder than it already is."

Tom crossed his arms and focused on an oval package that hung high up in a tree. Shaped like a football and bandaged in stringy grey gauze, the wasps' nest looked like a piñata made by colour-blind monks. For his birthday last year, Mom had bought an orange piñata with green dots and a huge purple bow. She had strung it up in the tree in their backyard and handed him one of Dad's baseball clubs. Tom started to swing but before he could get to the hidden treats, his father made him stop.

"Slow down, Skipper," he said, and pulled out a bandana. "Let's do this properly. You're a big boy now."

Then he spun Tom around and around and around and then around some more. Blindfolded and now dizzy, Tom swung the club, hitting nothing but air. More air. And then, yet more air. After enduring Dad's swearing and Mom's pleas, after soaking the bandana with tears and soiling his birthday outfit with sweat, Tom never so much as scraped the stupid thing. Dad, his face stiff with disappointment, picked up the club and split the piñata open with one stroke.

It was empty.

"How was I to know?" Mom whined, as Tom slipped away into his room. "For that kind of money, you'd think they'd fill it up."

"LISTEN," Aunt Sonya's voice now had become too insistent for Tom to tune out any longer. "I know it's hard to believe right now, but no matter how we feel about it, life goes on. The trick is to ...." She fastened her fingers tightly around the steering wheel, and a network of blue veins popped up across the back of her hand. "The trick is," she repeated, and let go of the wheel, "the trick is to make the best of what we have."

She moved over, closer to Tom, but thankfully the seatbelt yanked her back into place. She smelled funny, Aunt Sonya did. Familiar but yucky, too. Tom wedged himself against the door and closed his eyes, wishing his aunt, this car, everything to disappear. Waking up in the morning hurt. Leaving his bed hurt. So did washing, dressing, eating, moving. He spent his days longing for night to return, for sleep to come, for nothingness to settle upon him.

Not that he slept much in that weird purple room. Every day something new showed up, like the blue curtains Aunt Sonya claimed were the colour of the Maple Leafs (not), or the Spiderman socks to match his bedding (really?). He used to love Peter Parker, the most fantastic crime fighter ever, an orphan forced to live with his Aunt May. At first, she was worried that the boy's presence might ruin her marriage, as she and her husband could not have children, but in the end, she grew to love Peter like he was her own son. Now that Tom was an orphan himself, he understood just how stupid that story was. How totally unrealistic.

To keep oncoming tears at bay, Tom wedged his index fingernails into the cuticles of his thumbs, pressing hard. When a bit of loose skin tried to escape, he angled his teeth and clamped down harder yet.

Agony. Stillness. Relief.

"Oh, look," said Aunt Sonya, so excited that Tom couldn't help but open his eyes. "Isn't that your buddy?"

Even though they had been best friends since kindergarten, it took Tom a moment to recognize Saanjh, standing right next to the car, waving shyly, his feet turned in. Way back when being apart from his parents for a week was the saddest thing Tom had ever endured, he and Saanjh had been bunk mates at Camp Pinewood. The two had hidden behind the boathouse and scared each other with ever more spooky tales. Saanjh's were about werewolves and ghosts, but Tom preferred horrors inflicted by nature. Hikers trapped in a snowstorm, sailors shipwrecked by hurricanes, miners buried alive. Later, after the two friends returned to the city, Tom swiped Dad's worn-out pocketknife and they became blood brothers in the ravine behind Saanjh's house. Like in the movies, they pricked their skin and rubbed their wrists against each other's, watching their blood mingle. United forever, they swore, totally unaware just how silly such a pledge was. How meaningless and dumb.

"Let's go," mouthed Saanjh now, but Tom returned his attention to the wasps' nest above. If only he could trigger its cargo. Make it explode on Saanjh's head.

"It'll get easier," said Aunt Sonya, her voice now starting to break. "Ms. Lipinsky said it's important to get back to your routines, even if at first it seems harsh. Sooner or later—"

Maybe he could beam himself up into another dimension? Live by himself in a place where there was no school and no Saanjh and no jabbering aunts. A place where—

"Tom? Are you listening?"

Maybe Rhinox would do the trick, a massive warrior with Chainguns of doom.

Aunt Sonya's door popped open. "Stay," she hissed at Saanjh, who had turned to leave. Then she yanked open the passenger door. "That's enough, Tom. I told you school's not a choice. If you don't go, I'll get into trouble with Children's Aid, and who

41

knows what would happen then."

Tom curled himself into a ball. One, he started to count. Two. Three.

Then he felt Aunt Sonya's hands hook into his belt.

"One, two, three," she counted aloud. Then she lifted Tom up, yanking him out of the car and onto the sidewalk. He landed on the pavement like a beached turtle, inches away from Saanjh, who was backing away.

"I told you, don't leave," Sonya hissed. "He'll be with you in just a sec."

★

"Do you understand why you're here?" asked Dr. O'Donnell, barely waiting for Sonya and Tom to settle onto his couch.

"I thought it might be a good idea to speak to somebody—" Sonya began. But Dr. O'Donnell cut her off, saying, "I was talking to Tom, thank you."

The next twenty minutes passed in silence. Sonya picked the last piece of lint off her charcoal linen pants before allowing herself to look up. Under framed certificates for this, that, and the other, the doctor sat, doodling away. His eyes shadowed by heavy lids, his cheeks floppy like a mastiff's. A lifetime of listening to other people's troubles etched unattractively into his face.

Dr. O'Donnell had been recommended by Sandy and Dick Moore, who worshiped his every utterance since he rescued their daughter from the tyranny of pharmaceuticals. Melanie had been trouble for years. At first it was Ritalin for hyperactivity, then Valium for excessive fretting, a bit of Prozac for depression, Ativan for anxiety, Sonata for sleep and Dexedrine to get her going again. As if there was a quick fix for life. That's what their mother had been after—and look where that got her. No, Sonya would not allow Tom to take drugs. Not under her watch. No way.

Perched on his side of the leather couch, Tom looked like a bird whose wings had been clipped. His head wedged between his shoulder blades, the tips of his toes barely reaching the floor. The sleeve of his hoodie was pulled all the way over his wrist, unsuccessfully trying to hide the thumb stuck in his mouth.

It had taken eight days until Tom had finally relented and walked off into school on his own. Watching his solemn figure being swallowed up in a sea of brightly clothed children, all so full of joy and energy and hope, had made Sonya cry. What if Tom had been right to resist? Maybe she should have fought harder to keep him at home.

Thankfully, the kids' initial curiosity waned fast, or so Tom's teacher said, and after that, the boy sat in class largely undisturbed, passing his days hidden in his hoodie, waiting, breathing, sucking, waiting, sucking.

"Stop it," Sonya hissed, struggling hard not to slap Tom's hand away from his mouth. "This behaviour," she asked once she steadied her breath, "this kind of behaviour isn't normal, is it?"

"No," said Dr. O'Donnell, without bothering to look up. "But then again, neither is his situation."

No kidding, Sonya almost said but she managed to keep her mouth shut. Instead, she counted the cracks in the wall.

They stepped out into the bright sunlight thirty-five silent minutes later, and Sonya vowed never to return. "Selective mutism," Dr. O'Donnell had finally diagnosed, something she already had figured out on Google. A disorder in which a person, often a child, is suddenly unable to speak.

"But he'll snap out of it," Dr. O'Donnell added cheerfully. "Sooner or later, he'll start to talk."

Until then, Sonya vowed, she was done with paying a grown man to draw pictures.

*

On Facebook, distances felt tiny, inconsequential even. But now, stuck in the Tokyo airport for a six-hour layover after having spent the last eighteen hours in transit, Will started to question if he had really needed to flee quite this far. Splashing water on his face revived his senses, not that he liked what he saw in the excessively clean washroom mirror. His hair was a greasy mess, his skin itchy and dry, his body bloated. Less beer, more swimming, he vowed, grabbing his knapsack.

In a nook near his departure gate, Will lay down. The carpet smelled of dust and chemicals, but stretching his stiff legs felt luxurious. Using his bag as a makeshift pillow and his jean jacket as a blanket, he closed his eyes, instantly calmed by the buzz of humanity that settled over him like a down duvet. There was comfort in being surrounded by a sea of travelers, all like him stuck between the here and the there. Garbled, incomprehensible words, mixed with determined, yet unrushed, movements forward produced a monotonous, oddly pleasant din, soothing like the Ukrainian lullaby his mother used to sing for him. Her normally assured voice turning delicate with girlish innocence, like she herself was yearning to be held, in need of solace faced with the meanness of the world.

The Dream passes by the window, she would sing. *And Sleep by the fence. The Dream asks Sleep: Where should we rest tonight?*

The bustle of the Narita airport slipped away, and along with it Will's doubt. He had been right to leave Toronto, where everything reminded him of his poor taste in friends, a lack of judgment that had led to his sister's murder. And to think that the last time he'd seen her, Mona had worried about him. "I'll die before you ever grow up," she had said. How right she had been.

Will pulled his jacket around him more tightly. Swaddled now, like his mother used to swaddle him when he would lie awake terrified of monsters lurking in the darkness. "Fear not, my dear little boy," she'd say and gently stroke his cheeks. "We are here for each other. That's what families are for."

Sleep, sleep, my little falcon,
Sleep, sleep, my little dove.
And so he did.

July

Two weeks passed. Two weeks of different shades of diddlysquat, accompanied by wet, sloppy, disgusting slurps. Sonya watched as Tom gnawed his fingers, bit his nails, sucked his thumbs. Bandages disappeared as quickly as she could put them on, bribes were as useless as pleas and threats. "This should do the trick," the pharmacist promised, handing her yet another vile-tasting cream. "Guaranteed." Only, as soon as Sonya could apply the ointment, Tom licked it off like it was vanilla ice cream.

"Give him time," said Marcie, the latest counsellor, this one from Sydney, Nova Scotia, her sweetly freckled face not yet marred by life's disappointments. Then she squeezed Sonya's hand, musing wistfully about how winter always turns into spring.

You try staying positive when an unresponsive alien invades your home, Sonya wanted to scream. Instead, she grabbed the boy and left. No point in arguing with the immature. Life had its way of getting to them; all one had to do was wait.

"You promised to take him fishing," Sonya reminded Alex later that same day, but Alex refused to look up from his computer.

"It's pouring," he finally said, withering under Sonya's unrelenting stare. "Not ideal."

Sonya pushed a crumpled bag of chips off his sofa and sat down. With all their extra rooms, there was no reason why Alex should not have this office, but really, what did he need it for? He hadn't written in years, giving up on his literary dreams, along with running the Boston Marathon and making a million bucks before turning thirty. Alex referred to what he was doing up here as work, but Sonya knew it was mostly playing solitaire and scouring Facebook. She did not understand what Alex saw in social networking. Socially sanctioned stalking was more like it. Who cares what Eli ate for lunch? How many years Dayna has been happily married? What Rilke had thought about life?

Sonya noticed a bottle of Laphroaig behind a pile of books. Next to it, two glasses.

"Well, how about a movie, then?" she asked, and poured herself a good-size shot. "I need the afternoon off. The house has got to be dealt with now. The real estate agent's getting cranky."

Actually, what the agent had said was: "I can't sell this place unless all the personal effects are gone. With people having died here, it'll be tough, even at a discounted price."

"I'm not sure those glasses are clean," Alex said, but Sonya didn't care. The whisky had already started to smooth out some of her indignation. Plus, she knew the agent was right. They couldn't afford for a potential buyer to imagine what life had been like in that house. Why the door to the closet was gone. Where Mona had been clobbered. How far Russell's blood had splattered.

"Will's such a jerk," said Alex, "Taking off like that. It was his job clean out the house, instead we're stuck with that, too."

"Anyway, Alex, you and Tom should bond. Movies are great for that."

"I take it you've noticed that the kid's not into bonding."

"Still, you need to try. We need to try."

"Why?"

"Because," Sonya said, pouring herself one more glass, "if we don't, Russell wins."

★

Tom's head hurt. So did his bones and joints, his eyes and skin, his stomach, throat, teeth, ears. And now, he was stuck in a smelly car with Uncle Alex.

"Alright, let's get this show on the road," said Uncle Alex, swiping a take-out coffee cup off the back seat onto the floor, where it joined a neon-coloured nest of interlaced bungee cords and sneakers.

They pulled out of the driveway, and Uncle Alex cranked up the CBC news. A black man killed in North York, migrants drowning somewhere in Europe, violence in Central Africa.

Tom closed his eyes and started to count. He had zero interest in the Science Centre—or in getting to know his uncle better—but now that school was done, Aunt Sonya had ramped up her push for activities. Draw a picture. Let's go for a walk. How about a movie? I hear *Kung Fu Panda* is good. Like he hadn't already seen it five times. Like he cared. Like it mattered.

Having reached 123, Tom stopped. He liked 123. Three small numbers that climb up toward bigger, better things, or one large sum made out of three little pieces. Added up, one, two, and three made six, Tom's second favourite number. There are six strings on a guitar. Ants have six legs. He was six when they visited Old Orchard Beach.

The car came to a stop, but it was the smell that made Tom open his eyes. Greasy, delicious, and until recently, forbidden: Mom hated all American chain restaurants, but especially McBarf.

"A Big Mac and fries for me and … " Uncle Alex turned to look straight at Tom. "What's it going to be, dude?"

49

Tom shut his eyes and continued to count: 85, 84, 83. Numbers are what he wanted. They were pure and delicious and easy to follow. 75, 74, 73.

As they pulled out of the drive-through, Uncle Alex dropped a Happy Meal on the back seat. The mouth-watering smell made Tom's tummy rumble. Mom would be disappointed, he was sure of it, but then again, she would never have to know.

Tom opened the bright red box, insulted to find a Hello Kitty set. Did the woman really think he was a she? Tom pushed the stupid toys to the floor and ripped a slippery plastic pouch open, squirting ketchup over his fries. Next, he took a giant sip of Coke. Sweet, tickly, and great.

"See, what Sonya doesn't understand," said Uncle Alex, "is that kids eat if you give them what they want."

Biting into the burger, Tom suddenly remembered the time Dad had gobbled up eleven of them. Sometime last summer, they had played in the park until a Border Collie caught their Frisbee and ran off with it. Tom was distraught, but Dad and the dog's owner laughed hysterically. They finally managed to retrieve the red disk, but by then it was all gross and slippery from the dog's spit. Dad offered the guy one of his beers and they settled underneath a big tree, bringing tears to each other's eyes with every more silly stories, proving just how ridiculous they could be. Like Dad jumping off a cliff so often, he bruised his butt black, or the time the guy had gotten stuck in some cave for a week. Tom, having heard his dad's stories already a gazillion times, had been bored out of his mind. Eventually, the two men came up with a bet: Whoever ate ten Big Macs would get the eleventh for free. Remembering his father's satisfied burp after the last bite, Tom shoved his Happy Meal onto the floor.

1 time 6 is 6. 2 times 6 is 12. 3 times 6 is 18.

"Shit, Tom! What do you think you're doing?" yelled Uncle

Alex, hitting the brakes, swerving off to the left. "This car isn't a dump."

6 times 6 is 36. 7 times 6 is 42. 8 times 6 is ...

If he kept counting, Uncle Alex's voice would fade away, and with it the dread that came from being alive.

August

"I saved this for you," said Sonya, presenting a blue ceramic mug to Tom, as if it were the latest action figure, impossible for any nine-year-old to resist. "Please."

But Tom did not so much as glance up from the TV. As if it mattered who *Canada's Worst Driver* might be. As if he cared. Instead, the boy kept sucking his thumb. Slurp. Slurp. Slurp. But then, Tom's refusal to engage was, by now, a given. In the last two months, he had rejected hot dogs, lemon cake, waterslides, go-karts, paintball, even the zoo. He proved to be the only kid uninterested in rides at Canada's Wonderland. In the ice cream shop, he solemnly shook his head, preferring his thumb to vanilla soft serve. Last week, Sonya had dragged Tom to the pool, but he refused to take off his hoodie, never mind joining the hoards of kids who had been thrilled to cool off on this brutally hot summer day. Not once since his parents' death had Tom smiled. Or looked into her eyes. Nor made a sound, aside from his slurps.

"Your mom made it," Sonya said. Tom shifted his gaze to look at the mug. A victory, Sonya told herself. Of sorts. The mug was crooked and the handle had been glued, but on one side Mona had etched TOM, and on the other side a heart.

"It's for you to keep. Here."

A blink, another, and then one more, but finally Tom took the mug, moving his scabbed fingertip over the jagged ridge that spelled out his name.

Mona's interest in pottery had been sudden. In the months after Tom's birth, when sweltering days merged into torpid nights, she had felt trapped in a relentless cycle of feeding, burping, diapering, napping, feeding, napping, crying, feeding. By September, she had felt obliterated by the onslaught of her child's needs. She loved Tom, of course, but in a voice so tiny Sonya had a hard time understanding, Mona admitted to aching to get away from this creature that had taken over her life, every fibre of her body, her brain and soul. So, when a few weeks later Dr. Gerschenfield inquired about returning to her dental hygienist job part-time, Mona had been thrilled. By then, her maternity benefits had run out, and this was a perfect excuse to escape. But Russell had intervened.

"I provide for us just fine," he argued. "Plus it's selfish to spend your life poking around people's rotting teeth when you have a kid that needs you at home."

Sonya had been suspicious of Russell's motivations. How 1950s, she thought. But Mona had acquiesced. "It's how he shows his love," she said. "And anyway, childcare would probably cost more than I could make." The pottery classes were a compromise, a chance for Mona to get out of the house, but countless misshapen mugs later, she quit those, too. Another lifeline to the outside world broken, Sonya realized now, leaving her sister even more isolated.

Tom closed his eyes and pressed his nose into the mug. Was he hoping to find his mother's scent? Did he even remember it?

"It will get better," whispered Sonya. "Trust me, it will."

The boy's eyes popped open, staring Sonya straight in the eye. She sat up, startled. Had she just found a way to unlock the door?

Had her silence about Mona, her inability to face her sister's death head on, made the boy's grief worse? Should she share more, rather than less?

Slowly, Sonya leaned forward, hoping for a first, gentle touch, but before she could reach Tom, he jerked away, hurling the mug across the room, where it smashed into the wall hard, shattering into pieces.

Sonya barely made it back to the kitchen before tears started to flow. What a miserable loser she was, no closer to reaching Tom now than she had been on day one. If anything, the boy was slipping further away. Fate was right to refuse her children of her own. Clearly, she did not have what it takes. Unlike the movies with their bow-tied endings, this tragedy was not pulling her family together. There was no new perspective on life. Just despair over what was lost. A family splintered, broken.

The first time she'd met him, Russell was fifteen. Sonya, only twenty-one back then, had just returned from Montreal to raise her siblings. Too old to be one of them, yet too young to befriend other parents. Neither fish nor fowl, stuck somewhere in between—just like in high school when she had not been pretty enough to be popular, too stylish to be called homely, and just a little too good at math to be considered fun.

One day, Will brought Russell over after swim practice, and then he just stayed. He called her brother a "mollydooker" because he was left-handed, took "doona days" after partying too hard, and ended every third sentence with "mate." But it was his poise that set him apart from the rest of Will's pimply-faced friends. Russell complimented Sonya on her cooking, even if her first attempt at Mama's lemon cake ended with half of the batter burning on the oven floor. He helped with the dishes. Laughed at her jokes when the others groaned. Soon he ate over, more often than not, and in the summer, when the city was stiflingly hot, Sonya invited him to join them at the cottage.

Mona was sixteen then and dismissive of her young brother's friend. She made fun of Sonya for laughing at Russell's jokes, and ignored his antics even when it became increasingly clear that most of them were staged for her benefit alone. But all that changed after Russell returned from his trip to South America. Now a grown man with worldly experience, the two discovered their shared love of canoeing and before long, Mona and Russell would set off for hours at the time, exploring the far reaches of the lake and soon after, Sonya suspected, each other.

Sonya splashed her face with icy cold water, washing away her tears but not her regrets. She had been swayed by Russell's easy charms, lulled into trust by his attentiveness. She had allowed him to join her family, to fall in love with Mona and take her away. But then how are you to know who to let into your world and who to keep out?

★

Back in the living room, Tom waited for his heart to stop racing, for his breathing to calm, for his mind to stop spinning. He reached down and found the carpet beneath him. Woolly and soft, like at home, bringing back the night he walked toward his parents' bedroom, the moment before opening the door.

Tom grabbed a piece of ceramic that had ricocheted off the wall and landed right by his foot. Mom had moulded this mug, written his name into the wet clay. But Tom could no longer remember the shape of her hands. Disgusted, he curled his fingers into a fist, savouring the pain as the shard dug into his flesh. The harder he pressed, the deeper the cut, the better.

"What's this?"

Tom opened his eyes to find Aunt Sonya hovering by the liv-

ing room door, her shoulders collapsed, fresh tears clouding her
eyes. Unwilling to let her sadness take over his, Tom clenched his
fist even more tightly. Bright red blood dripped on the beige carpet, leaving a trail like strawberry syrup splattered over vanilla ice
cream. Panicked, Aunt Sonya leapt across the room, trying desperately to pull away the shard. To ward her off, Tom curled into
a ball, pressing harder yet. Pain, delicious and real, took over his
mind, numbing his agony.

And then he was spent. Tom let go of the shard, dropping it
onto the ground. There was blood now splattered on Aunt Sonya's
shirt, and her face was smeared with mascara and fear. "Why?"
she kept saying. "Why? Why? Why? Why? Why?"

Aunt Sonya walked off, returning with bandages and a super
stingy liquid she poured all over the gash in the palm of Tom's
hand. "This is just too awful for words," she said, and yet she kept
on talking, dabbing off the blood before wrapping his hand in a
thick layer of gauze as if he were a boxer about to go into a fight.

Once done, Aunt Sonya grabbed her phone and disappeared
downstairs, letting Tom watch TV undisturbed. Next thing he
knew, Aunt Rose showed up. He heard the two sisters arguing
first in the kitchen, but when Aunt Sonya began sobbing again,
they moved into the back yard. Then Uncle Alex returned and,
after yet more arguing and pleading and tears, Aunt Rose came
into the living room and turned off the TV. In her hand, Tom's
backpack, his suitcase by her side. "Looks like we'll get to hang
out for a bit," she said, not that Tom believed her fake cheer.

"I'm sorry, Tom," Aunt Sonya said just before they drove off,
"but I'm at my wits' end. I need a break, and it looks to me like
you do, too."

And so Tom moved again. This time in Uncle Alex's smelly car,
heading downtown to live with Aunt Rose. Outside, rows and

rows of houses flew by, each filled with boys who had no clue about how horrible life could be, how mean and totally unfair. Like when he was young and stupid, bursting into tears because of a piñata. Dad was right: He had been one silly boy.

Tom wedged the thumb of his bandaged hand between his teeth. It tasted salty, like the tears he would not shed. Unable to calm himself, Tom pushed the thumb up further into his palate, scraping the broken nail across the tender skin. It took focus not to gag, determination to control the pain, but he was a big boy now, able to keep those useless tears at bay.

"You want one?" asked Aunt Rose, twisting around in the passenger seat, dangling a bag of Liquorice Allsorts. Her lips smiled, but in her eyes, Tom recognized dread.

"Oh, come on," she said, the bag of candy now inches away from Tom's face. "How can you not love them? They were your mom's favourites."

But Tom knew that was a lie. Mom never ate candy, or anything with ingredients she could not pronounce. "It's disgusting," she'd say. "An attempt by the food industry to reap profits while making us sick."

"But Mom," Tom would argue, "do you have any idea how delicious Doritos are?"

"Nope," she'd say, giving him an apple instead. "And quite frankly I don't care."

"Fine then," said Aunt Rose now, popping a bright coloured Allsorts into her mouth. "Your loss, not mine."

★

But that was another lie. Rose wanted Tom to engage. She wanted him to look up, to let her partake in his grief. After all, they were in this together. Mona was dead. A fact that had not stopped Rose from imagining that it was her sister when only last week she got a call from an unlisted number. Her heart had started racing with irrational hope, only to be confronted with a survey about cannabis.

"Thanks for the lift," Rose said, genuinely grateful. She had known Alex for over a decade, yet until she had gone up to his office he had barely registered. Then everything changed. Unlike her panicky sister, her flighty brother or her overly concerned friends, Alex offered no tears, no silver linings, no meaning where clearly there was none. Instead, he was simply there when Rose needed it most.

"I'm glad you're taking him," Alex said as quietly as possible. "She was way over her head, though of course, Sonya wouldn't admit it until her precious carpet was ruined."

By the time Rose had arrived at her sister's house, Sonya had been in full-blown hysterics. "It's too much," she kept sobbing, "I've tried everything, I really have, but nothing sticks. Nothing changes. Not for the better anyway."

"Give him time," Rose tried hard to sound more reassuring. "Remember how long it took us to accept that Mama was not coming back?"

But Sonya was not to be calmed. "It's my fault," she said, over and over and over again. Taking on the weight of the world, like it was her fault that Mona had died. Like she was the only one riddled with guilt.

Alex got off the highway at Strachan Avenue, driving past Liberty Village, one of the many new neighbourhoods that had mushroomed in Toronto over the last few years. Seemingly overnight, glass towers and megastores replaced long-abandoned warehouses, bringing in a whole new, much more affluent crowd into the downtown core.

The adjacent neighbourhood of Queen West, where Rose lived, had not been spared progress, either. Igor the bike thief had long been hauled off to jail, his once decrepit building turned into yet another shop selling overpriced sunglasses, joining an ever-revolving bunch of splashy but mediocre restaurants alongside boutiques selling fashions to anorexic teens. Most of the old-timers were long gone. Like Ernie, the cigar-smoking antique dealer, or the ever-smiling Chungs from Square Fruit Market, and Gay, who had sold penis-shaped bread. Even the Prague Deli closed after forty years in business, its Eastern European counter ladies replaced by hipsters making drinks served with a side of fried pig's ears.

At Bellwoods Park, they turned onto Queen and got stuck behind a streetcar. Rose turned around to check on Tom, who was still staring out the window. Silent, detached, and utterly lost. To think that from now on, she would be responsible for this boy. A boy she barely knew. Absorbed in her own daily dramas, Rose had spent little time wondering why Mona had shown up less and less at the cottage, why the invitations for Tom's birthdays stop coming, what had happened to her sister's love of Christmas dinner.

"You'll stay in Will's room for now," Rose said, unable to bear the silence anymore. "When he gets back, you'll have to share a room with Nick. Unlike Sonya, we don't have billion bedrooms at our disposal but really, it's not that bad. Sonya and I used to share that very room, and we managed just fine."

"Now *that* I find hard to believe," said Alex. But he just did not understand. Rose had loved sharing a room with her older sister, who was a six whole years wiser to the world. It was Sonya who had hated having an audience, even if it was an adoring one.

But Rose's joy and Sonya's purgatory did not last. Tato's plumbing business took off, and the family upgraded to a brand-new, fully detached house north of Highway 7, with a bedroom for each of the four children and one more to spare. A dream come true for her parents, who'd arrived in Canada with little

60

more than their will to succeed. Rose had felt diminished by the empty space around her, frightened by the silence, lonely even, but Sonya had adored their new, squeaky-clean home, and refused to live downtown ever since.

"Did you know that traffic in Toronto is worse than in LA?" asked Alex, as he honked at a cyclist trying to turn left, blocking the way.

"Please, Alex, don't be an ass," said Rose.

"Why doesn't the moron move over or better yet cross at the light? It's jerks like him that create this gridlock."

"Cyclists, obviously, are not the problem. Drivers are."

Alex rolled his eyes and turned on the news. More atrocities in Syria, arrests in Turkey, the far right on the rise again in Europe. Rose finished the Allsorts and turned off the radio. Life was already tough; no reason to make it tougher by imagining the misery of others.

"Is there anything in particular that you like to do, Tom?" asked Rose, determined not to let the boy's silence get to her. She would succeed where her sister had failed. "What do you like to eat? Make? Watch? Listen to? Play? Read?"

"Nice try, Rose," said Alex, gunning the car to escape Queen. "Sonya went through all those at least once a day."

On Claremont Street, the level of activity dropped immediately. Here, crappy, yet-to-be-renovated, turn-of-the-last-century homes stacked tightly as if they needed one another's support not to fall apart.

Just north of Robinson, Alex pulled up onto the sidewalk. The black-clad Portuguese widow from next door shook her head and returned to sweeping her already swept yard. In Rose's own front yard a cracked planter stood at the end of an equally cracked walkway, all of it blanketed with dandelions and clover and last year's decomposing leaves from an unpruned linden.

46 Claremont was a narrow, two-storey sliver of a house, the first in a row of four once-identical homes built for immigrants from the poorer parts of Eastern Europe. Now, after years of neglect and ill-advised upgrades, each of them had acquired a distinctive look. Next door, red paint flaked off the brick façade, a scattering of flyers indicating that Colin, an eccentric impresario, was off on yet another tour of the Far East. Another door up, the house was clad in angel stone bricks to match the paved-over yard, and next to that, a pair of young professionals hoped to give their home cachet by wasting money on cedar siding.

"Home sweet home," Rose said, relieved like an exhausted explorer reaching port. It was thanks to Tato's most surprising spurt of generosity that she had been able to return to Claremont, her childhood home, eight months after giving birth to Nick. To the surprise of no one, Eugene failed to rise to the challenge of being a father, never mind a provider. "Why rent the place to strangers when my grandson needs a home?" Tato had said, allowing no dissent, not even from Sonya, who complained bitterly about deserving a fair share, too.

"Want to come in for a drink or something, Alex?" asked Rose, reluctant to face time with Tom alone.

"Traffic's going to be a bitch," replied Alex, "But I will take a rain cheque. Please."

Rose got out of the car and pulled Tom's bag from the trunk. "Well, you know where to find me."

By the time she opened the front door, Tom was still staring off into nowhere, sucking his thumb. Saliva was now dripping from his mouth.

"You can stay with Alex," Rose said, "that's fine. Me, I'm going in."

Immediately, Tom jumped out of the car and dashed inside the house.

"Good luck," said Alex just before driving off. "You'll need it. Both of you."

"Better eat it while it's hot," said Rose, as she settled down in front of the TV. "This stuff won't improve with age."

Tom curled deeper into the velour recliner that used to be Tato's favourite, refusing to even look at his Kraft dinner. Rose had been warned about that too. "He eats," Sonya had said, "but never when you think he will." Leftovers would disappear from the fridge, cookies from the jar, "but put a plate in front of him," Sonya complained, "and he'll wrinkle his nose as though it's shit."

"That's one awesome chair, right? Your grandpapa's girlfriend didn't like it, but it's comfy and in furniture as well as in men, that's what counts."

No reaction. None.

"Is there something else you'd like to eat? A grilled cheese sandwich? Peanut butter and jam toast?"

No reply.

"How about a drink? Hot chocolate? Tea? I'm thinking Tension Tamer."

Rose stopped. Questions clearly weren't getting her anywhere.

"When I was a kid, I was a bit of a loner, too. So it's okay to be quiet. Really."

She paused.

"Do you like to read? Reading has always done it for me."

Rose waited some more.

"How about going to the Science Centre? I hear they have a great exhibit on lizards and snakes."

Again she waited.

"Wanna check out the nude beach on the island?"

Finally, a glance.

"Cool, we'll go tomorrow."

Tom slid his thumb into his mouth. Suck. Suck. Suck. Suck. Suck.

"I was kidding. Obviously." Rose picked up the remote and started to flick.

She'd be damned if she'd repeat Sonya's mistakes. She would not get all frazzled and mad. Take personal what was not. Impose her will on the boy. There was no point. It took nerves to raise a kid. Rose knew, after all she had not only survived Nick's projectile vomiting but also lice (thrice).

Nick returned at 9:30 p.m., wearing his "I'm not a hipster" T-shirt, paired with his equally ironic, if contradictory, trucker hat that spelled out "LOSER" in red capitals.

"I know you're on holidays," said Rose, muting the TV, "but we agreed on nine o'clock. Remember?"

"Ryan lost his wallet, so we didn't get to his place 'til five, and then we were starving, so we got snacks. And anyway, he gets to stay out 'til ten, so it's totally not fair that I've got to be home so early."

At fourteen, Nick had become a full-blown teen almost overnight. His voice had dropped an octave, his smell turned funky, and he now towered over Rose. Yet sometimes he still reverted to being her sweet little boy—telling her about Steve, who snorted Ritalin to lose weight, or Ms. Chapman, a teacher he adored, even if it was deeply uncool to excel in math. But those moments of easy intimacy were growing rare. And sadly, unlike a book she could put down to make the good parts last longer, there was no stopping her son's trajectory out into the world, away from her.

"What's he doing here?" Nick asked, pointing at Tom.

"He's going to stay with us now," said Rose. "It's for the better, and anyways, I think we'll have fun."

"Cool," said Nick, pre-empting Rose from going on. "Hey,

you're done with that, am I right?" he asked, grabbing Tom's untouched plate without waiting for an answer.

Tom did not even blink.

Nick, taking Tom's non-reaction as a sign of approval, dug in. Like his father, whom he had not seen in years, Nick balanced his fork awkwardly between middle and index finger. Thankfully, he had not shown any interest in juggling eggs, painting rabbits, or pyramid schemes.

"*Murdoch Mysteries*," said Nick between hungry bites, "blows, Mom. It's Canadian."

"How's Carmen?" asked Rose, flicking over to *Destroyed in Seconds*.

"What are you talking about? I was at Ryan's, and anyway, she's not even at my school anymore."

Rose decided not to mention the hickey just below her son's left ear. She had put him on alert, and that was enough.

★

The smell of bacon made it impossible for Tom to wait any longer. He opened his eyes and looked around at what used to be Uncle Will's room but was now his. Dappled light streamed in through a thick layer of vines that grew outside the window facing the backyard. All four walls of the small, almost square room were covered in wood panelling painted yellow. Dustballs gathered along the baseboards. A radio sat in the corner with its innards exposed, next to it a bass guitar with two strings missing, though still connected to an amp.

Tom slipped out of bed to pull off his damp pyjamas. After struggling for hours to fall asleep, he had woken feeling all warm and cosy and perfectly at peace. A sensation so unreal, so unburdened and free, he knew it could not be true. And sure enough, before long, his pee turned cold, serenity gave way to panic, and then, for the rest of the night, he was condemned to wait yet again in his puddle of shame.

Tom pulled his suitcase out of the closet and a pile of sweaters tumbled down on him. He stuffed them back as best he could, though it was unlikely anyone would notice. None of Uncle Will's clothes were folded right. "Are you a pig or are you a human?" Mom would have asked, making Tom fold the sweaters one by one. Mom couldn't stand disorder. It made her sad.

Tom opened his suitcase. Underneath his Maple Leaf sweater (which was already too small for him) and Mom's blue album, he found his army of Transformers. Somebody, probably Aunt Sonya, had thrown the whole lot into the case, and now wings and guns and limbs and swords were all mangled and weird. Not that Tom cared. He was long past hoping to be saved by stupid toys.

Tom ditched his wet pyjamas and slammed the suitcase shut. Then he pulled on his hoodie and ventured out into the hallway. The wooden floorboards creaked with every step. Nick's bedroom was closed, but the bathroom door stood open, revealing the toilet seat up, a mirror freckled with long-dried toothpaste spatter and an abandoned sock on the floor. "People who live in a mess are a mess," Mom would have said. But Tom wasn't so sure. After all, Aunt Sonya's place had been spotless.

Tom walked past Aunt Rose's room—bed unmade and the floor strewn with clothes—before making his way down worn-out stairs to the kitchen, where he found Nick cracking eggs into a bowl.

"What's up?" asked Nick, when he noticed Tom hovering by the door. "Mom's out, but don't worry, she'll be back soon." Then he slid the eggs into the pan and buttered his toast.

"Sit. You're making me nervous," said Nick, turning his attention to flipping his omelette, leaving Tom to check out the kitchen. It was a narrow room with double glass doors opening out into a small, fenced backyard. Above the kitchen table, a window looked out onto the cracked brick of the house next door. The windowsill was crowded with stained cookbooks, sun-melted candles, rocks, and a hairbrush. The huge, old-fashioned gas stove was dirty with grease. In the sink onion peels bonded with soggy pieces of charred toast, joined by an assortment of dirty dishes and pans. A fork slimy with raw egg had escaped onto the floor. Mom was wrong, Tom thought. There was something cosy about this mess, something just right.

★

When Rose got home, she found Nick fiddling with his phone and Tom sitting across the kitchen table, watching.

"Isn't that nice? The two of you bonding … Hey, what's this?" Rose put down her four bags of groceries and pointed at the lone dirtied plate. "Nick! Where's Tom's breakfast?"

"I didn't know it was my job to feed him."

Rose kicked her son's chair: "I told you to be nice."

"I offered."

"And what? He said no? Did he say no?"

"Mom," said Nick as he stood up, "he's not going to starve to death, so just let him be."

Rose watched her son leave. He had a point. Still, she plonked down a bowl of Captain Crunch in front of Tom. Just to be safe.

Then she put away the groceries and got busy with washing the dishes. Pretending not to care that Tom hadn't so much as acknowledged her presence, Rose built a two-foot-high pyramid of freshly rinsed cups and bowls and plates, topped by a spatula, three knives and a whisk. "Mount Dishmore!" she declared, turning around with a proud smile.

Tom didn't even look.

67

"Really? You're not going to check out my feat of dish engineering?"

Not a blink.

"Not even for a second?"

How was it possible for a boy to sit still like that? Nick had never been able to stay put for long, unless it involved a movie featuring aliens or hobbits or both.

"A millisecond?"

"A picosecond?"

Was that a smile? Rose waited one more minute before conceding. There was no smile. No nod. Nothing.

"Not sure if you've heard," she finally said, bent now on getting the boy to engage, "but this ain't no hotel. Around here, you've gotta help out, or I'll have to send you back to Sonya."

Immediately, Tom jumped up, grabbed his bowl, and took Captain Crunch for a swim. Quickly, he added Nick's plate to the sink, followed by the cutlery and Rose's half-drunk cup of coffee.

"Tom, I was teasing," said Rose, instantly ashamed. For what did she expect? That the boy would snap out of his torpor just because she made a callous joke? That he would be impressed by her pile of dishes, start to speak just because she wanted him to? Whatever she had learned by raising Nick, clearly did not apply here.

"I'm sorry," Rose said. "I love you, obviously, and this is your home. We will never let you go."

Tom, unmoved by her pleading, swung around—on the lookout for more items to wash. Rose's teacup from last night. A spoon that had escaped under the counter. A bowl of mouldy peaches. Turning toward the living room to scour for more, Tom's sleeve caught on a wooden spoon that stuck out from under the pile of dishes.

One step forward, two steps back, Rose thought, as pots, pans, plates and cups slid off the counter and crashed onto the floor. She had wanted a reaction, and gotten what she deserved.

Tom stopped running only at the far end of the living room. Then he turned slowly, his eyes open wide, both hands curled into fists. Expecting violence, Rose realized with a start.

"Oh, please don't worry, sweetheart," she said, stepping over the mess. "It's just a bunch of old crap. In fact, this is a perfect excuse to get those matching dishes Sonya has been on about for years."

Then, instead of waiting for an answer she knew wouldn't come, she turned on the TV. "There," she said, putting the remote on the sofa. "You can watch whatever you want. For however long you want. No more questions asked."

Rose returned to the kitchen, discarded the shards and started mopping the floor. Now more than ever, she was in awe of her mother, who for years had managed to keep the house spick-and-span, despite four children and a husband who expected a meal on the table by six o'clock sharp. All the while she sewed dresses for the girls, knitted sweaters, ironed shirts, trousers, and underwear. She had also handled bookkeeping for her husband's expanding plumbing business, volunteered at the North Toronto Cat Rescue, and enrolled each of the kids in the sport of his or her choice. But then, Mama had buckled under the load. Spending days, sometimes weeks, without leaving the house only to bounce back miraculously, until one day, she did not.

Rose went into the basement, pulled a load of T-shirts out of the washer and tossed them into the dryer. She ought to hang them—better for the environment and for the fabrics, too—but she could not be bothered. The Homemaker-of-the-Year-Award would have to go to Sonya yet again.

Rose had long given up on perfection. Instead, years of sleep deprivation had given her a near-psychotic ability to imagine horrific outcomes of even the most mundane situations. Five minutes late to pick Nick up at school, Rose envisioned strangers stepping in to kidnap the boy. What if the swing's chain broke and Nick crashed to the ground, injuring his spine and condemning him to life as a paraplegic? What if she got hit by a bus, dying before Nick had learned to look out for himself? She had no plan B, all the more worrying because she was now responsible for two boys instead of only one.

Tato's Plan B had been Sonya. Rose still remembered when her sister had returned from Montreal. Pretending to be all grown-up and sophisticated, when really she was just as lost as them. A know-it-all who burned dinners and ruined Rose's favourite sweater by throwing it into the dryer. And things did not improve when Rose became a mother herself. "You do know that the nutritional value of gummy bears is zero, right?" Sonya commented, when Rose finally figured out a way to get Nick to bed without a fight. "Kids, especially boys, need to help out around the house, otherwise they will turn into sexist slugs later," she'd say, blissfully unaware that a teen's clumsy attempts at housekeeping produce more work, rather than less. And now, after years of armchair parenting, Sonya had lasted only couple of months. If only the irony wouldn't taste quite so bitter.

Rose was loading towels into the washing machine when Tom came down the basement stairs, his sheets dragging behind him like the train of a deranged bride's wedding dress.

"Wow, you do your own laundry? That's so sweet. Thank you," said Rose.

The boy dumped the load and turned to leave.

"Listen, Tom. What I said earlier, that was a joke. A stupid joke, obviously. It's just sometimes, I can't help myself. Stuff slips out of my mouth before—"

But Tom was already gone.

The boy's silence was eerie, unnerving even, but Rose respected his choice. None of her talking had brought her closer to understanding even the most basic facts. She knew her sister was dead. Killed by her husband, who then shot himself. But how could Rose relate those realities to the Mona she knew? The dancing, laughing, breathing sister she missed every single day? And she missed not only her sister. It was shameful to admit but Rose missed Russell, too. For he had been part of their family almost since she could remember. On Boxing Day he'd make a pancake breakfast; on Victoria Day he'd light up the sky with his fireworks, and now that he was gone, nobody had opened the cottage, leaving it abandoned for the first summer ever.

Rose picked up Tom's sheets and immediately felt the damp pee stain. She ought to be more patient with the boy, gentler too. Maybe she should take that yoga class her friend Martha had been on about, cut down on coffee, and... but before her thoughts of self-improvement veered further off course, Rose was interrupted by a knock on the front door. A sound so rare, she could not imagine who it could possibly be. It had been years since the last Jehovah's Witness tried to save her soul or Greenpeace pleaded for the whales. She dumped the sheets on a pile of whites and made her way up the stairs. This had better be worth her while.

"Hello, Ms. Micha ... Mickajo ... Michel ... ." Rose had opened the front door to a slender man in his early forties. He looked up and smiled awkwardly, before returning to his notes, determined to pronounce her name. "Ms. Mickela ... "

"Michajelovich, but whatever you're selling, I'm not interested, thanks," said Rose. She tried to shut the door, but the man jammed his well-worn boot into the doorway.

"I'm not selling anything," he said, extending his hand. "I'm

Raymond Lafond, Ray. I'm with Children's Aid. I've been calling but nobody ever answers."

Rose stepped back just enough to check Ray out. His hair was in need of a cut, his corduroy jacket a tad heavy considering the late summer heat, but his T-shirt and jeans were nicely worn in, just like those boots.

"Why would you call the landline?" said Rose. "Nobody calls the landline. I'm not even sure why I still have it."

"Anyway," said Ray, "I'm here because we've been advised that Tom no longer resides with his appointed guardian." Again his eyes shifted down to his folder. "Sonya Fleming," he read, with obvious relief at being able to pronounce the name. "It's our responsibility to ensure that the child is adequately housed, so I'm here to check in, to make sure Tom's safe."

"He's safe," said Rose.

"Good. But to be honest, I'd like to come in. Have a word with you and the boy. Discuss what to do next."

"Not sure if you heard, but Tom's not much of a talker."

"I've heard." Ray put away his file, waiting for Rose to let him in.

"I'm actually super busy right now," she finally said. "How about coming back later? Like sometime next week."

"Well, that's not how this works Ms. Mickle … . May I just call you Rose?"

"Sure."

"Great. Thanks. So yes," Ray pauses. Then, seeing that Rose was not about to budge, he shifted his voice into a darker, more authoritarian tone. "May I please come in?"

"Do I have a choice?"

"No," Ray said, his smile now sad, rather than kind. "Not really."

Under the gaze of a stranger, the bohemian chic of Rose's living room instantly lost all its allure. The travel trunk that doubled as a coffee table looked shabby, Eugene's triple-life-size oil painting of a rabbit just seemed bizarre. Undeterred, Ray settled into Tato's recliner, folding his slender hands as though about to lead them in prayer.

"Now, first up, let me assure you that we're aware that this is a very difficult situation for all parties involved," said Ray. He glanced over at Tom, who sat on the sofa next to Rose, still staring at the TV as if it had not been turned off. "There are numerous programs available to you, and your family," Ray continued, now focusing on Rose, "and I will do my best to help you navigate all that but if there's anything specific you are wondering about, please do not hesitate to ask. I'm here to assist you in this most difficult situation."

Rose nodded, hoping that would suffice. She was not going to ask a stranger for help, however well-intentioned, however handsome.

"Given the unsettled nature of your current arrangement, the Society will need to—"

"Really?" Rose asked, folding her arms, determined not to blink. "Society cares? Since when?"

"The Children's Aid Society," responded Ray, pronouncing *so-ci-e-ty* one syllable at a time. "In the coming weeks, the Society will conduct a home study to assess the suitability of the current situation. As you're probably aware by now, the Office of the Children's Lawyer will deal with issues pertaining to Tom's inheritance, but we will also conduct an assessment of your financial situation, to make sure that transferring Tom into your care is economically feasible. And then there's the question of his education. He will have to resume his schooling in September, and the last thing we want is for him to change schools during the term.

Once the home study has been completed, the Society will assess, in conjunction with a qualified psychologist, if the current situation is indeed suitable for the boy."

"Suitable? What do you mean by suitable? Of course we are suitable. We're his family."

"Family, as you well know, does not guarantee safety."

Rose pinched her arms, trying hard to remain calm.

"Rose, I know this must feel like an enormous invasion of your privacy, but please keep in mind that we do both want the same thing: to find an arrangement for Tom that will help him to heal. Unless there are blatant irregularities, a record of gross negligence, continued violence, or substantiated reports of misconduct, I'm confident that a mutually agreeable solution can and will be found."

Rose was just about to explain that the most mutually agreeable solution was for Ray to leave and never come back, when she felt Tom leaning into her. Surprised, she looked over just as he burrowed his hand into hers, like a baby bird cradled into its nest. A first.

"How about a cup of tea?" she asked Ray, as she closed her fingers around the boy's. She would do whatever it took to protect this child, and if opening her house to a perfect stranger was part of the deal, so be it.

*

Will's friend Jimmy had lied. Teaching pre-K at a Korean hagwon was no picnic, if keeping eight four-year-olds under control could even be called teaching. Child taming was more like it. Parental crutch. Time killer. These kids didn't even know how to sit still for more than three minutes. How could he teach them anything, let alone English?

Having scoured the Internet for tips, Will started to sing: "If you're happy and you know it, clap your hands!" Clap. Clap. Then got the kids to draw flowers, trees, moons, suns, and stars. Next he pointed to his nose and said: "Nose." His ears, "Ears." His mouth, "Mouth." Repeating those same three damn words until even lazy-eyed Angelina got them. This was nothing like working with adults, which Will hadn't loved either, but had endured for years to finance his travels. No surprise that Jimmy had taken off to Bali.

The free housing turned out to be a tiny room in a shared apartment, furnished with a threadbare futon and a stash of Jimmy's fake-fashion finds, in a neon-lit high-rise that reeked of rotten cabbage. His roommates, Jason, a six-foot-two slob from Texas, and Chastity, a cheery-faced do-gooder from Wisconsin, were pissed at Jimmy for running off. Totally not cool, they kept saying every time they saw Will, so totally not cool.

"I need you to understand that I'm doing this as a favour to Jimmy," the school principal, Ms. Yoon, told Will upon his arrival. The frown on her unyielding face looked as tight as the hair bun glued to the back of her tiny head. "The parents like Jimmy, and I suppose the children do, too—which is why I allowed him go on this holiday and let you sub in for him despite your obvious lack of credentials. But, in return, you will have to take on two extra classes."

"Jimmy told me I wouldn't have to—"

"If you want this job, comply. If not, feel free to leave, but you'd have to vacate your room immediately. There are plenty of qualified teachers eager to jump right in, and Jimmy will have to start from scratch."

Will shut up and returned to his airless classroom, the walls covered with cheerful posters, every corner stuffed with bright-coloured plastic toys. Sitting on their floor cushions, his gaggle of kids waited to be entertained. "If you're happy and you know it, clap your hands." Clap. Clap. Thank God for *Inside a Korean Hagwon: Managing Pre-K*. Praise the kids, recommended the shaggy-haired hipster in his YouTube video, give them compliments, compliments, and then a few more compliments. Thankfully, he was right. It worked like a charm.

"Look at Jin, he's such a great helper."

"See how well Mary is drawing?"

"Slowwww aaaas aaaa tuuuurrrrttttle, quiiiiiet aaaas..."

After finishing his two extra classes, Will set off on foot. Every night, he explored the city, nestled on the southeasternmost tip of the peninsula between the mountains and the sea. Far from being the quaint little town Will had imagined, Busan was an urban jungle of concrete high-rises plastered with garish neon signs and billboards advertising plastic surgery and online dating. After centuries of deprivation, this was a nation caught in the thrill of consumerism. Markets stayed open all night, crammed with stalls hawking electronic gadgets, cheap fashions, trinkets, and of course, food. A lot of it. Everywhere. Ramshackle restaurants frying up mouth-watering pork, pushcarts offering spicy rice cakes on sticks, plastic tubs filled to the brim with phallic-looking worms, baby octopuses (to be eaten alive), raw abalone (not that bad), and stewed silkworm larvae (revolting).

Finally, Will reached the beach. The din of the city dropped off sharply the closer he approached the shore. Beyond a strip of darkness, the horizon was aflame with lights of fishing boats, hauling in their daily loot to slake the insatiable appetite of a seafood-obsessed nation.

Not far from the north end of the Gwangalli beach, Will arrived at his destination, Millak Raw Fish Town. Maybe because he no longer was interested in getting drunk every night, he had yet to make friends. And so, for the eighteenth night in a row, he faced dinner by himself.

The busy fish market took up the entire first floor of a glass-clad, ten-story building. Mullet. Flounder. Scallops. Eels. Will wondered around aimlessly until two middle-aged women with identical yellow aprons and perm-curled hair zeroed in on him, trying their best to peddle their wares, despite Will's inability to respond in Korean. He settled on raw sea bream to eat upstairs. Hwe, the Koreans called it. Like Japanese sashimi but served so fresh it sometimes still wiggled on the plate.

Will wedged his feet under the low plastic-covered table and dug into the banchan, colourful side dishes he had come to love. Seasoned seaweed, steamed shishito peppers, spicy squid, kong-namul muchim, and of course, kimchi. Pungent, garlicky, and oh so delicious. A table away, a girl, cute in that Birkenstocks/ripped jeans kind of way, smiled.

"Hi," she said.

Will looked behind him, before realizing she was talking to him. "Hi?" he responded. Unsure.

"Where are you from?" she asked.

"Toronto. You?"

"Iowa."

"Cool."

"You're funny."

Will laughed. "Well, thank you."

"You alone?" she asked.

Again, Will looked around him. "You mean aside from my imaginary friends?"

"I'm Marissa," the girl said, "How about a Soju bomb? I hate drinking alone."

"Sure," said Will. "Why not?"

"두 개의 폭탄 소주 하십시오," said Marissa, ordering their cocktails and laughing when she noticed Will's surprise. Her laughter came up from deep within her, like water gushing forth from a broken pipe. "I pick up the basics wherever I go," she told Will, who could not believe his luck: an American girl who spoke Korean. "It makes travelling so much more fun, don't you think?"

Three Soju bombs later, they stumbled out into the street. The world so much softer and fun.

"I bet my place is cosier than yours," Marissa said, after their first sloppy kiss. In her apartment overlooking the beach, they fell onto the funky-smelling sheets of her unmade bed. They laughed and drank and fucked and laughed until night turned into day. And then, instead of getting up and going to work, Will closed his eyes and fell asleep.

*

Back in Toronto, dressed in her favourite grey suit and new heels, Sonya scanned through the 800-plus emails that had accumulated in her absence from work. Most of them were spams, scams, and outdated *New York Times* news bulletins, plus a few belated condolences. Mona's death had made the papers, so nobody at C&C Consulting was surprised when Sonya stayed away from the office. "You want another month off? Please, take two," J.D., the head of HR, said when she asked for additional time to look after Tom. "Of course," he said. "Anything you need to tend to that poor child." But her gratitude had been spoiled when she called last week to announce her early return. "You sure you're ready?" J.D. had asked. "Because, really, we're managing just fine." He sounded squirmy, reluctant even. As if her presence might bring the stench of death into the office.

"It's so awesome to have you back," said Kiara, as she entered Sonya's office without bothering to knock. Clad in a perfectly tailored suit, she dropped off a cup of coffee, just as she had every morning Sonya had worked with her. At the beginning, Kiara had been Sonya's assistant. Now, not even thirty, Kiara was her boss.

Maybe to soften the blow, she kept delivering the coffee; and to-day more than ever, Sonya was grateful.

"Okay, so here's the scoop," Kiara said, as she parked herself on the corner of Sonya's desk. "Raheem's giving up on that Internet dating thing. Too many space aliens out there looking for love, he says, though I'm not sure if he's looked into the mirror lately. Oh, and speaking of space aliens, we're pretty sure Cheryl got another boob job. And Leila from HR is back with that jerk, even though he still won't move in with her."

Sonya tried not to feel bitter about Kiara's promotion to head accountant, a position that by all rights should have been hers. Kiara was married to one of the partners, and as Mama used to say, jealousy gives you nothing but ugly lines around the mouth. She was right, of course, but as Sonya grew older and doors started to close, it proved increasingly exhausting to remain kind.

"It's great to be back," said Sonya, surprised to find that that really was the truth. After Kiara left, she took a sip of her coffee, kicked off her pumps, and opened up the Ferguson account. In an ever-shifting, uncertain world, Ferguson's haggling about their payment schedule was balm for her weary soul. A rock upon which she could rest for the remainder of the day, far away from Tom—and even from thoughts of Mona.

But the thrill of reclaiming her professional life quickly crumbled under the weight of averted eyes, embarrassed hugs, and clumsy, ill-considered condolences. "I'm sorry that you lost your brother in a car crash," she told Leila, making it to the wash-room before bursting into tears. Why did people feel the need to compare? Mona had been murdered, by her husband, in her own home, nothing to do with drunk drivers on icy roads. "Yes, Raheem," she said, but only after he had left her office, "life goes on, but what on earth for?" And then Cheryl assured her that everything would be okay, the trick is, she said, to keep breathing!

Somehow, miraculously, Sonya managed not to scream: "No, Cheryl. It's not going to be okay. My sister is dead, dead, dead, dead, dead!"

At five o'clock sharp, Sonya let out a sigh of relief. She shut off her computer and snuck out of the office without saying good-bye. By the time she made it down to the subway, the blister on her right foot had popped. Wearing new heels had been stupid; not bringing a backup pair of loafers? Idiotic. She found a bench and pulled her feet out of her shoes, luxuriating in the flow of blood rushing back into her crushed toes. All around her, people hurried home to make dinner, commuting to a second job, going out for the night to eat, dance, have fun. Full of purpose and hope, something Sonya suddenly felt without. Across the tracks, she noticed a woman who, like Sonya herself, sat alone in the midst of rush hour. Her head bopped along to the unheard rhythms on her phone, her youthful face open, unaware of just how cruel life could be.

When Sonya got home, her house felt like a big empty shell. So many rooms, and no one around to fill them with. She slid her favourite frozen pizza—spinach and cheese—into the oven and opened a bottle of red wine. It's practically medicinal, she rationalized, if you keep it to a single glass. Plus, she deserved it.

Ever since they'd met, Alex had insisted on his Thursday Night Out with the boys. Sonya would never admit it, but she enjoyed this weekly evening by herself. No dinner to cook, no conversation to initiate, no compromises to endure. No expectations to be lowered, no disappointment to hide.

Glass in hand, Sonya walked into Tom's room and sat down on his bed, gently stroking the Spiderman sheets, already soft from needing to be washed so many times. Not once had he sat at his desk, or played the board games she had bought. How silly that she'd bothered to paint the walls. It had done nothing to make the boy feel more at home, and now she would have to redo the décor all over.

The oven's beeping made Sonya return to the kitchen. The crust of her pizza was thin and perfectly crisp. With the chilies from Terroni's this was a perfect, if nutritionally questionable, treat. To atone, she would wear sensible shoes tomorrow, get off the subway five stops early, and walk the rest of the way to work.

After a bath and two more glasses of wine, Sonya settled into the far corner of the living room sofa, Tom's former spot. On the carpet below, she noticed the birthmark-like smudge that his blood had left behind. Sonya had tried to clean it away. She had sworn, she had cried, she had cursed and cried some more, but the stain would not come out. Finally, she resigned to let it be. A reminder that at least she had tried.

To fill the void that had settled all around her, Sonya turned on the TV, but no matter how high she turned up the volume, it did nothing to assuage her feeling of gloom. How silly to long for a person who had been so impossible to live with. A slurping volcano of pain. A vortex of misery. Unresponsive. Sad.

Embarrassed by her unkindness, Sonya switched to CNN. A fake blonde with an even faker smile droned on about the latest suicide bomber blowing up a bus somewhere in the Middle East, killing fifty-three. With so much anger in this world, how was it possible not to let it wear you down?

Sonya slid her hand into the pocket of her bathrobe and found a small tube of Ste. Anne's foot cream. A thank-you present from Mona for taking her to the spa on the shore of Lake Ontario. It had been a freakishly warm day in March. The kind that gives you hopes for an early spring, even though snow still covered most of the frozen ground.

"Everything's fine," Mona had said, while buckling her seatbelt, but Sonya had a hard time believing it. Her sister's eyes were red, and Russell had just lost his job. Which one, Sonya was not sure. It was hard to keep up with his ever-evolving attempts to strike gold. The more strident Russell became about the injustices of life, the more Mona had pulled back, spending hours, days on the sofa, concocting elaborate dinner menus that she never managed to cook. Instead, surprised that Tom was already back from school, she'd scrambled to pull something, anything, out of the freezer.

The sisters' trip to the spa was Sonya's attempt to get Mona off the sofa and out of her funk. Sonya was hoping for a heart-to-heart talk, the kind they used to have before Mona married Russell and everything changed. She knew that Russell lost his temper from time to time, about a hole punched in the wall, a light switch broken. She had been worried, of course, but each time she broached the subject, Mona had pulled back further. "It's fine," she'd say. "It's just how he is."

At the spa, Sonya had been lulled into complacency by the serenity of the surroundings, the overwhelming kindness of the staff. Instead of talking with her sister, instead of probing more deeply into what was going on, Sonya closed her eyes and let the hands of strangers massage away her fears.

By the time they returned to Toronto, winter had reclaimed its rightful place. Hail was followed by sleet, followed by twenty centimetres of snow. Shorts were put away for another couple of months, mitts and hats retrieved. Just as the unseasonable warmth had made the oncoming cold all the more bitter, the sisters' brief spell of serenity seemed reckless in light of what was to come.

The foot cream felt soothing on Sonya's aching feet. She replaced the cap and weighed the tube in her hand, a token of Mona's love.

The TV news broke for commercials, prompting Sonya to flip through the channels. A rerun of *Murdoch Mysteries* on CBC. Guys talking about fishing. Brides freaking out over finding the perfect dress, as if one could buy a perfect day, or that would guarantee a charmed life.

Sonya muted the TV. What if Tom really was better off with Rose? It wouldn't be the first time that Claremont had turned out to be a safe haven. Her own parents had found refuge there after a long journey that took them from rural Ukraine through Eastern Europe, a yearlong stint in Essen, Germany, and finally to downtown Toronto. They had loved that crooked house, despite its creaky stairs, draughty windows and a basement full of paint cans dating back to the 1930s. It was the first home they had ever owned, and the one Tato had refused to sell. A good investment, he rightfully claimed. But Sonya suspected that he kept it because it was a door to the past, a reminder of a time when his wife's ups outweighed her downs, when their future still felt open and bright.

What would have happened to the family, to Mama, Sonya wondered now, if they had stayed downtown? Withstood the temptation to buy-up? To live in a place that revealed their new-found wealth rather than conceal it? What if they had kept in touch with the people who had become surrogate family in this new country? People like the Sawatzkys, who never managed to save enough money to buy a home, or Uncle Andriy, who wasn't really an uncle at all, but who came over most weekends to play *durak* in the backyard. A community of fellow immigrants replaced after the move to the suburbs by people with names everyone could pronounce, who had no accents, no shared stories of survival.

Sonya finished her wine and got up from the sofa, overcome with a sudden urge to speak to Rose. Maybe being miserable together was better than to endure alone. Maybe there was something she could do to help out, *should* do to help out. She grabbed her phone and dialled, but then she hung up. What if Tom was now eating his dinners, doing his homework, laughing out loud? What if there were living happily ever after on Claremont while she was stuck in this empty place, still alone, a failure yet again. No, Sonya decided and poured herself another glass of wine, she would not call, she could not.

★

Marissa, the girl from Iowa, decided to go for a swim, but Will wasn't sure. Haeundae Beach, so busy during the day that sometimes it was hard to find a spot to lay down, now stretched out empty before them in both directions.

"Come on, scaredy-cat," she yelled, already in the water up to her knees. "If I can do it, so can you."

Emboldened by liquor-induced invincibility, Will shed his clothes and followed her into the frigid water. That girl had no right to call him timid. Immediately, his penis shrivelled to the size of a baby carrot. Unsure of where Marissa had gone, Will inched forward into the darkness that was broken only by the distant lights of fishing boats and the stark moon above.

These had been strange, but exhilarating, weeks. Every night, Will met up with Marissa, and they had sex. In his apartment, with his roommate Skyping next door, turning up her volume to drown out Marissa's moans, or her apartment—preferable—even if it took Will almost an hour to get there after work. And then they'd go out. For beer, food, beer, soju, and yet more beer. By nine o'clock, their speech would slur and by eleven it was hard not to sway. After more food, and possibly more sex, they'd go for another round of drinks, falling into bed at three in the morning. As excruciating as teaching had been before Marissa, Will's near constant hangovers made the children's sharp little voices worse yet, each shriek causing more pain, pushing him closer to towards the edge.

84

"Where are you?" Will yelled now, but the only answer he got was the sound of breaking waves. The drunken haze was suddenly all but gone. Bits of plastic floated by, a stone jabbed into his left foot, and when he turned back toward the beach, a stray dog barked at the water's edge. "Marissa," he called out, "this isn't funny!"

That's when he saw a foot jutting out of the water, ten meters away. "What the fuck kind of game is this?" Will yelled, rushing toward the spot, only to have Marissa disappear before he got there. He scanned the rough surface of the jet-black sea, but around him was nothing but the waves' unrelenting crash and roar. This was no game. Not anymore.

Then, just to his left, a mass of long blonde hair bobbed up to the surface, floating like loose algae, only to submerge yet again. Will splashed forward into the darkness, moving as fast as he possibly could through the choppy sea, the salty water making him gag, his heart feeling like it might burst apart, his muscles screaming out in pain. When at last, he reached Marissa, her body swayed in the waves, limp, barely alive. It took three tries to get her onto her back and into a Cross Chest Carry, a technique Will had practiced in the water-safety classes he had taken as a teenager. Holding onto the slippery body of a girl he barely knew, he pushed as hard as he could towards the shore. Feeling her life drain away despite all his efforts, he experienced a feeling so lonely, so disconnected, so sad, that it made him want to give up, to simply be swallowed up by oblivion, to just let go and drown.

But then Mona appeared in his mind's eye. Her broken body sprawled on the bedroom floor, Tom trying to shake her awake, not letting go until the paramedics pulled him away. Determined to not fail the girl he had laughed with, drunk with, slept with, Will pushed forward, adrenaline dulling his pain, along with all doubt.

Then, at long last, he felt the shore beneath his feet. An old woman in gum boots helped to pull Marissa's blue-tinted body out of the water. She yelled at him, shaking her head, pointing at his naked body and the unconscious girl at his feet. Will didn't need to know Korean to understand that she thought he was a stupid fuck-up. And of course she was right. As the woman ran off to get help, Will tilted Marissa's head back and placed his stacked hands at the centre of her chest. Pushing down hard, he started compressions. Then, pinching her nose, inhaling deeply, he put his lips back onto hers, exhaling hard into her mouth. Inhale. Exhale. Inhale. Exhale. Push. Push. And on it went until Will started shaking with pain, until his head was spinning, until the skin of his knees scraped on the sand and blood smeared up his thigh. He kept going, until finally, white liquid gushed from Marissa's mouth.

Then, she shook herself back to life. "Far out," she said between gasps, as if what had just happened were just another joke. Sober now, just like him. "Who would've thought I got myself a hero?"

But Will knew he was no hero. He had done what needed to be done, just like Tom, who had clung to his dying mother. Only Mona had not been as lucky as Marissa, she did not get a second chance. And that's when Will knew that he was not going to stay. What he needed right now more anything was to be with his family, with Tom.

★

Back in Aunt Rose's kitchen, Tom swirled limp bits of pasta in a bowl of murky instant soup.

"It'll be great for Tom," said Nick, between spoonfuls. "It'll give him something to do, instead of moping around the house all day."

"Seriously, Nick? Leave him out of it, okay!" Aunt Rose said, as she got up to slide her plate into the sink. There was something different about her tonight, Tom thought. She seemed distracted, giddy almost, and even less willing than usual to put up with Nick's nagging.

"But everybody has one. It's just totally embarrassing not to."

"Wanting stuff because somebody else has it is consumerism at its worst. And anyway, which part of 'We don't have money for useless crap' do you not understand? Especially now that I'm on a leave of absence."

"It improves visual and motor skills, so it's, like, perfect if you want to be a pilot."

"If you want to be a pilot, how about enrolling with the cadets?"

As thankful as Tom was that Aunt Rose stood up for him, he was with Nick when it came to buying a PS4 Pro. His parents had been equally reluctant. "We don't need any more time traps in this house," his father had said and, for once, Mom agreed.

Thankfully, Saanjh's father didn't agree. In fact, he happily added to his son's already massive collection whenever he returned from one of his many trips. "Guilt games," Saanjh called them, pretending not to care that his dad was away more often than not. Then the two boys would go to Saanjh's room and play until their eyes ached and their fingers felt numb.

"I'll be back not too late," said Aunt Rose, "And thanks for looking after Tom, Nick. I owe you one."

"Oh yeah? Well, I just know what—"

As soon as the door slammed shut, Nick grabbed Tom's uneaten soup. But Tom didn't mind. Eating was a drag, though he had forced himself ever since that man had come by to check up on them, threatening to take him away. No point in giving Ray any extra ammunition, Aunt Rose was good at doing that all on her own.

Nick finished eating and went to watch TV, leaving the dirty dishes behind on the table. Mom would not have been pleased. "Excuse me, your Royal Highness," she would have said, "but the staff is on strike."

Tom picked up the bowl and slid it into the already full sink. Hopefully Ray would not return anytime soon, because this kitchen was still a mess. Overripe plums sat next to unopened mail and two bottles of half-drunk wine. The fridge was plastered with stickers and postcards and bills. Drawn in by a collection of class pictures, Tom stepped closer. Over the years, Nick's hair had gone from short, to shaggy, then shaven, to short. Tom picked up the latest (shaggy), only to uncover a photo of Mom and him at the cottage, taken after they returned from paddling across the lake to Bigwin Island. Tom had loved being alone with Mom, surrounded by nothing but water and air and the sounds of their paddles hitting the water. How quiet the lake had been, how peaceful and safe. He loved it even when his arms started to ache, and his legs went numb, tingly, and finally stiff. This was the first time they had ventured out in the canoe on their own. It would also be the last.

Tom slid onto the floor and buried his head in his hands, his racing heart willing his mother to disappear and to leave him be.

"Not the greatest place for a nap," said Nick, who stepped right over Tom to get to the fridge. "Move, and I'll get us a treat."

Tom opened his eyes and watched as his cousin retrieved two glasses from the freezer, covered in frost. Then he pulled a bottle of Coke out from under the sink and poured equal amounts.

"Don't tell Mom. She thinks pop is the root of all evil."

Nick exhaled deeply and then started to drink, downing the whole glass in one long gulp. Mom would have thought it impolite, Dad a waste, but Tom was impressed.

"That takes years of practice," said Nick, "so don't even try."

Tom waited until Nick disappeared upstairs. The frosting on his glass had started to melt, creating tiny rivulets along the side, lacy like the curtains at Aunt Sonya's.

The first few gulps were easy enough, delicious even, but soon his throat started to tingle. Still, Tom pushed on, past the itching, into ache. One more gulp, he demanded of himself, and another, but then the pain erupted and dark syrupy liquid spurted out of his mouth and down his chin, followed by uncontrollable coughs and tears.

Tom closed his eyes and steered his mind back to the canoe, to crouching on his knees in the front of the boat, his paddle hitting the water in a precise, steady rhythm, undeterred by the stinging sweat, the burning sun, his aching bones. Behind him, his mother, steering the boat, proud of their achievement, and like him, happy.

When at last the glass was empty, Tom let out a sigh. His mission was accomplished, a challenge met.

*

The elevator door slid shut behind Rose. There was no turning back now. The smudged mirror distorted her features, but she was fine with what she saw. Her short, spiky hair gave her an edge, without being edgy. Her lips were still full enough and the lines around her eyes came from laughter, rather than frowns. The straps of her new sandals dug into her feet, but she loved the way her toes peeked out from under the rainbow-coloured strips. And anyway, they weren't going to be trapped much longer.

On the sixteenth floor, the elevator door opened with a cheap ding. Rose straightened her spine and continued toward Room 1616. The hotel carpet was patchy, the brass tacky, and the walls dotted with offensively inoffensive reproductions. Landscapes, seascapes, horses, and trees. Turning the corner, Rose passed a half-eaten dinner tray, abandoned in front of a door with a Do-

Not-Disturb sign. Pretty clear what was up for dessert. She continued along the corridor, knowing she should not be here.

A week ago, Alex had called her to cash in on his rain cheque. But instead of a drink, they went for a walk in High Park. The hot midsummer heat was vibrantly heavy, the air fecund. Without saying a word, they had veered off from the path into thickening shrubs. A rogue branch hit Rose in the eye and when she stumbled over a root, Alex had caught her hand, not letting go until they found a clearing. It was there that he had leaned in for a kiss. Tentative yet with confidence. Assured but not assertive. Rose closed her eyes, allowing for the embrace to calm her aching heart. Then they scrambled back to the path and walked back up to Bloor. It was only after saying good-bye, and one last kiss, that they made a plan to meet up again. Today.

Rose stopped at room 1616. Taking a deep breath, she knocked.

Alex opened the door immediately. "Oh, I'm so glad you came."

"Why? You didn't think I would? Should I not have? I could always…"

Alex pulled Rose into the room and into his arm. He felt warm, exciting, and oh so alive.

Less than an hour later, her want sated, Rose moved her head onto Alex's chest. She closed her eyes and let quiet settle upon her. Feeling safe, she allowed Mona into her thoughts.

"Why didn't she tell us how crazy he was?" she whispered. "We could've helped."

"Rose. Please. Don't," said Alex.

"I just can't stop thinking about her. About her last days. Her last night. What it must've felt like to suddenly know that there was no way back, that this time—"

"Rose, this kind of thinking will get you nowhere."

"Maybe nowhere is a good place to be."

Alex sat up and pulled on his pants. His body was lean, with strong, muscular legs, the imprint of his socks still visible around his calves. He grabbed his watch from the bedside table. "Shit," he said. "It's late. I've got to run."

Stumbling over Rose's discarded dress, he grabbed his shirt. His socks. His tie.

Rose rolled onto her back. A crack ran across the ceiling and the image of the hotel collapsing invaded her brain. Windows shattered, shards dancing in the vortex of the implosion, steel melting like candy. Dust filled her lungs.

"Do you think Mona saw it coming?" she asked.

Alex pulled on his jacket and sat down again. He touched her face and wiped away her tears.

"Of course not. Why else would she have stayed?"

Why indeed?

The next morning, Rose was jerked awake by a loud thud. She ran out of her room, finding Tom sprawled out at the bottom of the stairs. Tangled in yet another set of wet sheets, a pile of books scattered around him.

"Are you okay?" Rose asked as she scrambled down but before she could reach, Tom got up and limped away. Anything to avoid human touch.

"How about breakfast?" she asked, when she caught up to Tom in the kitchen. "Milk? Toast? Cereal?"

"Sounds awesome, Mom. How about some eggs, too?"

Rose swung around to find her son standing in the doorway, dressed in nothing but boxers three sizes too big, his hair tousled, rubbing his eyes.

"How often do I have to tell you not to leave crap on the stairs?" Rose asked.

"What's that one about the kettle that's black, calling somebody else something?" Nick answered, as he pulled a bowl out of the cupboard and filled it up to the rim with cereal. "Plus I don't think it's right to call books crap."

Rose missed her brother. Will would have known how to set Nick straight. After years of staying with them on and off, he was the closest her son ever had to a father figure, albeit another reluctant one. Still, during that awful time when Nick got the chickenpox, Will had managed to make the poor boy laugh, even though he was covered in welts. Later, when Nick lost three teeth in a day and was convinced he was going to die, Will had shown him his own complete collection of baby teeth stored in a dented tin box labelled *Sweet Delights*. Nick, gap-toothed like an eighty-year-old sailor, promptly set out to build up his own collection.

"Halli, Hallo, Hallu?"

Rose stopped in her tracks. What was she hearing?

"Anybody hi-ha-home?"

She raced to the front hallway and found Will standing in the door. His shirt was as greasy as his hair, but the smile on his face huge. "Are you for real?" Rose asked, sounding harsh despite her joy. "You've never heard of a phone? Texting?"

"I went standby," said Will, as he put down his backpack. "And anyway, I thought you like surprises."

"And you're planning on staying here?"

"Well, yeah. Why?"

★

"I know, it's not ideal," Aunt Rose said, pushing a long-abandoned art project into the corner to make space for the inflatable mattress. "But it'll do for now."

While she got the air pump, Tom looked around Nick's room, which he was to share from now on. The floor was strewn with clothes and stray shoes, and on the walls hung an Italian flag, a purple Raptors T-shirt, and a poster of a long-haired kid jumping high into the sky, holding onto his skateboard as if it were a magic carpet. Under his cousin's unmade bed, Tom noticed the Bart Simpson snow globe.

Tom had bought it at Old Orchard Beach, a present for Nick, but then, on their long drive home, he had changed his mind. He wanted to keep it as a souvenir of their time at the ocean, a vacation that had been fun even though his parents hadn't spoken to each other in two days. But Mom had put the kibosh on that idea: "You intended it to be a present," she insisted, "so a present it should stay."

Looking at the snow globe now, abandoned and covered in dust, Tom knew that Mom had been wrong. Things never stay the same, no matter what you wish or say.

"Alright then," said Aunt Rose, when the mattress was inflated, a small bedside lamp installed. "I think this is super cosy. Let me know if you need anything else."

As soon as she left, Nick drew an imaginary line across the floor. "Don't cross this, or you're in trouble. Got it?"

Tom slipped into his new, squeaky bed. He had no intention of trespassing into his cousin's territory. Just like he had no intention of laughing, swimming or canoeing, ever again.

"And that not-talking business," said Nick, who had settled into his own bed across the room, "are you planning on snapping out of that sometime soon or what? 'Cause to be honest, it's getting a little tired. Make that a lot."

Tom pulled the blanket over his head and started to count. 1. 2. 3. 1. 2. 3. 1. 2. 3. 1. 2. 3.

"I will give you an A for consistency though," Nick said and turned off his light. "Sleep well."

After that, life on Claremont life settled into a new kind of normal. Uncle Will entertained Aunt Rose with crazy stories about some girl named Marissa and delighted Nick with elaborate meals. All the while, Tom sat back and watched. Content to be left alone. Trapped, just like them, in his own world.

"I should be back by nine," Aunt Rose said one Thursday evening. She'd been buzzing around upstairs for an hour, finally coming downstairs in a slinky dress and bright red lipstick. "There're leftovers in the fridge, unless you feel like making something fresh, Will. The tomatoes need to be eaten."

"Can't do. Sorry. I'm meeting Burt," said Uncle Will, without looking up from *The Deadliest Catch*.

"Nick?"

"It's Ryan's birthday, Mom. I told you. I'm leaving right after dinner and then I'm sleeping over."

Tom, who slumped on the sofa between Uncle Will and Nick, slid even lower. Please forget all about me, he thought. Pretend I'm not here. Please. Please. Please.

"Sorry, Will, but one night of babysitting is not too much to ask. You do owe me rent."

"Tom's not a baby, Rose, therefore no babysitting needed."

"Don't be an ass, Will. I'm late as it is."

"Late for what?"

Aunt Rose was gone for less than ten minutes before Uncle Will caved to Nick's whining about wanting something more fun to eat than three-day-old leftovers.

"Onions, mushrooms, tomatoes—and the secret ingredient is … " Uncle Will's face popped up over the door of the fridge, a knobbly little root in his hand. "Nick? Tom? Anybody have any idea what this is?"

"I don't know," said Nick. "Garlic?"

"Oh boy, you've got a lot to learn. No, it's ginger. A root that tastes fabulous and is good when you have stomach troubles, sore throats, nausea, loss of appetite and even cancer."

"Fascinating. Call me when you're done," Nick said, turning to go back upstairs.

"Slow down, buster. This ain't no resort with an all-you-can-eat buffet. If you want dinner," Uncle Will said, grabbing an onion and taking aim, "you've got to help out."

The onion only narrowly missed Nick's head, leaving behind a trail of dry, papery skin.

"What about him?" Nick pointed at Tom who had settled at the kitchen table. "It's not fair that he always gets special—" Before Nick could finish his sentence, five mushrooms landed in front of Tom, along with a knife.

"There. Happier now?"

"Also, can he wash his hands before smearing his saliva all over our food? Have you seen what he does with his nails? It's disgusting."

"Seriously, Nick? It's just about time for you to mind your own frickin' business. Just because he doesn't speak, does not mean he can't hear." But Uncle Will did drop a wet towel in front of Tom.

"So, what exactly am I supposed to do with this?" Nick asked, inspecting the onion as if it were a thingamajig from outer space.

"Take it for a walk, Nick, and make sure to scoop the poop. What do you think? Peel it. Chop it. Sauté it. And Tom, I need those mushrooms sliced now, not sometime next week."

Tom picked up the knife and let the blade gently slide over his palm, along the scar that had formed from smashing his mother's mug. The skin was still tender and the metal felt sharp, exciting. But before he could probe deeper, cut into his flesh, see how far he could push without flinching, Uncle Will grabbed the knife and repositioned it in Tom's hand.

"Timing's everything in the kitchen, Tom, so don't let the team down by dithering. Mushroom slivers are what I'm looking for. Chop. Chop."

Dinner, a vegetable stir-fry with rice, took forever to make, but only minutes to eat. Tom finished his plate, but neither Uncle Will nor Nick bothered to comment. After ditching their plates into the sink, they settled on the sofa to watch TV.

"This is the stupidest show ever," said Nick.

"No, it's not," replied Uncle Will.

"It is so. The music's stupid, the outfits are stupid, the numbers are stupid, the moves are stupid, the judges are stupid, the—"

"Nick! I get it. It's stupid. But for Pete's sake, do us all a favour and expand your vocabulary."

But Uncle Will did switch through the channels until he finally settled on *How It's Made*. Huge, gleaming machines sorted, washed, peeled, sliced, fried and salted potatoes until they became chips, ready to be bagged. A deep, foreboding voice droned on about how many chips an average potato yields (thirty-six) and other, equally obscure minutiae of chip production. "This show sucks so bad," said Nick, "it hurts my teeth."

"How about flossing?" said Uncle Will. "And anyway, if you don't stretch your mind, you'll wind up a retard."

"I'm pretty sure you're not supposed to use that word."

"Don't you have a party to go to?"

"Whatever," said Nick and grabbed his skateboard. "Have fun."

"How about you?" said Uncle Will, turning to Tom. "You don't mind expanding your horizons, do you?"

Hoping for the unwanted attention to go away, Tom closed his eyes.

"Suit yourself," said Uncle Will. Then he returned to watching his show, which had now moved on to microprocessors. Only this time, nothing made sense to Tom. How did the infrared light know where to place each microchip? How was it possible to store memory, and why would anybody want to? All Tom wanted to do was to forget.

As the voice on the TV went on, drowsiness, thick and delicious, settled upon Tom, like the mid-summer heat that would lull him to sleep in the hammock at the cottage. He closed his eyes and drifted away. Water splashed over his skin, refreshing and cool. But then the lake in his dream turned into a river, flowing through a ravine. The current strengthened, the sound of the water soared and he remembered that there was a waterfall just past the bend. Jolted into action, he tried to paddle toward the shore, but the undertow pulled him away. Then, the water turned into mud, into goo, and finally concrete, and Tom was stuck. He tried to scream, but there was no sound. Air ran out. Darkness took over—until he startled himself awake.

Tom looked around, unsure for a moment where he was. Next to him lay Uncle Will, asleep and purring like a cat. On the TV, ugly old men with huge bellies went on about their ugly cars. Tom needed the remote to change the channel, but it was firmly ensconced in Uncle Will's clasped hand.

Carefully, Tom unfurled the fingers, one by one. Uncle Will's nails were ridged, with sharp, jagged edges. Mom would've never let his nails go messy like that. She used to trim his nails with her special scissors after he'd taken a bath. "That way they're softer," she'd say, "much easier to cut." Maybe she had never told Uncle Will about this trick. Maybe one day, Tom would.

It took ten minutes, but Tom finally extracted the remote. Clicking through the channels, he found the Blue Jays were playing the Yankees. Next, people talking. People dancing. The weather. Singing. Talking. Chocolate. Talking. Talking.

Then a bare-chested fighter, his entire back covered in a dragon tattoo, kicked a guy in star-and-stripes-shorts in the chest. The American stumbled across the mat, but somehow he remained standing until the dragon guy jumped up into the air, landing another blow with his right foot. Sweat splattered off the American who promptly collapsed, wriggling like a fish, unable to escape. Still the dragon guy fought on, landing blow after devastating blow. Blood squirted and the crowd's jeers reached a feverish pitch. Tom gasped.

"What the hell?" asked Uncle Will, woken by the announcer shrieking with excitement. He grabbed the remote and muted the sound. "What the hell happened to the chips?"

September

Sonya stretched out across the bed, but it was empty. Before disappointment could settle in too deeply, she smelled coffee brewing. Maybe not all was lost. Maybe Alex would remember the croissants she'd put in the oven last night, to be baked to buttery perfection this morning for her birthday breakfast in bed. Sonya turned on the radio and waited for the hourly news. When she awoke next, Mary Ito was already giving the weather: fifteen degrees and sunny. Perfect for a fall barbecue.

Without opening her eyes, Sonya went through her mental checklist. She had already stocked up on wine, cleaned the house, prepped the dips. Today, only last-minute touches were left: making Mama's famous potato salad (no mayonnaise, no pickles, no bacon, instead homemade bouillon, parsley and rapeseed oil); chopping condiments for Alex's burgers; swinging by Cyndy's Bakery to pick up the cake.

"Have a good one," said Alex as he set down her coffee on the night table. "I'll be back in an hour."

"How about a snuggle?" asked Sonya, in her most alluring voice. How embarrassing having to ask for sex, especially on her birthday.

"I can't, hon. I still need to get charcoal and beer."

"Now? Why didn't you...?" But Sonya stopped. Unlike her, Alex was a crammer. Looming deadlines made him feel alive. So what if his approach sometimes backfired? Like the time when his—granted, charming—idea of celebrating their anniversary in Prince Edward County ended with driving home through the night because all the hotels were full. Or the countless IOU's he'd given Sonya, instead of real presents. Or the croissants that lay forgotten, as Alex rushed off to do what he could have done days ago.

Sonya's morning did not improve from there. When she arrived at Cyndy's Bakery, somebody had misplaced her order, and all they had left was a pink monstrosity with purple flowers. She decided to skip that toxic excuse for a cake and then got stuck in traffic all the way up to the cemetery.

Sonya loved visiting her mother's grave on her own birthday. A perfect place to review the past year and set goals for the one ahead. Only this time, standing at the graveside after cleaning away the fallen leaves, all Sonya felt was her mother's disapproval. Like it was her fault Mona had died, that their lives had turned to shit, that yet again she had failed to become a mother.

This was not the first time Sonya had felt the brunt of her mother's displeasure. She had been inconsolable when Sonya enrolled at McGill. "Why Montreal? Don't they offer math at UofT? Won't you miss me? I'll miss you."

Sonya hadn't said so, but getting away from her mother's increasingly erratic moods had been a big part of the appeal of leaving town. At first, Mama had called her daily, worried that her eldest child might starve, freeze, or die of loneliness. It took months to convince her that she was doing just fine, that surviving on her own was possible. Preferable even.

She'd lived in a third floor walk-up on Duluth that was decrepit in a way only young people find charming, her roommates an impossibly earnest astronomy student from B.C., and a good-natured but malodorous political science major from Nova Scotia. Even all these years later, the smell of burnt milk reminded Sonya of mornings in their under-heated kitchen, discussing Monica Lewinsky, the last Seinfeld episode, or quantum physics.

And then there was McGill. How exhilarated she had felt the first time she entered the storied campus off Sherbrooke. Just like James McGill, the fur-trader-made-good, she felt poised for a better, grander future. Taking a left, she arrived at Burnside Hall, the home of the Department of Mathematics, a thirteen-floor brutalist building that stuck out from the otherwise genteel campus like a misshapen mongrel in a litter of purebreds.

Patronized by the pimply, the insecure, and a few ultra-smart nerds, Sonya felt instantly at home. Here problems were solved through logic, deduction, and abstraction. Answers were either right or wrong. Conclusions, once understood, satisfied Sonya with their simplicity, their inevitability, and their irrefutable truth. She loved the ridiculously convoluted course descriptions, and picked whatever she understood least: Linear dependence and independence, bring it on. Inverses and determinants, absolutely.

Then, she met Xavier and everything changed. Xavier, who smelled like the ocean, like wood, like life. Xavier, whose touch took Sonya out of her head and into her body, who made her feel beautiful and oh so desired. Lying in his arms, she no longer saw the point of the Jacobian matrix, conditional probability or Bayes' Law. Previously enticing equations now proved unintelligible, enigmatic, impenetrable, and by the end of the year, she failed most of her exams. Not that Sonya cared. Listening to Xavier's lilting Québécois accent, and his hip, if mostly incomprehensible, friends, it was easy to imagine herself as a renegade student in 1920s Paris, rather than a Math undergrad gone astray in Montreal.

But then Xavier moved on, enchanted by someone new. Dumped and wrapped in self-pity, Sonya retreated to her bed, until her roommate shook her awake one afternoon, tears in her eyes: Sonya's mother had died. Found by Rose in a puddle of vomit, next to a one-word note: Sorry.

In the end, Sonya's stint in Montreal was short-lived. A year and a half of life on her own terms was all she got. The story she told herself, and anyone who cared to ask, was that she gave up her studies, her future, to help guide her rudderless family. The surrogate mother of three at the age of twenty-one. Imagine. Not once did she utter Xavier's name. Instead, she settled for a man who made her feel safe. A man who was steady. A man who was there.

When Sonya got home from the cemetery, she found Alex in front of his computer, watching something explode on YouTube. *FailArmy*, Sonya suspected, or his latest favourite, *Idiots at Work*. Sonya could not pinpoint the moment when her husband had turned into a cliché. A small belly bulging from his admittedly still lean frame, addicted to videos of men hurting themselves, waiting for her to nag before getting off his ass.

"Alex," said Sonya, already hating the sound of her voice, "the garden's still a mess."

Alex rolled his eyes, but went off to rake the leaves. Sonya pulled out her apron and got to work. Her mood lifted instantly as she mixed the ingredients for her mother's lemon loaf. *Beat 200 grams of butter with 200 grams of sugar*, she read in Mama's rushed handwriting, the page stained with flecks of butter and crusty bits of flour. The low purr of the mixer was firm and reassuring. *Add three eggs, one at a time, and then 25 ml of lemon rind*. Sonya's movements were quick and precise. Numbers dissolved into pleasure, uncertainty gave way to purpose. *Add 40 grams of flour, plus 140 grams of ground almonds, beat until smooth* and voilà, she was done. Happiness.

Sonya slid the pan into the oven and set the timer for forty-five minutes. How embarrassing to have to bake your own birthday cake. But then it could be worse. There could be no birthday at all.

★

Rose loved Saturday mornings. Already, she had spent two luxurious hours reading about Amina, an obedient wife in 1917 Cairo who devoted her life to raising children and appeasing her philandering husband. A life so small, even confined, yet at the same time so deliciously structured and clear, it made Rose yearn for more certainty in her own unruly world.

Growing up, books had been her escape, her way of finding peace in a house full of people. At first, it had been mysteries only Nancy Drew knew how to solve. Later, she moved on to the convoluted quest to recapture *The Moonstone*, and then, when she was fourteen, *War and Peace*. Tato had sneered. "They talk a good talk, those Russians, but try living under their rule."

Rose closed Mahfouz's *Cairo Trilogy* and went downstairs. In the kitchen, she found Will reading *The Globe and Mail* and Nick devouring peanut butter toast. Tom sat at the far side of the table, seemingly counting the cracks in the wall. "Here," she said, as she put down a bowl of Captain Crunch in front of him. "And," Rose said turning to Will, "shouldn't the person who pays for the paper get first dibs?"

"Life ain't fair, my dear darling sister. You should know that by now," said Will, without looking up from the paper. "You snooze, you lose."

Rose picked up the travel supplement. "All Aboard the Marrakesh Express," she read now. Unlike her brother, she had not ventured beyond Niagara Falls since becoming a mother at twenty-one. "The Foodie Renaissance in Wales." More useless information for a brain that was already crammed with secrets of friends who had long moved away, the password for Eugene's ATM card (not that there had ever been much money in Nick's father's account) and phone numbers no longer in service.

A knock on the front door brought Rose back to Claremont. "Will. You promised to fix the bell," she said.

"So sue me."

More knocking.

"Please. Somebody. I'm not really dressed." And she wasn't. All she was wearing over her worn out pyjamas was a threadbare bathrobe with once vibrant green and brown stripes. On her feet, beloved but sad looking brown slippers.

The knocking continued while Nick devoured another toast and Tom moved from staring at the wall to staring at Captain Crunch.

"Sounds to me like whoever that is, they're not going away," said Will, flipping the paper. "But as you keep pointing out, Rose, this is your home, not mine."

Giving her unruly hair a last pointless pat-down, Rose opened the front door to find Ray standing on her walkway. His usual grin changed to a look of alarm, before settling on a friendly, if somewhat uneasy, smile. "So sorry to wake you," he finally said.

"I've been up for hours," Rose replied, as she tightened her already tight bathrobe. "What can I do for you?"

"We had an appointment, Rose."

"Shit, how could I forget?"

"How could you indeed?"

Rose parked Ray in the living room while getting dressed. When she returned, Ray was studying a drawing of two Mounties holding hands that Will had bought years ago from a homeless man on Queen Street.

"So, what's up?" she asked, hoping that Ray had yet to notice the oversized dicks that bulged in the Mounties' snazzy black pants. She resented these regular visits, hated having strangers examine her life, judge every choice she had ever made. Where were these do-gooders when it actually mattered?

"Really, Rose, do we have to go through this every time?"

"No," she lied and bit her tongue. Until the home study was complete, and Tom's fate was decided, Rose was determined to play along.

"I'm afraid anger does not make this situation any easier."

"And forcing Tom back to school does?"

"Don't blame me, Rose. Summer's over and in Ontario, all children must attend school. And anyway, I spoke to the guidance counsellor yesterday, and she tells me he's doing just fine."

"Just fine? Really? That's what we are going for now?"

"It's a start, Rose. So why don't you tell me how it went?"

Last Monday, Rose and Nick had walked Tom over to Charles G. Fraser Junior. Nick babbled on about his own time spent at the school: a soccer tournament won in the pouring rain, a trip to the zoo to see the new baby gorilla. Rose remained quiet, because what she remembered most about Nick's time at Fraser was an Art teacher correcting his delicate drawings with a red felt marker and her son crying in distress.

"Let me show you your locker," the school's stern but well-seasoned guidance councillor had said to Tom, "and we'll take it from there."

Without any resistance, the boy had followed her down the long, squeaky corridor, past pictures of classes long graduated, his head bowed, his frame tiny. Just as Tom disappeared around the corner, Nick reached for Rose, making it impossible to hold back her tears any longer. The law is the law, she resolved, fine, but anytime that kid wanted to stay home, she would let him. No questions asked.

"So, I've been doing some research," said Ray, "and I believe I found just the right person to make this situation a whole lot better."

"You found somebody who will clean up the place for free?"

"Rose, therapy. I'm speaking about therapy."

"Oh please, not another one. Which part of 'He's a mute' do you people not understand?"

"This is someone who works with non-verbal techniques. She comes highly recommended, Rose, and getting a spot for Tom was tough. As for verbalizing, I'm not worried, he'll talk when the time's right."

"Speaking of which," said Rose, "what time is it?"

"Just past eleven."

"Oh no. Sonya's going to kill me. Guys," Rose was yelling now, "we've got to go."

An hour later, they emerged from the subway at Young and Sheppard, surrounded by ugly glass towers and cranes poised to build more.

"Just because a team doesn't win, does not mean it sucks," said Will, when he and Nick finally caught up with Rose and Tom at a red light. Somehow the two had managed to argue about sports ever since leaving the house. What a waste of time to watch, never mind discuss, grown men run after a ball. And what was the thrill of seeing it land between two posts? Why not use that energy to do something that matters? Like clean up your room? Figure out a way to make Tom laugh? Or better yet, talk.

The light switched to green and Rose grabbed Tom's hand, dragging the boy along like a balloon on a string. He didn't like the touch, but she had no choice. They were late, and at Tom's natural pace, a twenty-minute walk could easily stretch into an hour.

"Happy birthday," said Rose, when they finally arrived at Elmwood, dropping her present on Sonya's kitchen counter. "Hope you like it."

"Appetizers are already served," said Sonya, without looking up from tossing her trademark watermelon salad, made with basil and feta. "But I guess I should be grateful that you made it up here at all. How's Tom?"

"Fine."

"Fine?"

"Yes, Sonya, he's fine. He eats. He sleeps. He even goes to school now. But no, he hasn't started speaking, if that's what you are really asking. And yes, he still wets his bed. Though less and less, which is progress, I suppose. Now where can I get a drink?"

Rose noticed a hot lemon loaf on the kitchen table. Her mother used to bake it, when she came back up for air after one of her episodes. The smell of butter and lemon was often the first sign that her downward cycle had been broken, that brighter days, maybe even weeks, were ahead. Rose pinched off a bit of golden crust, savouring the taste of childhood. It brought back memories of her mother's kitchen engulfed in a cloud of flour, sneaking her finger into the batter for a delicious lick, smelling of butter and lemon and nuts.

"Stop it, Rose. It needs to rest."

Through Sonya's spotless kitchen window, Rose saw Will, beer already in hand, debating Nick on whatever nonsense they'd glommed onto now. Off to the side, Tom had buried himself in a pile of leaves. A BMW pulled up onto the sidewalk, and the teenage girl from next door emerged with a backpack strapped to her slender frame, her hair flowing down past her waist, a tank top cropped inches above her skin-tight tight jeans.

"That girl's a slut," said Sonya. "Just like her mom."

"Wow, you *are* harsh."

"Sometimes, Rose, the truth is harsh," Sonya said, as she washed the last of the dishes, her movements as efficient as her kitchen, home, and life. "Nice wrapping job," she said, picking up Rose's present. A purple box bound by an oversized green bow. "I'm impressed."

"The clerk at the store did it, not Christo."

"Christo?"

"The artist who wraps islands and stuff. Whatever, Sonya, just open it."

Sonya untied the ribbon, rolled it up for later use, carefully peeled off the Scotch tape and folded the paper, before finally opening the box. Inside, she found a red candle embossed with HOPE.

"Oh, it's perfect! Look," said Sonya, disappearing into the dining room, waving Rose to follow. There, next to their sister's urn, sat three similar candles inscribed with TRUST, LOVE and FAITH. Purple, beige and green. "Penelope gave them to me. Isn't this neat? Now I have the whole collection."

Shopping at the Bay is lame, Rose decided. Picking stuff up on sale, stupid.

"You made it."

Rose flinched at the sound of Alex's voice. She spun around to find him standing in the doorway. He looked strange here in his own home, so much more real, so much less appealing—as if a layer of wonderful had been removed. "Sonya was worried that you guys got lost."

"I said no such thing, Alex. Why would you say that?"

Rose turned and grabbed an item from Mona's shrine, a card

embossed with white roses. " 'When someone you love becomes a memory, the memory becomes a treasure,'" she intoned, with the hollow gravity of third-rate poets, " 'With deep-felt sympathies, The Husby's.' Wow, that is deep."

"Rose," said Sonya. "Please."

Encouraged, Rose grabbed another card: "'If there's something I can do/ Anything at all/ Think of me thinking of you/ And don't hesitate to call.'"

"That's quite enough."

"'Although it's difficult today to see beyond the sorrow, may looking back in memory help comfort you tomorrow.'"

One by one, Rose pitched the cards into the fireplace, not that flames would ever devour them. Like so much else in her sister's house, the hearth was a fake.

"Who writes this shit? Who prints these inane cards? Who buys them? And then displays them, as if these clichés have anything to do with Mona or what happened or how we feel?"

"You ladies up for a drink?" asked Alex, who still hovered in the doorway.

"Seriously," said Rose. "How can you stand it?"

"I," started Alex, but then he changed tracks. "I've been on her to take this down for weeks."

"At least these people are trying to help," Sonya said and bent down to retrieve the cards.

"Wine, beer, a Caesar? Come on girls, lighten up. It's Sonya's birthday."

"Gin and tonic," said Rose. "And make it a double."

★

Tom hated being at Aunt Sonya's, and the smell of rotting leaves made him want to throw up. Each fall, he used to hide in the mountains Dad used to make, waiting patiently until Mom came running, sweat streaming down her face, her voice quivering, her love for him so strong and clear. Now, buried underneath a pile of leaves, nobody came looking for him. Not even Aunt Rose.

Across the street, a group of teenage boys played ball hockey, screaming like the Stanley Cup was at stake. A girl rode by on a BMX, her skirt hiked up so high that Tom could see her pink undies. She smiled at the hockey players and disappeared around the corner. Tom used to love riding his bike, and only now did he realize that it was gone, along with so much other useless stuff he used to own.

Tom dug his fingers into the soil. Pebbles, roots, and rocky clumps of earth held promise, but he kept searching until he chanced upon the rugged edge of a stone. He dragged his hand back and forth, along the scab in his palm, the one he wouldn't let heal. Deeper and harder with every stroke. Faster and stronger. Finally, the boys and their shouts disappeared, as did the smell of rotten leaves, the yellow house, the two-car garage. The harder he pushed, the further away he got. Old Orchard Beach. The cottage. Home.

"GOAL!" screamed one of the boys, too close and too loud to ignore.

"Not fair," yelled the goalie.

"Off sides."

"Screw you."

"Rematch."

"Pussy."

Tom scurried to the backyard, past a dozen or so strangers, to find Uncle Will by the grill. Uncle Alex was scraping off burnt meat, a black smear ran across his cheek, sweat dripped off his forehead and his apron was stained with grease. Twenty or so patties sizzled above scorching hot flames.

"Charred on the outside, raw in the middle. Not a winning combination, Alex."

Uncle Will took a sip of beer, relaxed if in a weirdly intense way.

"You need to wait 'til the flames die down before putting on the meat. Otherwise, you'll be serving E.coli on charcoal again."

"So, you decided to come back," replied Alex, pretending not to have heard but moving the patties to the cooler side of the grill. "Hopefully with better results this time around."

"Excuse me?"

"Gallivanting around Korea, sleeping with nineteen-year-olds, showing up broke, gambling—it's not cool, Will. Not at your age."

"Who told you all that?"

"Does that matter?"

Tom instantly tensed up. Moving closer to the barbecue, the heat felt comforting, inviting even. Maybe, if he got close enough, his uncles would fade away.

"Rose. It must've been Rose. When did you talk to her?"

"I hope," Uncle Alex said, lowering his voice but still loud enough for Tom to hear, "I hope you understand that you're putting your sister in a tricky position. She's got enough on her plate. The last thing she needs right now is more hassle from you."

Tom extended his hand closer to the red-burning coals. It was a challenge not to pull back, to stay the course, to finish what he had set out to do.

"You're one to talk, Alex."

"What's that supposed to mean?"

"Don't play me for a fool. You know what I'm talking about."

"Actually, I don't."

Actually, thought Tom, you do. But instead of piping up, he pushed his hand closer yet toward the coals.

"Brent tells me you've been missing Thursday nights."

"He what? When did you see Brent? He—"

The heat was burrowing into his skin, red hot. Fierce.

"What the fuck!" yelped Uncle Will and pulled Tom away from the fire. "What on earth are you doing? You could've hurt yourself. And what the hell's going on with your hand? Is that blood?"

Tom had never seen such fear in a grown man's face. For a moment, he considered reaching out, telling Uncle Will that this was just a game. But then he thought better of it. Because this was his secret—and secrets were not for sharing.

"Why don't you ... " Uncle Alex scanned the yard. By the back fence, he spotted the boy from next door hitting a tree with a three-foot stick. "Why don't you wash your hands and then... I don't know, go and play?"

"Yes," said Uncle Will, for once in agreement. "Why don't you?"

★

Will pried open another medicinal bottle of beer. This was one hell of a journey to make for a couple of burned burgers and a side of reprimands topped with a shitload of tension. Every year, Will came up with fifty brilliant excuses to miss Sonya's party. But then, swayed by some misguided sense of family obligation, he overruled his own better judgement only to resent every minute spent in Sonya's pretend-perfect world.

Sonya's friends, most of them comfortably settled into their boring, middle-of-the-road lives, milled around the backyard. Penelope, Sonya's barrel-shaped friend from kindergarten, laughed at some stupid joke like she'd never heard anything more amusing ever before. Time, Will decided, to check up on Nick.

"It's not what it looks like!" exclaimed Nick, when Will

tracked him down behind the garage, with the cute girl from next door. Neither could stop giggling.

"This might be a good time to educate you kids about dope's long-term effects on the teenaged brain," Will said, as he picked their still-smouldering joint out of a bed of pink petunias. "Seeing that yours already functions only part-time, Nick, this might be a lesson you don't want to miss. I, on the other hand," Will said, as he took a deep, satisfying drag, "I need to chill."

Will closed his eyes and flopped down onto the lawn. Why had he come back? To this tedious family, this ridiculous house, in this dull country with its constraining rules and smug people who did callous things while smiling and saying Oh, thank you so very much. Korea hadn't worked out as imagined, granted, but he could have gone somewhere else. He could have taken another loan from Rose and run off somewhere affordable, like Merida with its colonial homes and cheap cervezas at Tequila Rock. A few years back, Will had spent six delicious weeks exploring Hammock Sutra with Geatanne from Sept Îles, who was irresistible with her perky boobs until she left Will just as suddenly as she had come into his life, off teaching some new guy the ins and outs of sex suspended in mid-air.

"Hey? Are you really going to pass out right here?"

Will opened his eyes to see Nick shifting nervously from one foot to the other, a strand of chewed-out hair clinging to his cheek, a throbbing pimple above his lip. This kid deserved a break, too.

"Here," said Will, as he returned the joint. "But for fuck's sake, make sure nobody else catches you."

The upstairs washroom was almost double the size of Will's room on Claremont and only one of four in the house. Will didn't understand. "Let's share our life, our money, our bodily fluids—but don't make me take a dump in the same place as you?" But even when he and his siblings were kids, an invisible line had been drawn across the family table. On one side sat "Why-have-you-been-suspended-again-Will?" and "You-should-not run-around-like-that-Rose;" while on the other side were "Always-so-nice-and-sweet-Mona" and "Perfectly-responsible-if-a-bit-dull-Sonya."

On his way to get another beer, Will stopped by Mona's shrine. Several of the cards had toppled over, while others had been pushed aside to make space for four gaudy candles inscribed with clichéd messages about healing. In the middle of it all, Mona still laughed out of a framed photograph: Her forehead was covered in freckles, first crow's feet barely visible around her eyes, tiny lines that would never deepen, hair that would not grey, eyes that would not cloud over with grief.

Will fled to the kitchen, where he found a lemon loaf hiding on top of the fridge. Perfect, especially with three glasses of milk.

★

Rose hated the subway. It was stinky and shrill, with unflattering light. Across the aisle, Nick's eyes were glued to his phone. Next to him, Tom was busy biting his nails, and next to her, Will had folded himself into a pretzel, apparently trying to sleep off a few of his beers.

Rose pulled the Expos cap off her brother's face and squeezed closer. This was a conversation best had *sotto voce*.

"You shouldn't talk to Alex like that."

"He started it," Will replied, squirming to wedge himself into a more comfortable position. "Plus, who's he to judge me?"

"What are you talking about?"

"I know where you go on Thursdays, all dolled up and excited like."

Rose's heart dropped, making her want to throw up. How was it possible? Was it possible? It was not possible for her brother to know. Not until they got off the train at the Bloor Station, could she speak: "Well, it's not what you think."

"Always the lamest line in the book."

The following Thursday, Rose returned to the hotel determined to do the right thing, to end her deception before drowning in her puddle of shame. She knew that being with Alex was wrong; that even if this had started in a moment of somewhat understandable weakness, it ought to have stopped long ago. But then Alex arrived, lifting off his shirt, and then hers, sliding her down onto the bed before even saying hello.

So she waited until they were done, relieved for a moment of the heaviness that threatened to smother her ever since Mona's death.

Then she told Alex what Will had said.

"Are you kidding me?" Alex said, jumping out of bed. "You're fucking kidding me, right?"

Rose bit her lip and pulled the sheets up to her chin. "I'm not sure how he figured it out, but somehow he did. Contrary to popular opinion, Will's pretty perceptive. There was the time when he—"

"FUCK FUCK FUCK FUCK FUCK!" Alex zipped up his pants and grabbed his coat. He was almost gone, but then he looked back: "What about Nick?"

"What about him?"

"Well, if Will could figure us out, couldn't he?"

"They'll never tell Sonya. No way."

The door fell back shut and Alex paced the room, trying to justify the unjustifiable. Then, he sat down on the bed, struggling to look Rose in the eyes, "Time has come for reason to prevail."

"I know."

But when she took his hand, he did not resist. Nothing, it turns out, fans passion like impending doom.

Twenty minutes later, Rose pushed the sheets aside and sat up. This would be her last time in this hotel. She would never kiss Alex ever again. She got dressed and was almost out the door when she noticed that the bedside lamp was still on. Next to it sat Alex's watch. It was big and clunky, with three different dials. Designed for divers, which was odd, given that Alex had ever been much for the water, forever the last to dive into the lake.

Rose weighed the watch in her hand. This was always the first item Alex had taken off and the last he put back on. As if he was taking a break from time, a vacation from reality and from whom he had become. Here, in this room, time had been fluid, the way it was when Rose was a child and hours stretched out to infinity, languid and still. She remembered counting down the days, hours, even minutes for something exciting, anything, to happen: like her birthday, or to be allowed to swim without floaters, size six shoes, weighing fifty pounds, sitting in the front of the car, turning twelve years old, driving the car, getting drunk, having sex—yes, especially having sex. None of what she had wanted could ever come soon enough, though reality all too rarely lived up to her expectations.

And now her gear was stuck in reverse. She could no longer stay up until three a.m., eat without gaining weight, or provoke young men to whistle. Her back was hurting. Was it pothole season already? Time to close the cottage? Her son's thirteenth birthday? Thank God (or whoever) for stretch jeans, Vitamin K, and low lighting in bathrooms.

Rose pressed Alex's watch against her cheek and gave into her tears. But unlike when she was a youngster prone to hysterical weeping, today her sorrow was silent. Ever since her sister had died, everything felt wrong. Twisted. Unreal. And to think that now, instead of making things better, instead of trying to heal, she had gone ahead with making things even worse.

★

Sugarplum Spice, perfect. Sonya poured steaming hot water over the teabag and took her owl-shaped mug, grey with big round eyes, into the living room. Thursday night was hockey night— Sonya night.

She grabbed the remote and settled onto the sofa. For days now, she had felt out of sorts. Tomorrow, she would go to the gym, buy kale, maybe call Penelope to grab lunch. But tonight, she would allow herself to succumb to instant gratification, to watch Netflix and forget all about yet another shitty wasted day at work. "She who rests rusts," their mother used to say, a German expression she had picked up along their trek from Ukraine toward Canada. As often, her mother had been right. During Sonya's absence, Kiara had fastened her grip on the department. Underneath the smiles and the morning coffee routine hid a predator ready to pounce. To think she had hired that woman. Blinded, yet again, by a pretty façade.

Surprised to hear the front door open, Sonya checked the time. "What's wrong?" she asked Alex, as he walked in. "It's not even eight." In all the years that they had been married, Alex had only rarely cancelled his game: Once on Sonya's birthday. The time he was out with bronchitis. The week after Mona died.

"The ice machine's on the fritz, so the arena was closed."

"And you guys didn't go out for drinks?"

"Look what I got," said Alex, as he pulled out a box of chocolates. "For you."

Torn between suspicion and the need to feel loved, Sonya chose to accept his gift.

"Up for a beer?" she asked.

117

"I am," said Alex, as he plopped down onto the sofa. "I most certainly am."

★

Saved from school by a slight fever and an only vaguely exaggerated cough, Tom spent his morning waiting. Across the room, Nick changed his shirt four times, before settling on the same one he'd worn yesterday. Then he put his pencils, one at a time, into his backpack, followed by books and folders. When finally he left the house, Tom began to count. At 35, Nick returned for his skateboard; at 72, for his lunch. But Tom was not in a rush. He would have all day to explore Nick's large, if forbidden, collection of books: *Spiderman*, *Asterix*, *Daredevil* and the *Bone* series, which Tom had loved ever since Nick gave him *Out from Boneville* for his birthday last year.

The door downstairs swung closed again and Tom reset his count to zero. At 123, he added another 50 for safety. And then 50 more, just to be sure. And then another 23 to make it even. Tom was just about to slide out of bed when Aunt Rose came into his room.

"I'm sorry, but sadly, unlike school, work's not optional," said Aunt Rose, as she sat down on Nick's bed. "You sure you don't want to go to school?"

Yes, Tom was sure and just to make sure she knew he nodded his head. He hated school, hated having to leave the house, hated being alive. Though Fraser wasn't nearly as bad as his old school had been. At least now nobody bothered to be extra nice, or looked at him like a pickaxe was growing out of his skull. At Fraser, after the first rush of interest had passed, Tom spent his days unbothered, watching time click forward one second at a time.

"I'll be back by two, and then we'll check out Ms. Colter, okay?"

Ms. Colter? Tom could not recall that name. But then, he'd been dragged off to see so many experts, it was impossible to keep track. Like the old man with the tiny glasses who drew pictures, until Sonya left in a huff. Or the lady with the orange hair who made him pick shapes for his fears. Or the one with the chirpy voice who wanted him to meditate, which he did, until he fell asleep. Thankfully, that time he had woken without having wet his pants.

"Will's around, so you guys can hang out. He loves Monopoly, but whatever you do, don't let him have the bank."

Aunt Rose, like Nick, took forever to get out of the house, and sometime between staring at the ceiling and counting backward from a 1000, Tom fell back sleep. The kind of deep, heavy slumber that comes in the morning, especially after a sleepless night. Delicious, until that dream returned. The one he'd been trying to avoid by not falling asleep.

At first there was nothing but joy. He sat on a swing, pumping as hard as he could toward the sky. How he loved the wind rushing through his hair, the slide up into the clouds, the fall as he returned toward earth. But then, as the torque increased, the chain started to creak and tears pushed into his eyes, blurring the world, making his stomach jerk up and drop down, his fingers clinging to the metal chain so hard, they turned white and numb. And then he remembered that he had to jump, and just like that, thrill gave way to dread, gravity asserted its pull, and joy turned into panic. And then he woke, in a puddle of shame.

Tom sat up and found fresh sheets at the bottom of his bed. Aunt Rose must have dropped them off after he had fallen back asleep. He slid out of bed, changed his bedding, got dressed, and opened the door.

The hallway was dark. He stopped to listen, but there was no Nick whining, or Rose shouting, or pots banging. No TV. No radio. Nothing. Tom pressed his ear against the door to Uncle Will's room, but again, silence. No typing, no music, no snoring, either. The quiet was sharpened by a car that raced past the house, blaring music. Its heavy beat set off a car alarm somewhere down the street. Carefully, just in case Uncle Will was hiding behind the door, ready to pounce, Tom pushed the handle down slowly, waiting for a few more seconds before opening all the way.

But nobody jumped. Nobody laughed. Nobody growled. Uncle Will's room was empty, and for the first time since he arrived at Claremont, for the first time since his parents had died, Tom was alone.

★

When Rose returned home shortly after two o'clock, she was not surprised that nobody bid her hello. Will had always felt that social niceties were for those who were too scared to do without, and Tom had yet to say a word.

She tossed the day's harvest of junk mail onto a pile that was growing like a malignant tumour on her dining room table. For years, she had simply thrown the letters unopened into the recycling but then Martha, her colleague at the library, had set her straight. "Identity theft is not a joke," she insisted, and Martha ought to know. Some asshole had dug through her recycling, pulled out an offer for a new credit card and racked up five thousand dollars by the time she got the first bill. "A shredder's only a hundred bucks," Martha said. "Peace of mind is worth at least that." Of course Rose agreed, not that she would get to buying that shredder anytime soon.

"I've got a surprise!" she called out, as she crammed Styrofoam boxes into the fridge. Boneless lamb with spicy potato, chickpea chana, chicken Jalfrezi with cauliflower and peas. Rose loved Gandhi Roti, a hole-in-the-wall place on Queen, where West Indian roti met East Indian curry with mouthwatering results.

"Tom? Where are you? Check out what I got."

The only response was the faint sound of a harmonica somewhere in the house, possibly upstairs.

"Will?"

Rose hadn't heard her brother play since the summer he had turned nine, when Will had found a harmonica in the attic of the cottage. *Voor Huub* read the flowery cursive etched into its silvery side, though nobody knew who Huub was or what the harmonica was doing in the cottage their parents had just bought. All summer, Will had tormented the family with his determination to master the entire *Beatles Harmonica Songbook,* unwilling to move to the next song, until he had played the previous one flawlessly a hundred times in a row. Hell, until the spell was broken, and the harmonica joined Will's pile of discards: the Rubik's cube, his rollerblades and his once indispensable Game Boy.

Upstairs, the harmonica sounds flowed from moans and wails, at times tentative and meek, but always discordant and sad. Suddenly concerned, Rose raced up the stairs. She found her brother's room empty. "Shit."

Rose burst into Nick's room and found Tom squeezed into the far corner of the inflatable mattress, his lips pressed into the harmonica, his tiny body shaking. As she approached, his spindly arms grasped tightly around his legs, the harmonica now held tightly in his fist as if it could fight off evil spirits or neglectful aunts. Uncertain which might be worse.

"I am so sorry, Tom. Will was supposed to be here today. He promised."

Tom stared at her without a blink. His movements frozen.

Rose approached the boy carefully, as if he were a feral cat. Thankfully, Tom neither growled, nor hissed. Instead, his gaze remained unbroken. Strong. Encouraged, Rose advanced further, but just as she reached out, Tom brought the harmonica back up to his lips, producing a sound that was achingly shrill.

Rose plugged her ears and fled into the basement. She was not going to repeat Sonya's mistakes. Force the boy into compliance. Assert her will. No, this was something she could wait out. And she would.

"Why don't you bring the harmonica," Rose said when she returned from the basement an hour later, the laundry for once neatly folded. By now, the wails had transformed to nothing more than a drone, bearable if still unspeakably sad. "Because please, we need to go. I promised Ray we'd check out that Colter-lady and who knows, maybe she'll be fun."

When they finally walked up to the shrink's second-floor office, they were twenty minutes late.

"Call me Claire," said Ms. Colter, watching as Rose and Tom squeezed onto a couch intended for one. Rose picked a *Psychology Today* off the mahogany coffee table, but when she got to an article entitled "The Road to Familial Bliss," she put back the magazine. If it were that easy, why would anybody bother with shrinks? Next to her, Tom sat holding onto the harmonica as if it were a buoy that might prevent him from drowning, staring down at the space between his feet. Transfixed by nothing.

Across from them, Ms. Colter smiled. She looked spiffy in her Wassily chair, calm and composed. Somewhere in her sixties, she sported a shock of white hair and a silk blouse that hugged her still shapely breasts. The office was a room in an apartment stuffed with mementos from far-flung travels: woven bowls, wooden masks, and an entire shelf dedicated to elephants. A postcard of a young boy hugging an elephant sat next to a candelabra made of tusks and a brass elephant bank.

"As you're probably aware, many of the symptoms point toward selective mutism," said Ms. Colter, after extensively questioning Rose not only about Tom's health and behaviour but also about their living arrangements and even Nick. "But in my opinion, it would be a mistake to focus on the symptom rather than the underlying causes. It's important to understand that mutism is not a frivolous whimsy, but a form of self-preservation fairly common in victims of trauma. One day, when he's able, Tom will speak, but there's no predicting the when or the where or the how."

"How's that news? We got that much from Google."

"As you will know then, as well," continued Ms. Colter, "psychological care is confidential so if you don't mind, it would be great if you could leave us alone for the remainder of the session."

"Really? You're kicking me out? What's the point of that? It's not like he's saying much."

"I beg to differ. There're many ways to express one's feelings. Not just with words."

"You don't say."

"We all have a right to privacy," said Ms. Colter in a voice so calm it egged Rose on further, "and this boy deserves it more than most."

Rose was about to respond when she noticed Tom letting the harmonica slip into his pants pockets. When he looked up a smile, ever so faint, was on his lips.

★

Claire was like an island in the middle of a stormy sea. She was calm and quiet, and as soon as Aunt Rose had gone, she kicked off her shoes and dumped paper and crayons onto the floor.

"Draw anything you like," she said and picked up a pink crayon herself. "Me, I like trees, so that's what I'm going to draw."

Tom was of half a mind to tell her that there was no such thing as a pink tree, but then he remembered the pictures he had seen in the hallway. Photos of Claire strapped into a harness atop a steep cliff, posing in front of a gigantic turtle, laughing on a cart pulled by two bulls. She had seen all sorts of stuff, so best not to rule out pink trees.

After that, the hour passed quickly. While Claire kept talking, Tom drew Brawl crossing a mountain, his left arm ripped off for accuracy. Claire didn't ask why, which was good, because it was not like he knew why it kept coming off. All he knew was that it did.

At 4:55 sharp, Claire put her shoes back on. "I'll keep this, if that's alright with you?" she asked Tom, as she held up his half-finished drawing. "And I will see you again Monday, okay?"

On the way home, they stopped at a California Sandwiches to pick up dinner. A long line of men waited for veal sandwiches drowned in hot peppers and cheese. Two firemen, still in their thick padded pants, red suspenders dangling low, flirted with Aunt Rose. "No," she laughed. "I can't go for drinks. I've got to get home and put this one to bed." Still, she smiled all the way down Claremont.

But then they found the house locked. Aunt Rose knocked and kicked and knocked again. "Will's in so much trouble," she said, as she rifled through her bag, "He promised to look after you. He said he'd be here. He said he'd fix that goddamn bell. And where the hell's Nick?"

She kicked the door one more time, before dumping the contents of her bag out onto the stoop: two books, a pair of scissors, lipsticks, a half-eaten chocolate bar, used tissues, and finally, the keys. Tom didn't get it. Why didn't she just put them on a string? Faster, safer and what Mom used to do.

Finally, Aunt Rose opened the door and Tom slipped upstairs, pleased, unlike his aunt, to find the house empty.

★

Rose pushed the plunger down hard. That shrink had nerve to kick her out of the room, like she was a hindrance to Tom's healing, like her presence made things worse. Soggy bits of onion, bacon and pasta sloshed back and forth in the sink, as Rose put her frustration into each thrust. Making her feel bad about wanting to protect the boy. Brown, stagnant water splashed back and forth and onto the floor, but Rose was beyond giving a hoot. She was a single mom with two kids. She could not afford sitting idle in that office twice a week. She had shit to deal with. Like this sink that had been acting up for weeks.

Upstairs, Tom kept that harmonica going hard. Ever since they'd returned, he had produced nothing but screeches and howls. That shrink should spend a whole day with that child before starting to judge.

"Fine job you're doing there."

Rose swivelled around to find Will standing in the kitchen doorway. Under his arm a box from Sony, on his face a look of self-satisfaction. "We made a deal, Will! You promised—" she started to say.

"I just paid rent, Rose. Don't get greedy like the rest of the stinking world."

"It's not about the money, you asshole. You promised to look after Tom."

"Chill man, Tom doesn't need surveillance 24/7. He likes to be alone. And anyway, kids these days are totally over-patrolled and under-challenged. When we were kids, we were left to our own devices. We learned to be responsible by—"

"You're un-fucking-believable, Will. You really are."

"What? It's the truth. Remember the time Mama and Tato went to visit Aunt Myrna in Winnipeg? How old was I? Five? Six?"

"With three older sisters, Will. They left you with three older sisters."

"They were gone for a week."

A particularly shrill harmonica note pierced the air.

"What's that?" asked Will.

"A child left to his own devices."

★

Will ditched the box and scanned his room, but it was impossible to know if anything else was missing. To think that he had gone out of his way to cheer that little turd up, only to have him snoop around his stuff.

"That, my friend, is mine," said Will, as he snatched the harmonica away from Tom's drooling mouth. "You're plenty old enough to know the difference between what's mine and yours, and this is mine."

"Stop being a bully," said Rose, who finally caught up. "You of all people."

Like Will needed reminding of his years in purgatory. "Downtown Slut" the kids had called him, likely not even knowing what exactly that meant, taunting him after his family had moved from the city into the suburbs. Later came "Elephant Head" for his well-developed ears, and "Prissy Boy" for telling Miss Doniz about the teasing. It took two years to convince Tato to let him switch schools. But by then, Will had developed a skin so thick, they could have called him "Elephant" for real.

"What's wrong with you, Will?" asked Rose now. "Stop scaring the kid. Be nice."

"You're telling me to be nice, when he's the one stealing stuff from my room?"

"Actually, it was his room until you deigned to return. So, in fact, it's he who is being nice here. Not you. And since when do you even care about that stupid harmonica, anyway?"

"It's the principle of the thing," said Will, feeling silly as soon as the words escaped his mouth. Sounding like he knew what was right and what was wrong. Like there was a right and a wrong. To make up for his lapse in judgement, Will dropped the harmonica onto Tom's bed. "But it's a loan, not a present, have I made myself clear?"

Tom snapped up the instrument and brought it back to his mouth. Then he gave Will a long, grateful look before filling the room with yet more wails.

What did she take him for, an unpaid sitter? Will slammed the door shut and walked up Claremont toward Dundas. Nanny 911? Will kicked an empty beer can across the 7-Eleven parking lot and turned right toward downtown. A streetcar rattled by with sad-looking passengers looking out, trapped behind soiled windows like fish in a bowl. Will wasn't sure where he has heading, but with the harmonica wailing and Rose still upset, it was time to get out.

It was not that Will minded Tom. On the contrary, he had always liked the boy, who even as a young child was bright enough to appreciate fishing, even if Parks Ontario made them throw everything back into the lake. For hours, they would sit in the canoe, tucked away in Will's secret spot across the lake. Their peace interrupted only by the occasional bite, a respite from the constant chatter back at the cottage.

But that was then. Now, Tom had shut down like a seaside town at the end of the season, the once brightly coloured streamers faded, his silence a reminder of just how awful everything had become, of how incapable Will was despite his best intentions.

To make matters worse, Will knew he had been unreasonable with Tom. As a kid, he himself had routinely scoped out the house, especially around Christmas. Sadly, his siblings had hated to have their surprises spoiled. "Good things come to those who wait," Mona lectured, when he told her about finding the ugly rag doll she'd been whining about for months. Then she informed Tato and Will was sentenced to a week of shovelling snow. After that, he learned to enjoy the power of knowledge without the need to share.

Will passed a bunch of artsy stores that had popped up in the last couple of years, proving that even a street as ugly as Dundas could be gentrified. He still yearned for Caffe Brasiliano and the row of craggy Portuguese men who used to sit in the window, tiny cups of espresso in their thick worn hands, long fluid sentences overlapping, roaring laughter spicing up endless debates about, Will suspected, nothing. Now, there was yet another fancy restaurant, this one serving up West Coast cool. Just as Will reached Bathurst, his cell rang. It was Coco, the manager of The Supper Club. A party of twenty had booked last minute, and the forecast looked good, meaning that the patio would be hopping with kids eager to waste money on overpriced food and fancy cocktails.

"Let me check my schedule," said Will, not that Coco was fooled. For all her push-up bras and high heels, that one was on the ball.

"Tell you what," she said with that smooth voice she usually reserved for customers. "I know you're interested in cooking, so how about we split your shifts? Half out on the floor, the rest to apprentice with Chef Patrick."

"Thank you," Will said into thin air after hanging up. "Thank you, Lady Luck. Thank you!"

★

The next day, a small moan was all it took for Aunt Rose to let Tom to skip school. Lying under his covers, waiting for the house to clear out, Tom listened to Nick pounding the washroom door. "Hurry up, Will, or I'll tell Mom that it's your fault I'm late."

The door cracked open and Uncle Will scuffled back into his room. Just yesterday, Aunt Rose had told Uncle Will to grow up and behave like an adult. Not that Tom knew what that meant. As far as he could tell, adults were just as clueless as kids, except that no one made them finish their food or send them to school or told them that everything was going to be fine, when clearly it wasn't. "Life ain't fair," Dad used to say, when he ran out of reasons. Now, Tom knew that Dad had been right.

Across the room, Tom noticed *Scott Pilgrim*. He and Saanjh had loved the movie—about a guy who has to fight off his girlfriend's seven evil ex boyfriends before winning her heart but Tom had never even seen the graphic novels the film was based on. He slid out of bed and grabbed one of the tattered paperbacks. Flipping through it, he recognized the CN tower, the Pizza Pizza up on Bloor near Claire's and many of the stores along Queen Street West. All set in downtown Toronto, where he now lived. The place that was becoming home.

"I told you not to mess with my stuff," said Nick, entering the bedroom. "That's a first edition. A collector's item for sure."

Tom dropped the book on the floor, slid back under his covers and grabbed hold of the harmonica that lay hidden underneath the pillow. There was something comforting about holding onto it. Something solid and real.

1, 4, 9, 16.

"Really?" Nick dropped the book back onto Tom's bed. "That was a joke. How can you not know that that was a joke?"

25, 36, 49, 64.

"Whatever makes you happy, dude. I've got to go."

By the time Aunt Rose and Nick finally left the house, Tom had finished *Precious Little Life*, in which Scott Pilgrim gets into a martial arts duel with Ramona's first evil ex-boyfriend, this one called Matthew Patel. Tom opened the door and tiptoed down the hallway. Only once did his foot land too far to the right, causing the tiniest of creaks. Tom stopped, but behind his closed door, Uncle Will was still snoring away.

Tom found the PlayStation in the living room, next to four empty beers and a bag of chips. But where were the controls? He rifled through papers, sweaters, scarves and socks. He lifted the crocheted blanket off Grandpapa's chair, poked behind the French doors, and scanned under the sofa, where he found nothing but a lone yellow mitt. Frustrated, he stood up and frowned.

Every possible surface was cluttered with stuff. On the dining room table sat a mountain of unopened mail, a three-legged teddy bear and, of course, books. Tom had never seen so many books scattered all over one house. In the bathroom alone, next to the toilet, he had found *Growing Older is Not for Sissies,* about wrinkly athletes, *Maus,* a comic that made no sense at all, and *Joy of Cooking, which was* held together by a rubber band. Mom would not have been impressed.

At the far wall of the dining room, a row of cupboards caught Tom's attention. Behind the first set of doors, he found well-aged boxes of board games and a collection of *National Geographic* dating back to the 1980s, along with school assignments that looked like they might have been Aunt Rose's. The paper brittle, the writing crisp. Little hearts on top of the i's.

Tom slid over to open the next pair of doors. On the bottom shelf, among an assortment of candles and napkins, he finally found the missing controller. Just as he was shutting the cupboard door, something oddly familiar caught his eye. Uncertain if really he should go on, Tom stopped. Like that night when he had stood outside his parents' bedroom, that moment when he could've turned back, but did not. Slowly, Tom opened the door. Tucked in the far back of the cupboard, he found a marble urn. His father.

Grey bits of matter and chunky pieces of ash floated in the toilet bowl, daring Tom to finish what he had started. Yet what seemed so obvious just moments ago, felt wrong now. The lever, only inches away, was suddenly impossible to pull. Tom leaned back into the sink, relieved to feel the cool ceramic on his sweaty hand.

"What's going on here?"

Tom whipped around, and as he did, the urn slipped out of his hands, the sound of the marble hitting the tiles and piercing the stunned silence. Uncle Will's eyes darted from the toilet to Tom to the urn on the floor. His voice, when he was finally able to speak, careened between incredulity and respect. "You did *not*, did you really?"

And just like that, Tom's determination came back. He reached for the lever and watched his father drain away. Awash with a sudden feeling of strength, Tom turned to face Uncle Will. Ready now for whatever consequences lay in store.

Uncle Will grabbed the toilet brush and scrubbed the last bits of ashes still clinging to the sides of the bowl. Two more flushes, and Dad was gone.

★

Hunched over the rusty old hibachi, Will added a bit more cardboard to his smouldering concoction of kitchen trash, coals, chicken bones and hair from Rose's brush. "This," he said to Tom, who had been watching his every step, "this should do the trick."

Will sat down on the wobbly garden bench and Tom followed suit. It would take time for the debris to turn into the crushed-seashell-like texture that could pass for human ashes, but it had to be done. How could he justify sleeping as Tom snooped around the house, finding his father's urn, waking only when Russell's remains were floating in the toilet bowl? Even if that was an appropriate ending for a man who killed his sister, Will should have been awake. And he would have been, if he not had Jägermeister shots with Coco after his shift, then beers with Burt on his way home. In hindsight, he probably shouldn't have unwrapped the PlayStation either, played until sunup, and hidden the controls, even if at that time it had felt like pure genius.

Will got up and stirred the ashes again. The consistency was just about right. He grabbed the empty urn and filled it halfway. Unsure how much ash the body of a grown man would yield, he showed it to Tom, who shook his head, grabbed the spoon and added two more heaping scoops.

Will's plan to diffuse the morning's sadness with a bit of gaming might have worked, had it not been for Tom's infuriating ability to make his fingers bounce up and down the controller.

"Beaten again by a nine-year-old mute. Please, someone, anybody, have mercy on me!" wailed Will, but Tom's focus would not waver. There were terrorists to be killed, tanks to be destroyed, enemies to be rooted out. Eyes on the prize, just like Russell. Father and son, Will suddenly realised, were so much alike. Tiny ears, hidden beneath large tufts of hair, but also a lanky build and steadfast determination that had propelled Russell up mountains, across rivers, and away into the world.

"Your father and I ...," Will started, unsure of how to proceed along a path that, much like the one on screen, was full of landmines ready to blow up into his face. "We used to have so much fun. For years, we spent every summer up at the cottage, racing each other across the lake." Will stopped. Best not to mention that it was in the cottage's attic where Will had found the rifle that

Russell had taken back to the city. To have close by, he said, for his next trip hunting, somewhere out West. "Anyway," Will continued, "he was like the brother I never had, so when he started dating Mona, it all seemed so perfect. And for a long—"

Tom hurled the controller across the room, barely missing Will's head.

"Shit, Tom! I was only trying to..."

Tom flew out of the room, ran up the stairs and slammed the door so hard, the windows rattled in their frames.

★

Waiting rooms were depressing, but this one, Sonya decided, was the worst. The walls were mucus yellow, not one of the well-thumbed gossip magazines was less than three years old, and the only décor was a pinboard full of birth announcements and "Thank you, Dr. Blumenthal, you are a genius" cards. Thanks for rubbing it in. The three other women waiting looked as uncomfortable as sitting in the stylish grey vinyl chairs felt.

The door of the doctor's office opened, and a heavily pregnant woman exited. Judging by her tired skin, she was at least forty-three. At that age, Sonya's mother would have already been a grandmother.

"Ms. Fleming," said the nurse, "the doctor's ready to see you."

Sonya slipped her phone into her purse, Kiara's sixth email this hour would have to wait. She got up and walked down the all-too-familiar corridor. For years, Sonya had been Dr. Blumenthal's patient. She had come here first with hope, then with trepidation, then sadness, sudden hope, more sadness and lately, resignation. And now her body was undeniably changing. Aging. She was fatigued, felt bloated, and now was missing her periods altogether.

"So, it's perimenopause, right?" Sonya asked, even before closing the door. "What should I do? Find a new doctor? Clearly, we're done."

"Have a seat," the doctor said, a smile on his face. "In your condition, it's best to take it easy."

"In my condition? Perimenopause is not a condition."

"You're right. But you're not perimenopausal. You're pregnant."

Sonya gasped and sat down. "What are my chances of keeping this one?" she asked.

Dr. Blumenthal leaned back in his leather chair and let out a sigh. But what did he expect? That she would jump up in joy? Give him a hug? At this point, Sonya was keenly aware of all possible risks. She could bleed to death, burden the baby with age-related genetic diseases, die before the kid reached high school.

"Best to worry about things we can do something about," Dr. Blumenthal said, as he flattened his palms on his mahogany desk. Then he pulled out his fountain pen and wrote a prescription. "You know the drill: I'll put you on vaginal Progesterone, twice a day. You need to remain horizontal for at least half an hour after insertion to avoid leaking. Other than that, get lots of rest, keep a balanced diet and, of course, avoid stress."

Sonya had been surprised by Alex's suggestion of a date night at Barbarians, the venerable steakhouse on Elm Street, but now his timing seemed perfect. This was the right place to tell him the news; after all, this was where Alex had proposed, where they had celebrated his MBA, and later, her full-time position at the firm.

A rotund waiter, as staid as the surroundings, guided Sonya and Alex through the already packed restaurant. "This," he said with considerable pride, "This is the very table where Richard proposed to Liz, though I'm uncertain if it was for their first or second kick at the can."

Tonight, the place was packed with men in suits wolfing down slabs of beef and couples celebrating their special nights out. Coming here, Sonya now recognized, had been a bad idea. She should have told Alex about the baby when he came home, given him a chance to take in the news on his own, without waiters hovering about.

"I've decided," said Alex, as he raised his glass of red wine, "that we should have more fun. We should enjoy life. Travel more. Remember Connemara? The crazy lady at the bed-and-breakfast who insisted you were Nika, her long-lost niece? What was the name of that charming village again?" As he rambled on, Alex picked through the plate of pickled vegetables that had arrived unordered, along with a basket of garlic bread. He touched the carrots, the celery, the jalapenos, as well as the more traditional dill pickle, before finally settling on a small piece of chalk-white cauliflower.

Sonya opened her mouth to complain, but stopped, suddenly uncertain about a man who would pick the least interesting item on offer.

"Roundstone," he said. "That's it. Anyway, I've been thinking…"

They used to know everything about each other, Sonya realized, but now she was unsure about the most basic facts concerning her husband. What did Alex do at the gym? Did the sight of a father sharing a hotdog with his son still tear him apart? If he were stranded on a deserted island, would he wish she were there or would he rather have something more practical, like a matchbook or a metal pot? How was it possible that after living together for thirteen years, this man had become more of a stranger, rather than less?

"Anyway, long story short, I've decided that we deserve some more adventures."

"You have?"

"Yes! Like Italy. You've always wanted to go, and there're some great fares right now. I can totally take three weeks off work in May. What do you say?"

For years, Sonya had dreamt about visiting the Amalfi Coast, of exploring the ruins of Pompeii, swimming in the Blue Grotto on Capri, having coffees overlooking the beach in Positano. It was Alex who hadn't wanted to go. Italians don't speak English, he'd say. Driving would be insane. Thieves would rob them blind. So, instead of Italy or Paris, Costa Rica or Spain, they had travelled to Florida, Hawaii, and last year, to rain-drenched Ireland.

"To us," Alex continued, hoisting his glass mid-air, still oblivious to the fact that she had not touched hers. "May the good times return!"

Sonya knew, of course, that the baby would not be hers alone, that she would have to share her child with Alex. Still, she was surprised to find that telling him felt like an obligation, rather than a joy. "I went to see Dr. Blumenthal today."

"I thought we were done with all that. You said you were in menopause."

"I said perimenopause."

"Right. Peri. Meno. Pause."

"Well, turns out I was wrong."

Alex finished his glass before he could finally speak. "Really? You want to go through all that again?"

"The crazy thing is," Sonya said, "I'm already nine weeks along."

Alex took Sonya's hand: "You sure about this?"

"Of course," said Sonya, as she pulled her hand away. "It's what I always wanted."

October

Rose's eyes glided along the row of titles. *Death in the Middle Ages, Death and Dying in Central Appalachia, Maori Death Customs*. The library where she worked on leafy Palmerston Avenue might be small, but it was still home to tens of thousands of books, a surprising number of them obscure. Re-shelving was technically no longer part of her job, but seeing that her co-worker Vanessa had to bring her kid to the doctor with a suspected case of croup, Rose didn't mind filling in. *Irish Wake Amusements*, she read. *The American Way of Death*. And *Rejoice When You Die: The New Orleans Jazz Funerals*. Whatever.

"So? Tonight's the night?"

Rose turned to find Martha, her colleague and friend. Her loose orange dress was somehow flattering, her hair bound into an unruly bun, her lips soft, just like her smile. Martha, who was helpful to a fault, had two delightful kids and a house that was small, but like her, perfectly adorable. Even after five years, Rose had yet to locate Martha's dark side. And she had tried.

"Oh, come on, Rose. Don't make that face. It'll be fun."

"If you think it's so much fun to make small talk with a perfect stranger hoping to get lucky, why don't you go?"

"I'm married, remember?"

"Right. How could I forget?"

Rose liked Evan, Martha's husband, even though he, too, was too perfect for words. A painter who made money, a loving father, and an inspired cook. Flawless, aside from his penchant for silly facial hair patterns, which Rose, in a pinch, could overlook.

"You've got to start somewhere," said Martha, her face so sweet it was hard to stay grumpy. "And Fred's a great guy. You'll have fun."

Rose shook her head and went back to finding the right spot for the book in her hand. She should not have agreed to a blind date. Being single wasn't that bad. She could flirt with whoever she wanted, had time to focus on work and Tom and Nick, and if ever there was any time to spare, she could finally tackle *In Search of Lost Time*.

"I hear that one's worth reading," Martha said, as she glanced at the book Rose had been trying to shelve for the past five minutes.

"Thanks," said Rose, as she dumped *After the Darkest Hour: How Suffering Begins the Journey to Wisdom* back into the cart. "One set-up a month—make that a year—is enough."

It was Rose who had suggested Kalendar on College Street, but now she regretted it. She liked this old standby with its quiet European-like charm. How shortsighted to taint a place this dear for a date.

The hostess, a waif barely out of high school, immediately spotted the book in Rose's hand. "He's in the back," she said, "by the window."

Next time she would pick something less conspicuous, Rose thought. Something more current, less bulky.

Fred, in a polo shirt with khakis and square glasses, was leafing through his own pristine edition of *Too Much Happiness* by

Alice Munro. Way too pristine for him to have actually read it, no matter what he asserted in his admittedly funny emails. But then, who was she to impugn his claim, having proclaimed a love for hiking, which was true more in theory than in any blistered, sunburned, parched reality.

Rose dropped her book next to Fred's and sat down.

"Sorry I'm late."

"No problem," he said, his eyes involuntarily plunging down to her breasts. "I just got here myself."

The empty glass proved him a liar. A considerate liar, but a liar nonetheless. Rose took a sip of water and surveyed the man in front of her, who nervously bit his thin lower lip. He had a full head of hair, but his grey eyes were dull and his chin weak. Martha might think him charming and quite accomplished in microbiology, but this was not going to work. Rose was just about to get up and put an end to this charade, when Fred spoke up: "So, you've done this before?"

"No. You?"

"God, no. It's too weird."

In truth, Rose had been on quite a few blind dates, set up by friends, friends of friends and even Sonya. She had gone on one online date, too, but that ended when the guy asked, before dinner, if she would let him piss into her mouth. She had better luck with men she met on her own. Like the pharmacist addicted to skydiving, or the impossibly blond guidance counsellor from Sweden, who she met on the streetcar. Too bad that one was married. And then there was Nick's hockey coach, who was fun in the sack—until he moved back to Alberta.

The waitress arrived with Rose's Steam Whistle and Fred's Chardonnay, and they each ordered a scroll, the house specialty—her roti filled with beef and caramelized onions, his with ricotta and pesto. Across the room, a young man moved a strand of loose hair behind his girlfriend's ear. The woman smiled and continued to talk. The ease of the gesture made Rose ache. It took time to become that close to another human, to scale a mountain of compromise, forgiveness, tolerance, loyalty and love. The longest she had been able to stand a guy, Eugene, was three years. And that was mostly out of a sense of obligation to provide a father for Nick. Never mind that Eugene's idea of parenting included watching *Fear and Loathing in Las Vegas* with a two-year-old. Then, eight years ago, he had put an end to their pretend family by taking off for Alaska, never to return.

"Martha tells me you've got a son you've been raising on your own," said Fred. "As far as I'm concerned, single mothers are the unsung heroes of our time. It's so much work and such an incredible responsibility, yet there's so little respect. Truly, you've got mine."

Behind those silly glasses, Fred was actually rather cute. His arms were nicely toned and there was that full head of hair. Too bad about the polo shirt tucked into his pleated pants—but then those were items that could be removed.

Misinterpreting Rose's smile as an invitation to go on, Fred continued. "I have a son, too. He's seven. And a daughter. She's nine, Lyla. She's the sunshine of my life. My wife, I mean my ex-wife, Susie, she doesn't understand the special connection between a father and his daughter. She gets jealous at the stupidest things, like when we go—"

"Fred," Rose said, interrupting him before he could launch into a story she had no appetite for. Fred, on the other hand, was palatable, especially after a couple of beers. His smile after all was kind, and those hands looked capable.

"What?"

Rose loved this moment just before conquest. A feeling so intoxicating and real. To be a woman who could get what she wanted. Powerful. Strong. She remembered her younger, more fearless self. Full of desire and desirable because of it. Back then, conquests had been easy. A smile. A laugh. A twist of her hand was all that was needed to feel a stranger's hands on her skin, to smell new aromas and taste distant flavours. Now, more work was needed for ever-diminishing returns.

"How about … " Rose put down her beer and leaned forward, pushing her breasts up just so. Unable to take his gaze off her cleavage, Fred blushed. "How about I go down to the ladies' room, and if you're up for it, you come and join me?"

"Give me a drink," Rose told Will, when she got home an hour later. "I know you've got a stash somewhere. Please."

"Every heard of knocking?" said Will, as he slammed his computer closed. As if Rose cared about what her brother watched online. She sat down on his bed and held out her glass. "Don't make me beg. I deserve it."

"Why? Looks to me like someone already got lucky tonight."

"Whatever makes you say that?"

"Your hair. It's fluffy. Always a surefire sign."

Will pulled out a bottle of Jameson from behind his bedside table and filled Rose's glass up to the rim. The whiskey felt reassuring, even if it did nothing to erase the feel of the cold ceramic sink against her bare skin, the image of Fred's fumbling fingers unrolling the condom, his sorry face when he came after less than a minute.

"Anyways," said Rose, as she downed her drink, "luck has nothing to do with anything."

★

Sonya woke just as Alex's hand journeyed up her inner thigh. He pushed away her nightdress, came to rest for a moment between the folds of her behind, before leaving to grab hold of her breasts. Longing, deeply buried and yet instantly alive, washed through Sonya, making her yearn for more. She pushed her body up against Alex's, his penis hard and undeniable now. Cupping his hands tightly around her breasts, he pulled her in closer yet. Sonya opened her legs and his penis slipped into her already moist vagina, his movements ever mindful of how she responded to him, their bodies attuned in ways their minds simply were not.

It had been ages since they had had sex like this, without considering Sonya's cycle, calculating her chances of conception, or praying that this might be the beginning of the story she would tell her child. After years of riding second class on the train of human evolution, Sonya had finally moved up to first. This time, the ultrasound technician hadn't scurried off to get the doctor. Instead, she had smiled at the shapeless blob that expanded and contracted on the black and white screen, its heartbeat ever so loud and clear. Their child who was due on April 16th, a little less than a year after Mona had died.

Alex, with tears in his eyes, had jumped up to hug the technician as if it were due to her brilliance that there was finally a viable embryo nesting inside Sonya's womb. Then he pulled out his phone to spread the news. But Sonya resisted. "Let's wait," she said, feeling no need to share just yet. What if the baby had spina bifida, she argued, cystic fibrosis, Down or Turner syndrome, or some other yet unnamed chromosomal abnormality? Best to wait until after the amnio, she said, and Alex reluctantly agreed.

By now, the baby had already pulled through dreaded weeks ten, eleven, and twelve. This time, though, Sonya would wait with naming her child.

Getting ready for work the next morning, Sonya checked herself out in the full-length mirror. Her forest green blouse was becoming, especially with her newly hemmed grey skirt. Already her breasts had started to swell, justifying three new bras. Her stomach, too, had grown, not that anyone would recognize her plumpness for anything other than middle-age sprawl.

Sonya pulled out her suede pumps, but her feet no longer fit. Being pregnant was different than what she had imagined. She'd dreamt of living in a bubble of hushed contentment, cosy like when you're watching the first snow fall outside, enfolded in a woollen blanket, the world suddenly all magical and for once, at peace. Instead, she felt nauseated all day and so tired that, last week, she had fallen asleep on the toilet. She had expected bliss, but had gotten fear. An ill-considered step could lead to a devastating fall, a listeria-infested bite of cheese might prove lethal, every passing car had the potential to veer and crash into her unborn child. Her foetus was barely the size of a lime, but Sonya felt as if she'd been hijacked, like she was no longer in charge of her emotions. Tears rolled at the slightest provocation: a boy trapped in an elevator, a YouTube video by a singer without arms and legs, a cat that gave birth to sixteen kittens.

Giving up on the pumps, Sonya pulled out her boots, comfortable from years of use. As she laced up, she noticed a thread hanging loose from the hem of her skirt. Annoyed, she went to the spare room, reclaimed as her sewing room after Tom's departure. The purr of her mother's old machine and its perfectly straight lines had been calming, reassuring even. Over the past few weeks, she had transformed Tom's curtains into a blanket, Alex's sweater into a hat, and become expert at adjusting her wardrobe to her ever-changing frame. "This is a skill every woman needs to have," her mother had insisted. "I don't care how Old World that sounds."

Sonya snipped off the rogue thread and checked herself in the mirror once more. With her scuffed brown boots, the skirt suddenly looked dowdy, and she had forgotten to comb her hair. How was she to survive another day trapped in that stale office air, pretending to laugh at Raheem's unfunny jokes, to not care that J.D. was avoiding her? For nine long years, she had worked at C&C, where a marble reception area quickly gave way to windowless workstations with stained carpets and worn chairs. Having advanced up the ranks without any formal education in the field, she felt trapped in a life not of her choosing, watching as co-worker Lisa left to have twins, followed by Albina and then Stefanie and Savita, too. All of them claimed they would return, even if none of them had.

"I just spoke to the doctor," Sonya told Kiara, when she finally answered her phone. "He says it's contagious, so I'd better stay home for the rest of the week." Sonya hated the idea of lying, but today she hated the idea of going to the office even more. She replaced her smart-wear with sweatpants and grabbed the keys to the car. Rolling down the windows despite the cool fall air, she turned on the radio and sang along to the hits of her youth: "Love Will Tear Us Apart," "Time After Time," and "Don't You (Forget About Me)."

As soon as she entered Designer Fabrics, Sonya's spirits lifted. Rows of silks, cottons and brocades were spread over two glorious floors; guarded by fierce middle-age ladies, who each wielded a set of equally formidable scissors, all assured and knowledgeable and in no mood to humour the uninformed. Tempted by luscious velour, delicate linens and a crimson Italian wool blend, Sonya finally settled on the ox-blood wool as well as a delicious myrtle green rayon. Then she dropped by Neveren's Tailoring Supplies, idling away another two hours sifting through oodles of buttons: some round, others square, made of leather, metal, wood and stone. Overwhelmed by choice, she bought an assortment of brass that would work for pants as well as a skirt, leaving behind an adorable set of pink baby buttons.

On her way home, Sonya drove up Claremont. She slowed down, trying to get a peek behind the sprawling branches of the still unpruned linden. Sonya rolled down her window for a better look, but it was impossible to tell if anybody was home. She considered parking the car, going in to check on Tom, to offer up help, maybe even tell Rose about the baby—but she did not. She could not. What if Tom had no interest in seeing her, what if Rose managed just fine, what if they were living happily ever after, laughing at jokes, enjoying life? Sonya pushed down on the pedal and sped off. Keenly aware of just how much of a failure she was, not just to Tom, but for her dead sister, too.

★

Telemarketer. Nanny. Janitor. Will turned off his phone. None of those jobs would pay enough to afford moving out, so for now, it was best to stick with The Supper Club. Eventually Lady Luck would return. She had to. She needed to. In the meantime, Will would have to put up with Rose's ever increasing demands: clean the backyard, deal with the kitchen sink, escort Tom to the shrink twice a week.

Will pulled a *NOW* magazine from the box. How fun that someone still believed in paper. He scanned the job section (even more dismal than online), read his horoscope (Aries—first, still so totally flaky), and flipped through the reviews of bands he would never go to see. He checked the time: Tom would be done in ten minutes and then, after dropping the boy back at the house, the rest of the day would be his.

Will crossed Bloor Street to ditch his paper in the garbage.

"Excuse me, mister," piped up a little voice. Will turned to find a kid close on his heels. Eight, maybe seven, round glasses and an oversized backpack strapped onto his tiny frame. "Newsprint's not trash, sir. It's recyclable."

"I appreciate your concern, kiddo. Now how about you minding your own business?"

"This is my business, sir. I don't want to grow up on a pile of garbage, just because you're too lazy to recycle."

"Seriously?"

The kid nodded. Earnestness dripping off him like honey, sticky and cloying. Entirely unearned.

"Let's go, Carl," said the kid's redheaded mother, finally deigning to look up from her phone.

"But Mommy, newsprint isn't trash. It's recycling."

"Yes, Carl. I know. Everybody knows."

"That man," Carl said, pointing his finger straight at Will, "that man doesn't know that. That man is stupid."

Will retrieved the *NOW* magazine from the trash. "There. Happy now?"

"There's a recycling bin close by. I can show you."

By the time Will managed to extricate himself, he was committed to buying a Hummer, wearing fur, shopping at Walmart, and never, ever, recycling again. For a quick fix, he settled on McDonald's and ordered two Big Macs to go.

Rush hour was well on its way when Will walked back to his post outside Ms. Colter's office. Waiting for a lull in traffic to cross the street, he noticed a child, sitting on the ground, rolled into a ball, rocking back and forth.

"Damn!" Will said, letting his cheeseburgers fall to the ground. Unconcerned about cars, he rushed across the busy street followed by a cacophony of honks. Just as he reached the boy, Tom started to ram his skull into the wall. At first tentatively, but then with force. His eyes trained on Will, clenching his fist. Unblinking. A woman passing by stopped, stunned into inaction. A little girl screamed.

Vomit pushed up into Will's throat. "I'm sorry, I'm sorry. I was only—" But his voice failed. Swallowing the bitter bile, Will caught Tom's head with his hand, a patch of blood already clotting the kid's hair.

"What's going on here? Do you need help?"

Will looked up, surrounded now by three women, a teenage boy and a man in a pink suit. Concern mixed with curiosity and disgust, just like after Mona had died and crowds had gathered in front of her house. To protect the scene, the police established a security perimeter but curious onlookers held a vigil anyway, wanting to know more, wanting to know why.

"Where's his mother?" somebody asked now.

"Why is he doing this?"

"Would you like us to call 911?"

"Someone should call 911."

"He's having a seizure," Will snapped, "nothing the cops can do about that."

Shamed by his lie, the crowd dispersed. Will slid onto the pavement, coming to a rest next to Tom, who buried his head between his legs. "I'm sorry, Tom, I really am. But there was this kid, Carl, who made me walk all the way over to Bathurst and ... " But Will shut up. This was his fault, there was no excuse. He had promised Ms. Colter to wait just outside the door. "Trust me," he had said, and unwisely, she did.

Cars roared by, a dog sniffed Will's leg, a homeless man asked for change, and Tom curled even more deeply into himself.

"That was stupid. I should've waited here like I said I would. It was totally thoughtless. Irresponsible. Idiotic. And it won't ever happen again. Promise."

Will waited, but Tom did not move.

Trying to match his own breathing to the boy's, Will started to count: One. Two. Three. Four. Five and Six. "Okay, let's go!"

But Tom did not move.

Will stood up. His legs felt bloodless, his throat sore. "Well, that's enough of this. Let's get you home."

Tom looked up, but instead of taking Will's outstretched hand, he squinted into the setting sun and shook his head.

"What do you want me to say?" Will asked. "I'm a fool, a moron, a total shithead, and you're absolutely right to be mad at me. All true, except life's like that. Shit happens, and then we have to deal with it. Now please, can we move on?"

Tom closed his eyes and let his head fall back between his pulled-up knees.

"Please!" Will said, but still no reaction.

"Sorry. Sorry. Sorry. Sorry. Sorry. Sorry."

None.

"Fine, have it your way. Stay for as long as you want to. I'm leaving. I've got things to do, places to go."

Will turned and went on his way. Thankfully, it took only two steps before Tom jumped up, racing past to take the lead. Relieved that the kid was okay, that whatever damage he had caused was not going to last, Will followed Tom down Bloor, a street lined with crappy sushi places, coffee shops and dollar stores whose windows were already stuffed with skeletons and gravestones for Bea A. Fraid.

Will used to love Halloween. As a kid, the sugar had been the main attraction, but as he grew older, he revelled in being shocking. Last year, for Burt's annual costume contest, he had dressed up as James Dean (a Ford grille strapped to his forehead), but after experiencing death up close, Will abandoned his plan to dress up as Jackie (JFK's shattered brains were going to drip off the shoul-

der). No, this year, he would stay home with Rose, hand out can-
dies and forego mocking the dead.

Three blocks later, Will had enough. "Dude, the subway's
back there and please, can we slip into a washroom so that I can
clean you up?"

But Tom continued on, evidently unconcerned with logistics
or looks.

"Fine, you win. I'm an asshole and you're a saint. Congrats. So
now what do you want? A trophy? An invitation to the Sonya's
Club of Perfectitude?"

Tom slowed down, as if waiting for a more enticing offer.

"A soccer ball?"

Did the kid blink?

"A Swiss army knife?"

Was that a smile?

"What? Just tell me what you want, and I'll get it for you."

Tom opened his mouth, but before he had a chance to speak, a
taxi honked inches away, making Will jump.

"Move it, you moron!" yelled the driver.

Only now did Will notice that he had stopped in the middle
of the road.

"Listen," Will said, when he joined Tom on the sidewalk.
"I'm totally, completely and with all my heart sorry. I promised
to wait for you right outside the door and I didn't. I should not
have left. But there's absolutely nothing I can do to undo the past.
Nobody can. All we can do is muddle on and hope for the best."

Tom shrugged. Still waiting for a decent offer. And that's
when Will had an idea.

★

Tom could not figure out what Uncle Will's "favourite place in
the whole wide world" could possibly be. Sitting in the subway,

going east, he considered the waterslides, but in October? The Ghost Blasters Dark Ride in the midway at Niagara Falls? Maybe Canada's Wonderland? Possible, but they were going in the wrong direction for that.

The subway screeched to a halt at Old Mill Station, and a black girl with hundreds of tiny braids got off. Just before she disappeared up the stairs, she turned as if she could feel Tom's look and then she waved. Thankfully, the doors snapped shut and the train moved on before Uncle Will could notice. People were weird, especially girls.

Now only an old man was left in their car, studying a paper printed with nothing but numbers and charts. Tom slid his hand into his pocket, relieved to find the harmonica to hold onto. On the seat across, Uncle Will napped. His arms folded over his chest, feet sprawled out in both directions, his stained jeans ripped along the knees. Tom could not imagine sleeping like that, with strangers looking on, exposed.

At the next stop, three boys in school uniforms boarded, settling down on the other side of the aisle. They debated, each voice louder than the next, about a hockey game they had lost. Uncle Will still did not wake. The train gathered speed, shrieking as metal scraped against metal. Tom let go of the harmonica to cover his ears. Pushing down the palm of his hands, he waited for the comforting sound of the ocean to return, to bring him back to Old Orchard Beach. To the waves and the sand and his parents laughing under the striped umbrella. But it did not come. No matter how hard he pressed, or how fiercely he hoped, even that escape hatch was closed now.

Tom brought his thumb up to his lips, gnawing on a rogue piece of skin, pulling hard. One of the boys, his pimply face crowned by a shock of red hair, stared open-mouthed. But that only made Tom clamp his teeth down harder. Tears crowded his eyes, not that Tom would give in. "Let's move," the boy said to his friends, "That guy's a weirdo." Not that Tom cared.

"Isn't this something?" said Uncle Will when they finally arrived. Tom scanned the huge, almost empty parking lot, uncertain what exactly was so fantastic about a glass building that looked like a mall. Under an enormous red and green sign that said Woodbine, he read *Racing* and *Slots*.

"When Rose and I were your age," Uncle Will continued, giddy as if this were Christmas, Easter and Halloween all rolled into one, "we used to piss in our pants with excitement when Tato would take us to the races. This is the one place where we got to eat hotdogs and fries smothered in ketchup and mayonnaise."

Inside the lobby, curved walls were covered with paintings of tall, lanky horses, men wearing black hats and ladies holding tiny umbrellas. In the middle sat a round information booth, like a saucer without a cup. Beyond it, an old man, leaning into his walker, tottered into a room guarded by two uniformed men.

"Slots," snorted Uncle Will and hung a right. "Stupid electronic hocus-pocus baloney crap. Perfect for fools."

Rushing past posters of long ago races and a line of colourful flags, Tom struggled to keep up, his sneakers squeaking on the black and white floor tiles. He still had no idea where exactly they were off to and why. At the end of a long hallway, Uncle Will waited impatiently at the top of an escalator. *Paddock* read Tom, just as he caught up, only to trip over a man's foot.

"Mind your step!" the man shouted and pushed Tom aside.

"People are assholes," said Uncle Will and grabbed Tom's hand. "Yet another reason to stick to horses. And each other."

As they stepped onto the escalator, Tom did not let go of his uncle's hand. It felt warm, and strong, and reassuring—feelings the he hadn't missed until just now.

The paddock, located on the lower floor of the gambling complex, smelled of hay and animals and sweat and fear. Uncle Will said hello to a scrawny man who nervously bounced from one foot to the other, his gaze constantly shifting from the weird paper in his hand, to the TV monitors that hung suspended from the ceiling, to his cell phone, to the horses being paraded around for inspection, and then back to the paper. The same weird paper the old man had studied on the subway. "A racing form," Uncle Will explained when he noticed Tom staring, as if that clarified anything.

Tom drifted off toward the metal railing at the far end of the room, joining a row of men gathered like birds on a wire. A steady stream of horses walked past, along with their tiny jockeys in colourful shirts. Wanting a better look, Tom wedged himself between a man with an orange tuque and a bearded guy in a sweat-stained Nirvana T-shirt. "Fuck," the Nirvana guy grumbled without taking his eyes off the TV that showed a race on some other track, somewhere else in the world. "Fuck me and fuck me hard."

"Mind your language," said the man in the tuque, pointing to Tom.

"This is a racetrack, not a playground," said the man and walked away. "Not my problem, if people have wacko ideas about how to raise their kids."

"Proof number 53: people are assholes," said Uncle Will, turning back toward the escalator. "And just for the record, as long as you're not placing bets, it's perfectly legal for you to be here. Now, let's move it. They're about to close my first race."

Dashing back up the escalators and racing through the food court, they reached a long row of cashiers. Uncle Will surveyed the tellers and picked a bookish man who reminded Tom of Mr. Dukali.

152

"I didn't know you had a son," said the man, who on closer inspection looked nothing like Tom's former math teacher. This guy was intense, unlike Mr. Dukali who had been funny and kind and super smart, too.

"He's not my son. He's…" Uncle Will turned and patted Tom on the head. "He's my lucky charm."

"Always good to have one of those around. Especially for you, Will."

"Whatever, Madhu. Give me Woodbine at $50. To win. Number five."

"That's it?"

"I'm just getting warmed up, is all. Give me a break."

Madhu passed Uncle Will his receipt and craned over the counter to get a better look at Tom. "First time at the track, kiddo?"

Tom slid behind his uncle and started to count: 10 times 6 is 60, 9 times 6 is 54, and 8 times 6 is 48.

"He's not that much of a talker," said Uncle Will, turning to draw Tom closer, wrapping him under his protective arm. "Kind of cool actually."

In the end, the vortex of hope proved impossible to resist. As they shuttled between the red plastic seats of the grandstand, the betting area on the second floor, and the paddock in the basement, Tom, for the first time since that dreadful night, forgot about his parents for more than a minute at a time. Race after race, Uncle Will put down money, winning some and losing more, jumping up and jumping down, cheering, screaming, cursing, pledging to never ever gamble again, to better his ways, to clean up his act. And then they would return to Madhu, place another bet, and start cheering anew.

"You want to have a go at it," Uncle Will said after losing money three races in a row. "Beginner's luck is a thing, it really is." Then he explained the difference between straight, place and show. They studied the Beyer Speed Figures and considered special bets like trifecta, quiniela and daily doubles. But Tom bet solely by the name of the horse, winning $30 with Skip Away and $10 with Desert Prince, only to lose $15 on Dreamer.

In the end, neither Uncle Will's knowledge nor his superstitions made the slightest difference, and he lost everything on Tango in the Night. A name so silly, Tom almost laughed.

★

The time for action had come. After working intermittently for months, this morning the kitchen sink had stopped draining for good. Ditching the plunger, Rose grabbed the Drano, only to be confronted with instructions so tiny she'd need a loupe to make them out. Hoping for the best, Rose poured a generous amount into the sink.

The water still refused to budge.

Rose grabbed the industrial strength plumbing aid she found in a stash Tato had left behind in the basement. Her eyes began to water and her throat to burn. Still, she added three more shots but even those did nothing aside from creating more fumes. She was just about to turn to the Internet for guidance, when her phone rang. TD Bank, she read, before picking up the call. She poured the rest of the Drano into the sink and left for the living room to let the magic happen on its own.

"Yes, that's me," Rose answered. "Why?"

"We're calling to discuss some unusual activity in your bank account, ma'am."

Rose sat down and listened to a list of withdrawals she had no memory of making.

"I am such a fool," she finally said. "I thought my brother was losing his own money, not mine."

"Your brother," the man on the phone asked, barely able to suppress his incredulity, "has access your account?"

"We share a password. It makes things easier for the bills and…" Rose stopped, hoping for something brilliant to pop into her mind, but all she could come up with was "and stuff."

"Well, it's important to keep a close track of your transactions," the man on the other side of the phone offered up. "Especially if one chooses to share access."

"I'm a single mother with two kids and a full-time job. I barely have time to brush my teeth."

But Rose knew it was not a matter of time. She simply did not have the stomach for dealing with her finances, a legacy of growing up with a father who would go to great—mostly legal—lengths for even the slightest financial advantage. Especially when it came to avoiding taxes. "They'll be squandering my hard-earned money on fake expenses anyhow. Anyway, I'm not going to pay for anything unless I absolutely have to."

"So these are all legitimate transactions," the man on the phone concluded. "No action required from our end."

Reluctantly, Rose agreed and hung up. She was about to return to the kitchen when there was a knock on the door.

"What now?"

"Okay," said Ray when Rose had finally finished venting about her idiot brother, writing copious notes into his file, judgment oozing from every stroke of his pen. How had he already accumulated a file that thick? Who else had he spoken to? And why oh why oh why had she felt the need to tell Ray about Will?

Without looking up, Ray finally spoke: "What your brother's doing with his money, or even with your money, is none of our concern as long as Tom is safe and provided for."

"Good, 'cause Will's an irresponsible jerk, for sure, but that has nothing to do with Tom."

"Except," said Ray, now looking straight at Rose with his wintery blue eyes, "how can you guarantee that Will won't somehow access, and squander, money intended for Tom?"

"He wouldn't do that," said Rose quickly, realizing now where this was going. "Yes, he borrowed money from me. Fine, without asking. Not good. Obviously. But he always pays everything back. Eventually."

"So this isn't the first time that he has 'borrowed' money from you without letting you know."

Anger flooded Rose's body with such ferocity, she gasped. To keep calm, she pinched herself hard. "Why—" she started, but it took her another deep breath to find a level voice. "Why don't you busy yourself with real problems, Ray? Like those babies abandoned in garbage cans, or dads who paint swastikas on their sons, or how about those Native kids you guys keep taking away?"

"Rose, it's my job to make sure that Tom's interests are protected. Seeing that your brother has—let's be kind and call them 'idiosyncratic'—ideas about what's his and what isn't, why wouldn't he apply that same questionable judgment to Tom?"

"Will's immature, sure. And weird, okay, but he's not a thief. And he and Tom have been getting on really well lately, in fact, Will even offered to bring the kid to the shrink."

"Is that where they are right now?" asked Ray, looking at his watch.

"I ... " Rose started, but was stopped short by a toxic cloud. "Oh no," Rose yelped, jumping up, "oh no, no, no!"

Racing into the kitchen, Rose found the sink spewing noxious fumes like a cantankerous Icelandic volcano. Coughing uncontrollably, she retreated into the living room, bumping into Ray, who had followed close by.

"Wow, this is…" he started, but by now the stench got the better of him, too. Still, he managed to cross the kitchen, pushing open the patio doors to air the place out. "What a mess!"

"Your powers of observation are astonishing," Rose said, joining Ray in the backyard. "But seriously, you try to keep this place in order with three guys doing their damnedest to mess everything up."

"We're not aiming for perfect here," said Ray. "Manageable is more like it."

Looking back at her kitchen darkened by smoke, a new wave of anger flushed over Rose. This was a mess. Her life was a mess. And Will, what an unbelievable idiot! How dare he take her money without bothering to ask first? After all she had done for him, after all she was still doing for him. Rose took a step back only to stumble over the hibachi Will had promised to clear away ages ago. Unable to restrain herself, Rose kicked it so forcefully, its filthy contents spilled across the backyard.

Rose closed her eyes, willing her fury to fade away. Ever since Mona had died she had experienced these sudden bursts of rage. The first time this happened was when Suzanne, her hairdresser of fifteen years, made her wait for forty-five minutes. Rose had shouted at the hapless receptionist and went to the wake with her roots showing. Later that month, a Lexus had cut her off while she was crossing Bathurst and she banged on the car's hood so hard, it left a dent. Horrified, the driver took off without calling the police.

Rose sat down on the small wooden bench and lit up a cigarette.

"How about spotting me a smoke?" asked Ray, and Rose obliged, pleased to share her dirty habit.

Ray sat down. Close, but not quite touching. Silently, they watched as all around them autumn leaves fell, the chill in the air undeniable now. Before long, the days would be grey and rainy and short. Winter was coming.

"Listen," Ray finally said. "What happened to your sister, to Tom, to you, is unfathomable. What you're going through is the worst nightmare one can possibly imagine. Still, there's no undoing the past." Ray took another drag of his cigarette before he continued: "After my mother died, I was in denial for years. And there's comfort in that, I understand. But you need to be stronger. For Tom. It seems impossible at times, I'm sure, but you have to deal with what's been put onto your plate. It's a challenge, for sure, but also an opportunity to grow."

"So my sister had to die for me to grow as a person?"

"Rose. That's not what I said. Or not what I meant, anyhow. All I'm saying is that we need to create an environment that is healing, not just for Tom, but for you too, and your family as a whole."

Ray got up and made for the kitchen door but then he turned: "As a sign of respect for you and all the work you're doing, I will keep what happened today between you and me. But please, Rose, promise me to get your head out of the sand. Sometimes those we love most are not who they appear to be."

"Thank you," whispered Rose. But by then, Ray was gone.

★

It was embarrassing to have Tom pay for the subway ride home, but sometimes shit could not be helped. Lady Luck would return, Will was sure of it. Just a question of time. And then he would pay Tom back, and Rose too.

"Are you insane?" asked Rose as soon as they arrived at Claremont, her face flecked with red spots. Tom ran upstairs as Rose pulled Will right back outside. "I trusted you and you repay me by stealing money from me?"

"Who told you?"

"What does that matter, Will? You've been stealing from me. Why?"

"Technically speaking, Rose, I haven't been stealing. I borrowed some money, yes, but I will pay it back. I promise."

"You really think your promises mean anything to me?"

Will looked at his sister, and for the first time ever, he wasn't sure she'd give in. Something had changed. There was something hard about her now, something unyielding.

"What's going on, Rose?"

"Our first priority has to be Tom. What if Children's Aid finds out about you stealing my money and then gambling it away? What if they take Tom?"

"Oh that's bullshit and you know it. Where would they take him, anyway? And why? He's fine with us. Great actually. We had such a nice afternoon. I even got him to smile. Once."

"Right. Where were you? Weren't you done at the shrink's hours ago?"

"We went to Riverdale."

"The petting zoo?"

"Yup."

"And Tom was into that?"

"He didn't hate it."

"Really?"

"If you don't believe me, why don't you ask him?"

November

Something was up. Sonya wasn't sure what, but something was not as it ought to be. Alex had been getting up early and leaving for work even before having coffee, only to return home late, after the gym, a last minute meeting or an impromptu game of hockey with Bill and the gang. Last night, he smelled of cigarettes—odd given that he'd never smoked. In the movies, Sonya thought, this was when the concerned wife searches the pockets of her husband's jackets, examines the phone bills or calls in a private eye.

Except she couldn't be bothered. Sonya enjoyed having the house to herself, especially now that she no longer had to face the future alone. So what that Alex wasn't as excited about the baby as she was? Until he saw their daughter smile—and Sonya was sure that she was a she— until he smelled her delicious peach-skinned body, played with her adorably pudgy feet, she was just a concept. A concept as perplexing to him as black holes were to her.

Sonya turned off the taps and unbuttoned her shirt. A bath would wash away another day of dealing with self-aggrandizing emails and meaningless smiles. Whatever import her career once had, it no longer claimed any pull. As soon as Sonya left the office, her professional life slipped away, like a bad dream that dissolves into a vague feeling of discomfort the moment you open your eyes.

Sonya stepped out of her panties and cupped her hands around her small yet positively bulging belly. For sixteen long weeks, life had grown within her, undetected by the outside world, thanks to her prowess with her sewing machine, and strategic dressing. Her baby, who was now the size of an avocado, could already squint, frown, grimace, and pee.

Sonya checked the thermometer: 36 degrees. Safe. Taking this bath was her treat for making it out of the first trimester, but she was not going to take any chances. Then she set the timer for ten minutes. The water made Sonya's skin sting. Goosebumps ran up her thighs, making her shiver. As she submerged herself underneath a thick layer of bubbles, her muscles relaxed, her mind eased. If everything went well with the amnio, they would be safe in fifteen more weeks. Maybe things would be all right. Maybe the tide had finally turned.

"Wow, you're having a bath," Alex said, as he stepped into the bathroom. "Weren't you told not to?" Over his shoulder hung his hockey bag, on his face a sheepish grin. He kicked off his shoes and dumped his sweats into the laundry hamper.

"Do me a favour," said Sonya. "I'm dying for a glass of orange juice."

"Should I make it a mimosa?"

"Are you kidding me?"

"Why? Us making it out of the first trimester is something to celebrate and you love mimosas, so who's going to begrudge you one glass? We still have the case of bubbly I bought on sale in Vermont. Remember?"

Sonya took a deep breath and slipped back under the water. Yes, she remembered the trip to Vermont. They had driven down there to celebrate their 10th anniversary. Alex insisted on Stowe, a mountain resort where his parents used to celebrate their anniversaries, a place that still held a dear spot in Alex's imagination, even if they'd divorced twenty years earlier and had barely spoken since. Unsurprisingly, the trip down Alex's faulty memory lane was a bust. It rained for three days straight, the food was awful, the innkeeper rude. On the way home, they hit a deer, leaving its legs twisted, its white belly sullied with blood, eyes open, frozen wide.

Sonya re-emerged through the bubbles and said, "I'm not about to endanger the baby by drinking alcohol, just because you couldn't resist a deal."

But Alex had already left, and she was relieved.

★

"This is bullshit," Will said to Tom, who was trying his best to keep up. Will turned into an aisle full of cheap-looking faucets, oversized sinks, ugly toilets, and matching seats. "It's not like having a Y chromosome means that I'm into fixing things. How would she like it if I were to ask her to iron my shirts, just because she's a woman?"

But fixing the kitchen sink was part of the deal he had struck with Rose in the aftermath of "Borrowgate," so fix it he would. Will walked through the sprawling hardware store with mounting exasperation. "Where the hell is everybody? Does anybody work here? Hello???"

Finally, they stumbled upon the plumbing supplies at the far end of aisle eight. Will grabbed a snake, not that he knew what to do with it, and threw it into his cart. Then he added a clog buster, a drain bladder and three different liquid chemicals, just in case. This was a job that had to get done. Rose's threats to kick him out were getting uncomfortably real.

On the way to the cash register, Will added a can of WD-40,

gardening gloves and a set of bocce boules on sale. By the time they left the store, he was eighty-five bucks lighter, toting seven heavy bags in exchange.

"Tom, please, let's keep the dillydallying to a minimum today, okay?" said Will, as they set off toward the subway. "There's a game at the Done Right Inn, and I know that Lady Luck will be on my side today."

At the station, Will dropped two tokens into the box and pushed through the turnstile, but when he turned around, he found that a girl in an orange parka had snuck in behind him, instead of Tom. "My second token was for that boy," said Will to the TTC teller, "not her."

The teller shrugged and returned to reading his book. Will rushed onward but Tom followed at his usual glacial pace. Like a snail with its house attached, shutters drawn. Waiting by the stairs, Will noticed a man flinging his *Globe and Mail* into the garbage.

"Hey, that's recycling," Will said, startled at the words that had just come out of his mouth. Still, he continued, "There's a recycling bin over there."

The man trained his steely grey eyes on Will. Two hundred pounds of muscle, ready to pounce. In a suit two sizes too small.

"And how exactly," the man said in a voice that was surprisingly squeaky, given his massive frame, "is it your business what I choose to do with my paper?"

"Our world's drowning in shit," said Will, taking a deep breath before continuing, "just because people are too lazy to do their bit."

"Really?" The man closed in. His musky aftershave made Will recoil within inches of the stairs leading down to the trains. "You really think that you have the right to tell me what to do?"

Just then, Will felt a pull on his bags, and when he looked, he saw Tom anxious to move on. For a moment, Will considered letting the man pass, and leaving the teaching of life lessons to those more qualified. But then he remembered Mona and how he had stepped aside instead of stepping in, how he had stood silent, instead of speaking up, and his resolve to do the right thing returned.

"There's only one planet that we all have to share, and it's our job to make sure it survives."

"Well congratulations, then, asshole, on sainthood." The man made the sign of the cross and lightly tapped Will's forehead with his middle finger before taking off.

Surprised by the stranger's touch, Will swayed backward, his footing uncertain on the brink of the steep, slippery stairs. In an attempt to steady himself, he reached out for the railing, but with his many bags, it was impossible to grab hold. Trying desperately to restore balance, Will bent his body forward, only to have his right foot slip off the ledge. He tilted backward but instead of finding equilibrium, Will stepped into thin air, tumbling down, one step at a time, coming to a full stop only when his body finally hit the concrete floor at the bottom of the stairs.

*

If he hadn't been counting his steps, thought Tom, if he'd carried some of Uncle Will's bags, if he hadn't needed to see Claire, if he had managed to get on with Aunt Sonya, if he hadn't played with his stupid Transformers, if he had protected Mom, none of this would have happened. Tom reached for his harmonica, crushing it hard against his lips. The metal felt cold, unyielding, but his blood tasted true. This was all his fault. Again.

Unable to move, Tom stood at the top of the stairs, staring at the plunger that stuck upright among the scattered bags. Be-

165

low, Uncle Will lay sprawled across the concrete floor, his right leg sticking out to the side, disconnected like Brawl. Like Mom. Tom's knees slackened, but before they could buckle, before he could let go and follow Uncle Will down into the abyss, hands grabbed him by the shoulders, shaking Tom so hard, his eyes popped open. The face of a woman hovered too close for him to focus. Her mouth moved as she talked, but none of it made sense. Whenever Tom caught a word, the next five slipped away, like silvery fish in an unruly current. Shaking her head, the woman moved in closer, but her stale breath made Tom back away. He sensed the edge of the stairs behind him but her grip around his arm tightened, and then the police officer—he recognized her uniform now—pulled him away.

"Come with me," she said, guiding Tom out of the station and onto the street. "Let's have a chat."

The woman, Officer Dunkirk, kept asking questions Tom had no answers for. Just like last time, he thought, biting down hard on his tongue. "Where can we reach your mother? Do you want to go home or follow your dad? Where do you live?"

Then she repeated each question at triple volume, as if he was partially deaf.

"Where do you live?"

Tom closed his eyes.

"Would you like to go home or follow your father?"

His tongue slid along his front teeth, finding sensitive tissue that was already bruised.

"Where can we reach your mother?"

Tom bit down hard.

"Talk to me," said Officer Dunkirk, her voice now pleading. "Please."

Just then Uncle Will appeared on a stretcher. Tom tried to break loose, to beg for forgiveness, to hold onto his uncle and never let go, but Officer Dunkirk's grip held firm.

"You can't go with him, sorry," she said. "But we'll stay close. Promise."

Then the ambulance sped off. This time, at least, the sirens wailed.

Once they arrived at the hospital, Tom and Officer Dunkirk sat among the old and the injured, waiting for Uncle Will to come out of surgery. A man with a three-toothed smile made the rounds, asking for change, his dented paper cup filling up with nickels and dimes. A baby screamed at the top of his lungs, silenced only when his mother pushed her dark purple nipple into his mouth. Startled awake by the sudden silence, the old man next to Tom repositioned himself and nodded back off. Perfectly at ease with sleeping in public, just like Uncle Will when they had gone off to the races. A thought that now made Tom gag.

"Are you hungry?" Officer Dunkirk asked, and Tom nodded, hoping that food might help take away the stale taste in his mouth.

By the time Aunt Rose came running, her heels clacking on the tiled floor like a pair of wind-up teeth, Tom and Officer Dunkirk had shared a large bag of chips, leaving Tom feeling even more sick to his stomach. Aunt Rose, her eyes smudged like an owl, swooped him up into her arms.

"I'm here now," she kept saying, hugging him tightly. "I am here now."

Tom allowed her touch. Even pressed his face into her hair, comforted by the familiar smell, savouring it actually, because soon enough Aunt Rose would throw him out, and Tom knew he would have nobody to blame but himself. It was his fault that Uncle Will was all messed. His alone.

"I have no idea why this crap keeps happening to us," Aunt Rose said, her voice shaky with tears. "It's like we're a shit magnet. Seriously. It's fucked up."

"Could I see some ID please?" asked Officer Dunkirk, not impressed with Aunt Rose's language. "Any picture ID will do."

Aunt Rose looked up, but refused to let go of Tom. "You're kidding, right? This is my nephew. He lives with me. He knows who I am."

"I can't release a child into the care of an unidentified stranger. The law's the law, ma'am. Surely, you can appreciate that."

Before Aunt Rose could argue, Tom wrapped his arms even more tightly around his aunt, squeezing hard. Please, he kept saying in his mind. Please don't. Don't. Don't. Do not! Please. Please. Please!

Somehow understanding his silent pleas, Aunt Rose pulled out her ID, letting Officer Dunkirk copy down her information.

When they were finally allowed to see Uncle Will, he was asleep—his head wedged between two rubber pads, a belt strapped across his brow, plastic tubes growing out of his arm. There were beeping machines, a cast on his left arm and another on his right leg, hanging up in a sling above the bed.

Despite the injuries, Aunt Rose seemed relieved. "Bones mend," she said. "All they need is time." Then she left to use the washroom.

Tom looked around the room. Two of the other beds were taken. Closest to the door slept a man with a belly bloated to the size a basketball. His hospital gown was pushed up above his knees, revealing thighs covered in a network of dark purple veins. Across, a birdlike woman circled letters in a book of puzzles. Her wiry leg up in a sling, on her bedside table a framed portrait of a black cat.

Tom pulled his chair closer to his uncle's bed. The wedges around Uncle Will's head distorted his features and there were small flecks of blood on his cheeks. On his forehead, a large egg-shaped bump seemed to be still growing, the skin soft and squishy like an overripe peach. Uncle Will's inhales were long and slow, followed by an eternity without any breath at all. Tom was just about to poke him, when Uncle Will sputtered back to life like a cranky old car. Instantly, tears sprung into the boy's eyes. Maybe Uncle Will would get to live after all.

★

Rose stubbed out her cigarette and decided to take the stairs, hoping physical exertion would burn off some of her rage. Why on earth did Will get into a fight? In front of Tom? And why did they bring him here, to Sunnybrook, rather than to a hospital downtown? And *why why why* did that clueless cop have to spoil Tom's first hug? How she had longed for this moment that was now ruined by bureaucratic bullshit.

By the time Rose reached the sixth floor, her thighs screamed bloody murder and her heart felt like it might explode. Come on, old lady, you can do this, she kept goading herself. I must. I will. I can! She forced herself up one more flight, and then even one more, but once Rose reached the ninth floor, sweat ran down her spine and her head felt like it might explode. Conceding defeat, she took the elevator the rest of the way, her anger now worsened by her inability to endure.

In Room 1503, Rose found Tom standing by her brother's bedside. As she approached, she noticed the boy's left hand suspended above a large bruise that had formed on Will's forehead, hovering as if it were a button waiting to be pushed. Rose knew that she should intervene, but curious about what Tom might do, she stopped at the door. Slowly, Tom lowered his hand. Then, he waited. Lowered his hand some more. Waited again. Tom, his face transfixed, lowered his hand even more. Now, less than a couple of millimetres separated his hand from Will's bruise. Then, just before making contact, Will's eyes popped open.

"No touching," Will said, as he swatted away the boy's hand. "Nobody teach you that yet, eh?"

Tom leaned back into his chair, a small smile on his face. Never mind that Will was bandaged like an Egyptian mummy, Rose thought, that his ten-day stubble looked grubby rather than cool, that he was strapped into place like a lunatic needing restraint. Will's spirits had returned.

"Sorry it took me so long," said Ray, when he arrived at the hospital hours later. "But traffic's just unbelievable."

"It's fine," replied Rose. "In fact, I'm not even sure why you bothered. It's not like there's anything to be done here. Will's still sleeping, Nick's busy being social with his phone, and Tom and I are playing cribbage. Old school." Then, after considering her hand one more time, she played out the five of hearts.

Tom put down a ten, moving his peg into a twenty-three point lead.

"Impressive."

"Not really," said Nick, who was perched on the windowsill, texting without looking at his screen. "Mom sucks at this game, not that that would ever stop her from playing."

"Thanks, my dear, darling son," said Rose. "I love you, too."

"I've brought snacks," said Ray, pulling out chips, nuts, and three granola bars. Turning to Tom, he added: "What's your pick?"

"Cute," Nick said, as he jumped off the windowsill. "Like he's gonna start talking just like that."

"Nick, please. Not today."

Tom grabbed the chips, put down his Jack and moved his peg across the finish line.

"Holy crap! Jesus, not again," Rose said, throwing down her remaining cards. "This is unreal."

The man in the bed by the door turned up his TV.

"Sorry," said Rose, not feeling sorry at all.

"You've got to learn to count, Mom."

"I count."

"What evs."

Ignoring Rose's spat with her son, Ray walked over to Will, who lay unmoving in his bed. His eyes closed, his breathing steady. "So what's the deal here, Rose?"

"He's got a concussion and multiple fractures, but he'll be fine."

"Whatever fine is."

"Exactly," Rose agreed, unable not to smile. Glad now that she had called Ray, relieved not to be the only adult in the room. After weeks of visits, she had gotten used to Ray's calm presence, enjoyed it even. Despite herself.

"Sorry but—" Will's voice startled them all.

"Yes," said Rose. "What do you need?"

"I've got to piss."

"Let's get a nurse," said Nick, and for once, Rose agreed with her son.

"You okay?" asked Ray many hours later, standing on the stoop of Claremont, his hand settling lightly on Rose's arm. The Portuguese widow from next door shook her head and abandoned sweeping her already-swept yard, shuffling back into her house.

"Of course I'm okay," said Rose, shivering but unwilling to go inside just yet. The weather had turned cold these past few days, hovering at freezing, but she had yet to pull out the sweaters and coats, long johns, mitts, hats and boots needed to survive the harsh Canadian winter. "It's not like I've got a choice."

"Choice is highly overrated anyway." Ray smiled without removing his hand. His touch felt warm, reassuring. "Sometimes it's best just to go with the flow."

His hands disappeared into his coat, but he stayed close enough for Rose to smell his aftershave. Old Spice. Simple. Yet manly, too.

"Do you—" Rose began. She paused for a moment, considered if really she should, before taking the leap. "Do you want to come in for a coffee?" Followed by what she hoped was a most alluring smile.

"I—," Ray stumbled backward, almost falling onto the walkway. "I'd best be on my way, Rose. Sorry."

"Why? You told me you're single. I'm single. And if you can be discreet, so can I."

"There are so many reasons why that's a terrible idea."

"I can keep secrets."

"Rose," Ray said, straightening his back, as if the extra inch might help his cause. "Even if I were reckless enough to endanger my livelihood, I don't swing that way."

Did she hear this right? Rose took a small step forward and cocked her head: "Really? Not even a little bit?"

"Nope. That said, I'd love to hang out. Grab a drink maybe. Just not tonight."

★

Faced with waves of trepidation, doubt and doom, overlapping in ever shortening intervals, Sonya turned on her bedside light. She tried to read but her mind was not to be stilled. What if she got an infection? A fever? Uncontrollable cramps? All possible side effects of doing the amniocentesis, scheduled for first thing in the morning. Would she abort her child if she had Down's? How about muscular dystrophy? Cystic fibrosis? For hours,

Sonya's mind circled every possible fear, leaving her exhausted by the time dawn finally broke.

"I'll make us coffee," said Alex but Sonya declined. No point in agitating the baby. What if she moved just as the needle poked through?

Driving silently to Sunnybrook Hospital, Sonya suddenly knew, with a certainty that was as clear as a bright fall day, that the time had come, yet again, to say good-bye. Her days as a mother were over.

"Let's not do it," she said, turning to Alex. "It's a stupid risk to take."

"Sonya, Dr. Berger has done amnios for thirty-some years. She knows what she's doing. There's so little risk."

"With my luck, I might just be the one in five hundred."

"It's time for you to get a break, this might just be it. And—" Alex hesitated, but then he spoke on: "You'd never forgive yourself if you didn't make sure everything is okay."

When they arrived, Alex took Sonya's hand and did not let go. So she walked into the hospital with quiet resolve. They waited for the doctor without speaking, she cradling her belly like it might be the last time, he staring at the wall as if it were a TV.

"Ms. Fleming," the nurse called out and Sonya leaned over to give Alex a kiss good-bye.

"Oh, I'm coming with," he said. "It's my baby, too."

Clad in a hospital gown, Sonya settled onto the cold bed. Again, Alex took her hand. Squeezed it hard. After the nurse prepped her belly with an antiseptic, Dr. Berger walked into the room, chatting while slipping on her gloves and scanning Sonya's belly with an ultrasound. Then she inserted a needle that was just as enormous as all the websites had warned, though the prick itself was so much less painful than last year's flu shot.

"Best to take the day off," the doctor counselled when it was all over, and Sonya was only too happy to comply. A chance was what she had taken, a break was what she needed.

Back home on her sofa, Sonya had just settled down with tea, when her phone rang.

"Are you kidding me?" asked Sonya, but Ray was not.

"He's been at Sunnybrook since Tuesday, you didn't know?"

Sonya felt like smashing the phone. Rose was such a cow. Treating her like she was in the "We'll tell her when we get to it" category of relations. As if Sonya was just a spectator with no emotional stake in the outcome. Relegated to the nosebleed section of her own family.

"Well, communication skills have never been my sister's strong suit," Sonya finally said, surprised but pleased to hear Ray chuckle in response. She liked Ray. He had come by for a visit as part of his home study and seemed honest, and kind.

A sharp cramp made Sonya hang up. She cupped her belly with her hands, trying hard to breathe away the pain. To think she might end up in the same hospital as her idiot brother. Getting into a brawl in front of Tom, Sonya shook her head. How's that for taking unnecessary risks? But maybe Will's unwillingness to grow up was understandable. Being the youngest, he was only ten when their mother had passed on, living his life under the protection of his three older sisters, certain after each adventure that he could return to a safe haven. The pain finally eased, and Sonya started to breath more easily. How different things would be if they'd spoken to one another. She could have visited with Will after the amnio, told her family finally about the baby. But now, after this latest betrayal, Sonya felt justified in keeping her secret.

Sonya got up and went to the kitchen, peckish for something, though unable to put her finger on exactly what. Pickles? Eggs? Pizza? Tonight might be perfect to revive their old ritual of "date-night-in," even if she would have to skip the wine. Sonya pulled out her phone and called the new pizza place on Sheppard.

"A medium sundried tomato pizza with arugula," she said, then adding an order of pepperoni and cheese for Alex.

Only after hanging up did Sonya realize that she'd need cash to give the driver a tip. She rummaged through the glass jar on top of the fridge, but all she could scare up was $1.35. She patted down her coats, finding nothing aside from old receipts, a hairband, and an equally useless TTC transfer from last May. Then she moved over to Alex's jacket. What she found made her heart stop: a three-pack of condoms, with one of them missing.

★

Rose's heart skipped a few beats when she read the library's daily log: 28th of November. Six months ago today!

She heaved herself out of her chair and made for the library restroom. The ice-cold water stung her hot face, but she kept splashing hard. How was it possible that already six months had passed? Six months since her sister was bludgeoned to death. By a husband who then blew his brains out in the family kitchen, unconcerned with his son hovering upstairs.

For so long, everything had seemed to stand still, but then, somehow, life started moving again. Summer had come and gone. Leaves changed colors, then fell, but all along, her pain had not lessened. Mona was still dead. Tom was still lost—even if Ms. Colter claimed progress. Somehow, graduating from drawing pictures of Brawl to pictures of Mona was a major step forward.

"I'm running across the street for a coffee," said Martha. "You want one?"

Rose looked up to see her co-worker standing in the door, watching her with that "I-feel-so-sorry-for-you" smile that Rose was all too familiar with. After her sister's violent death had made the local news, Ming, at the corner store, started giving her discounts and the clerk at the bank had asked her into his office, instead of making her wait in line like everybody else. To this day, a hush fell over a room when Rose was recognized—like last week, when she got a pizza at Terroni's. You'd think in this era of the 24/7 news cycle, people would quickly glom onto a new horror to live through vicariously.

"You okay?" asked Martha now, pretending that Rose was not drenched in water and tears.

"I'm okay," Rose said, as she turned off the tap. Hoping to sound steadier than she felt. "Let's get back to work."

"Why don't you take the afternoon off?" asked Martha, without moving away from the door. "Go have a G&T at the Hyatt. You used to love sneaking out for an afternoon drink. I'll cover for you, no problem at all."

Martha had been an excellent friend. The shift-taking, casserole-making, tea-drinking-at-midnight kind of friend. The kind that so rarely existed.

"Thanks, Martha. You're too kind. But if I bugger off, how's that schedule gonna get done?"

"It's just— " Martha stopped and looked at Rose like a mother might her sick child. "You look so sad."

"And I am," said Rose. "We all are."

Unable to keep her mind focused, it took Rose two hours to finalize the schedule. Then it was time to pick up Tom from school, before doubling back to the subway to make her way up to the hospital.

Rose grabbed Tom's hand and marched down corridors that were lined with overflow beds, bins of used linens, and carts containing stacks of half-eaten food trays. An old man was snoring in his wheelchair. An orderly was soaping down a stripped bed.

The intercom blared. How was anybody supposed to heal in this place? Thank God, or whoever, that Will would be let out today.

Rose squirted disinfectant into her and Tom's hands before entering Room 1503. The patient by the door was asleep, his wife watching TV, while across from him, the bird lady was still searching for words.

"Sorry I'm late, but I'm here now, and—" Rose said, as she pulled open the blue curtain that surrounded her brother's bed, finding a different man lying there asleep. The cribbage board, the books and Will were gone.

"Where is he?" Rose demanded of the young woman manning the nurses' station.

"Who?" she said, without looking up from her typing. With the world-weary air of a sixty-year-old veteran, she craned her neck forward as if she needed glasses.

"My brother, Wilfred Michajelovich. Where is he?"

"From Room 1503?"

"Yes," said Rose. "The Wilfred Michajelovich from Room 1503, not the one from 1504."

"He was discharged as scheduled."

"Yes, and I'm here to pick him up. Where is he?"

"If you have an issue with our procedures," the nurse kept typing, but now looked Rose straight in the eye. "I suggest you contact the Office of Patient Experience. Here's their card."

"So you threw him out onto the street?"

"This is not a hotel with late-checkout privileges, ma'am. Now if you don't mind, I've got work to do."

Rose and Tom scoured the entire fifteenth floor, the gift shop and the pharmacy, but Will was nowhere to be found. At the information desk in the main lobby, a woman in a fur coat and three-inch heels was chatting up the attendant.

"Excuse me," Rose interrupted, "But I'm worried about my brother and I—"

The man behind the desk cut Rose off. "I'll get to you just as soon as I can," he said. "But one customer at a time, please."

Rose stepped back, looked around only to realize that Tom was gone. A minute ago, he had stood silently by her side and now he was nowhere to be seen. Shit.

She retraced her steps to the men's restroom, calling at the door for Tom. Then she rechecked the gift shop and the pharmacy. Panicky now, Rose raced to the cafeteria, passing cellophane-wrapped pastries and limp slices of pizza. She scanned the dining area. A large Asian family had gathered around their shrivelled-up matron, her head bobbing up and down, her expression unchanging, as two men, maybe her sons, talked. In the old woman's arms slept a baby, not three months old. Had something happened to its mother? Rose wondered, not wanting to imagine what. To the left, two men in tattered bathrobes played a game of chess, one of them connected to an IV, the other one strapped into a wheelchair covered in stickers, most of them rude.

Rose was just about to give the jerk at the help desk another try, when in the far corner, partly hidden behind a giant fake palm tree, she spotted a familiar head of curly black hair. Slumped into a wheelchair, she found Will asleep—and next to him, stood Tom. One of his hands firmly planted on his uncle's shoulder, while the other clutched the harmonica. On Tom's face, amazingly, a smile.

Back at Claremont, Rose helped Will heave his bandaged body out of the cab and up the stairs, a painfully slow ascent accompanied by moans and groans.

"I can't believe they let you go like that," said Rose for the umpteenth time. On his bedside table, she set up a pop-up pharmacy for the three different sets of pills (to be taken at precise intervals throughout the day), gauze, bandages and clips to dress the wounds. "I should sue them or something."

"Well," Will finally admitted, "I did sign a bunch of papers and promised you were waiting for me in the parking lot."

"Why on earth would you do that? I don't even know how to drive."

"I don't know Rose, I just need to get away from that germ-invested place. How was I to know you'd show up three hours late?"

After that, Will settled into his bed, and passed out. Despite his thirty years, he still looked like a boy. A boy who had smoked cigarettes laced with nutmeg, even if they made him puke rather than get high. Who got beaten up for not shutting up. Who ran away to explore the world. A boy who was still a boy, even if his body had long grown into a man.

Rose left to make herself a cup of tea. She craved something soothing, something that would take the edge off this shitty day. Rifling through her pile of tisane, she came across a fancy box of green tea, covered in dust. Mona had brought it back from her honeymoon in Bali, and here it sat, all these years later, still waiting for a special occasion. Rose ripped open the package and piled three spoonfuls of leaves into her teapot. She would honour her sister one sip at a time, no matter how tasteless that might be.

As she waited for the water to boil, Rose picked up the plunger. After working for the better part of the week, the sink had seized up again last night. Now, yucky brown water lay stagnant above the morning's dishes. How pathetic that she, the daughter of a plumber, could not take care of a clogged drain. Tato would not be impressed.

Moving aside the dishes, Rose began to pump. Why did this shit keep happening, she asked herself, pumping harder. The grimy water sloshed back and forth, soiling her jeans down to the ankles. But Rose did not care. She deserved to be covered in grime. What a joke she was. Pretending to have her shit together when everything around her was falling apart. Piss, she thought, pumping harder yet, crap, shit, fuck, motherfucker! "FUUUUUCK!"

Feeling a presence behind her, Rose turned to find Tom hovering by the door. His eyes were wide and completely still. Had she just sworn out loud? Had he heard her? Was he judging her? Rose followed Tom's gaze down to her feet, finding a banana peel stuck to her toes.

A loud sucking sound made both of them jump. Carefully, they approached the sink and watched as the water drained away. Rose turned on the tap, and the water flowed easily down the drain, as if there never had been a problem. As if months of congestion, of stagnant waters and disgusting smells, had only been imagined.

"I'm sorry," Rose said, when she finally could speak, "but life sucks."

December

The sun now set shortly after four, causing seasonal gloom, which this year Sonya could not offset with holiday cheer. The preliminary results from the amnio showed no abnormalities, but that did nothing to put her at ease. Even a cursory search of the Internet revealed that, given her age, history, and general lack of luck, a wide spectrum of catastrophic developments was still possible.

And then there were the condoms. Unable to confront Alex yet, Sonya had checked his credit card bill (no, he wasn't dumb enough to charge something incriminating), frisked his pants (loose change, wrapped up gum balls, crumpled receipts), even sniffed his shirts. But finding no unfamiliar fragrances, no further evidence of his obvious transgression provided no comfort. Alex did have sex with somebody else; the only question was: who did he fuck?

The phone rang. "I'm sorry I didn't call earlier," Rose said, pre-empting Sonya's lecture, "but it's been nuts around here."

As Sonya listened to Rose's list of complaints her heart softened. Will, still barely able to make it to the washroom, craved homemade food, Nick had started hanging around with a new, wilder group of friends, and then there was Tom, who only last night had woken up screaming, covered in cold sweat.

So, Sonya went over to Claremont to help out, not that her

sister had actually asked. But she knew that Rose was not one to solicit help—instead counting on and miraculously receiving whatever was needed when she could no longer do without. Like getting the job at the library exactly fifty-three weeks before having Nick, giving her full maternity leave. Or being able to live in this house, after Nick's dad turned out exactly as useless as Sonya had suspected from the first time she had laid eyes on him.

Sonya rang the bell, but of course, it was still not fixed. What would it take? A call and fifty bucks? Even Alex could have done this for Rose, if only she'd ask. Sonya knocked once more, but still there no response. She stepped off the landing to search for the spare key that had always been stashed behind the cracked cement planter. "One of you is bound to forget the key," Mama would say, "And what's here to steal anyway? Our stash of Alphagetti?" Sonya pawed through rotten leaves, but all that did was sully her new beige coat. Leave it to Rose to break with even the most sensible tradition.

Sonya knocked once again and waited some more. She pulled her coat tight against the chill creeping into her bones. What if she got sick standing here in the cold? Yes, Will craved company and Rose needed help, but Sonya's priority now had to be the wellbeing of her child.

Next door, below a fake pine wreath with flashing red lights, sat three once gleaming white plastic chairs stained with age. This is where the Portuguese man, who had lived there for the past fifty years, had spent his retirement years. First glued to a cigarette, then an inhaler, and finally, for the last three months of his life, tethered to an oxygen tank.

Behind Sonya, the door opened a crack. She turned to find Tom, clad in his hoodie, peeking out. Not moving aside, not asking her in, just waiting for Sonya to state her business. As if she were a stranger not to be trusted.

"I'm cold," she finally said. "Can I please come in?"

Without so much of a blink, Tom stepped aside.

For the next hour, Sonya cleared dirty dishes out of Will's room, returned his clothes to the dresser and watered the withered spider plant that miraculously survived years of neglect.

"Don't you ever get tired of living in a pile of junk, Will?" asked Sonya, as she tossed yet another empty bag of chips into the garbage.

"You need to learn how to look past the shiny appearance of things," said Will, who was ensconced in his bed like a pasha on his throne, right leg propped up in a cast. "Take that beauty, for example," Will said, pointing at a banged-up guitar. "It's worth eighty bucks on eBay for sure. All I need to do is to get around to posting it. Oh, and Tom," Will moved his attention to the to-be-recycled-pile, "would you give me that?"

Tom picked up a yellowed issue of *Barely Legal*, but Sonya snatched the magazine away: "Why would you keep stuff like this in a house, Will, with two underage boys? And what is the allure, anyway? Pink polka dot thongs, really? *Oral Education*, you've got to be kidding me."

"Oh come on, Sonya, it's fun."

"Fun for who? You really think any of these girls would agree to be photographed like that if they'd had access to a proper education, fair pay and something remotely close to equal opportunity."

"Really, Sonya, how old are you?"

"Anyway, what's the point of magazines? I thought the Internet now takes care of men's need for smut?"

"Sometimes, Sonya, it's just nice to have a hard copy. For old times' sake. And also in case of power failures."

"I'd put a flashlight, canned beans and a barbecue on my survival list, but I guess that's just boring old me. Now drink your tea before it gets cold."

"Bah," said Will and spat out most of it. "This is disgusting. What is this?"

"Dandelion, which will help your bones heal. I bought it special for you at BioWorld. Speaking of disgusting," Sonya pulled a mummified apple out from behind a stack of unopened mail, "one of these days you're going to regret cultivating all these bacteria in your room."

"What doesn't kill you makes you stronger, Sonya."

"Really?"

"Yup, remember what Dad used to say: 'Floaters are for sissies. My kids are smart enough to swim on their own, and if not, well, so be it.'"

"How about," Sonya said sharply, turning to face Tom, "you get me a broom from downstairs?"

Tom closed his eyes and started chewing his thumb. Despite her better self, Sonya felt relieved that not even Rose had been able to break that nasty habit.

"I bet," said Will, pulling out a stopwatch from his bedside table, "that you can't make it downstairs and back with the broom for Sonya and honey for my tea in under three minutes. If you do, I'll give you what's left of my Coke."

Tom did not move.

"But if you can't," Will added, "I'll have to take back my harmonica. Ready, steady, go!"

Sonya could not believe it, but bribery worked.

As soon as Tom was gone, Sonya sat down on the bed. "Will, I'm impressed but still, you've got to be a bit more careful."

"Oh come on, it's a game we play, nothing wrong with that."

"I mean saying 'What doesn't kill you makes you stronger' in front of a kid as traumatized as Tom!"

"Oh, please, it's fine. It's what people say."

"No, it's what Tato says. And it's not even true. Tom's no stronger for having survived. We're not stronger. And Mona is dead. Sometimes shit just kills. And the truth is, none of us did anything to prevent it."

"Really, you want to talk about all that now?"

"No time like the present, Will, just as Tato likes to say."

Will rolled his eyes, but Sonya was not deterred. "The thing is, Mona did call me. Several times. Telling me how jealous Russell was, and how frightened that made her. And I," Sonya said, as she straightened out her already straight hair, "and I, like a complete imbecile, told her that everything was going to be fine. That men get stupid sometimes, and that the best, the only thing to do was to give Russell space and let him calm down."

"So, you think what happened is your fault? That's ridiculous."

"Actually, it's not."

"Oh, come off it," said Will. "Mona loved Russell, and nothing you could've said or done would've changed her mind about that. Nothing."

Tom slid back into the room, handing the broom to Sonya and the honey to Will. The Coke, he downed in ten seconds flat.

"I wish you were right," Sonya said, getting up. "But you're not."

Faced with Rose's kitchen, Sonya couldn't help but recoil. Why leave butter out until it was rancid and bread until it was stale? Get a butter dish and a breadbox and discard the rotting fruit. How hard can it be? Sonya checked the time: 8:30 already. Where was Rose? The library must be closed by now. And what about Nick? What about supper? Bedtime? Order? Routine?

Sonya tossed the dirty rag into the overflowing garbage can.

Having already wiped down the bathroom, sorted the hallway clutter and straightened out the living room, she'd be amiss not the finish the job. So she took a deep breath and looked for a fresh rag. Their mother had kept her supplies in the slender cupboard that Tato had built to the left of the window. Rose, of course, had rearranged everything. Not to make things better—simply change to make them hers. Always needing to put her own misguided stamp on everything.

Sonya opened the cupboards above the radiator and looked under the sink, foraging behind the pile of discarded plastic bags. Nothing. Then she pulled open the drawer next to the stove. There, far in the back, something shiny caught her eye. A metal band so familiar it made her heart skip three beats. She briefly considered closing the drawer and moving on. She considered denying what in her mind was already forming into certainty. But then she remembered Mona, and how denial had cost them her life. Closing that drawer simply could no longer be done.

She slipped Alex's watch into her purse and left.

★

"Life's a bitch, isn't it?" said Rose, as she drowned the last of her beer. "Finally, I meet a halfway decent guy, only to find out that he's gay."

"I was going for fabulous, but I guess halfway decent will have to do."

"Halfway decent is actually pretty good, Ray. You should've seen some of the guys I was set up with. Anyway, I've got time for one more round. What do you say?"

Ray nodded, and Rose went to the bar to speed up the process. Clinton's on Bloor, a woodsy pub straight out of central casting, was empty aside from a few inevitable barflies. By the time the night crowd filled up the place, she'd long be home, putting Tom to bed. Until then, he'd be fine hanging out with Will. The bartender grabbed the empties and popped open two more Steam Whistles. The glint in his eyes made Rose over-tip.

"He's cute," said Ray, when Rose slipped back into her seat.

"Really? Now you're hopping on the 'Let's-set-Rose-up' bandwagon, too?"

"Just stating the obvious, is all."

"Sadly, that guy's just not going to happen. And sadder yet, I'm done hoping for that fairy-tale ending."

"But once you did?"

"Sure. What girl doesn't?"

"Not my area of expertise," said Ray, holding up his hands.

"Well, aren't you just the lucky one?"

"What are you talking about? I can think of a million reasons why it's great to be a girl. Like 'You can work without the pressure of success' or 'Your career might pick up after age eighty.' And the old: 'You don't get stuck in tenured teaching positions.'"

"You know the Guerrilla Girls. Cool," said Rose, impressed with Ray's knowledge of the feminist arts collective who'd been fighting for gender equality behind rubber guerrilla masks. "Those guys totally rocked."

"Rock, actually. They're still at it. The last work I heard about was to advise museums on how to deal with art by predators."

"Shit, you know your shit."

"I may work for the government, Rose, but I'm not an imbecile."

"I never said you were."

"Anyway, there're plenty of advantages to being a woman. There's fashion for starters—"

"And insane husbands to finish. Did you know that over fifty percent of all women killed are killed by their spouses?"

Ray leaned back, suddenly looking at her as if she were a

puzzle to be solved. Immediately, Rose straightened out. She had gotten this wrong. Again. Ray was not here for a friendly drink. This was work. He was here to close this case, so he could move on to whomever else might wash up at the shore of Social Services.

"You can't tough out grief, Rose. It just can't be done. At one point you will have to express your true feelings, even if they're ugly or angry or sad."

"Really? All I have to do is cry, and then all will be better. How wonderful."

"Sarcasm is easy, Rose. Dealing with trauma is hard work. It's like loosening up a sore muscle. Like massaging away a gnarl of pain. At first, your body wants you to stop, but if you persevere, if you breathe through the misery and let it pass, the tissue will soften and the ache will fade away."

"I better get going," said Rose and pushed away her half-finished beer. Why waste time on listening to trite clichés when really, she should be home, making dinner for Tom?

Ray cocked his head, taking a moment before speaking: "I'm here for you guys. You know that, right? Please reach out anytime."

"Except no amount of reaching out, no amount of talking, thinking, wishing, pleading, or whatever, will make my sister come back to life, will it?"

"No. It will not."

"So there's no point, then, of talking."

By the time Rose reached Queen Street, the snow was falling hard. As usual, the first storm of the season made Torontonians behave like they had never experienced winter before. The city, bustling only an hour ago, had shifted down to slow motion, restaurants sat empty, streetcars stalled. The few drivers who were obliged, brave, or stupid enough to hit the roads, crawled forward, uncertain of their traction like a novice on skates. At Manning, a snowball intended for a group of giggling girls hit Rose in the back. Her anger melted away when she turned to find the mortified face of the pimply boy who had thrown it. After a deluge of his apologies and her happily granted pardons, she watched as the kids disappeared down to King Street, off on another adventure, so energetic and carefree. Long ago, Rose had been just like them. With so many dreams yet to dream, so much hope not yet squandered.

The smell of household cleaner hit Rose as soon as she opened the door. The pile of boots that ordinarily cluttered the entrance had been sorted out, each pair matched and lined up. In the living room, yesterday's leftovers were gone, all four remotes neatly arranged by size. The pillows were fluffed.

"Sonya?" she called, taking the stairs up two at a time, hurrying past the gleaming bathroom sink, the sparkling mirror, and the hallway dresser that was closed for once. "Where are you?"

"Pssst," whispered Will and pointed at Tom, who was snuggled into the crook of his arm. "Isn't this cute? He just climbed up into my bed, closed his eyes and fell asleep. Who would've thought that was possible? Even yesterday?"

At any other time, Rose might have rejoiced. She might have sat down to take in the sight of Tom, so peaceful for once, even if his hand was still curled into a fist. She might have felt jealous that he'd chosen Will to snuggle with, rather than her, and might have even dared to imagine that better days lay ahead. But something felt off.

"What the hell! I invited Sonya over to keep you company, not to clean up my life."

"She just wanted to be nice, Rose," said Will, sounding every bit the grownup he wasn't. "You should be thankful."

189

"Yeah, well, she should deal with her own crap, before sticking her nose into my business."

Rose sat down, exhausted, on top of being embarrassed. She should be grateful. Sonya had done in a couple of hours what Rose had been meaning to do for months. But all Rose could feel was resentment, and a childish competitiveness she was not able to leave behind.

Will pulled out the whiskey and filled up his mug. "Where were you anyway?" he asked. "Doesn't the library close at eight?"

"Gimme that," said Rose, taking a long swig and enjoying the liquor burning right to her core. Then she stood up and made for the door, suddenly desperate for a smoke.

★

As soon as Aunt Rose stepped out of the room, Tom opened his eyes, at first unsure about exactly where he was. Then, he remembered an undeniable urge to crawl onto the bed with Uncle Will, who had been watching videos about surviving in the wilderness. There was something cozy about lying next to his uncle, something comforting about his smell. Tom remembered struggling to keep his eyes from falling shut, but then he let himself go and run off into the deepest jungles of India. Stumbling over knotty roots and slimy stones, he ran deeper and deeper into the forest, away from everything he knew and hated and feared. At a small clearing in the middle of nowhere, Tom stopped and slid to the ground. Surrounded by chirps and whines and squeals and squawks, he inhaled the thick, fecund jungle air. Ready now for whatever fate awaited him.

"I can't believe she's still hanging out with that jerk," said Uncle Will, waiting until Aunt Rose had gone outside. "But I suppose Alex must have positive qualities somewhere. Hidden. Somewhere. Deep down."

Tom shook his head.

"You're funny, kid," Uncle Will said. "You really are. There's a joker in there deep down, just waiting to pop out."

Tom smiled, even though he knew that there was nothing waiting to pop out. Nothing fun, anyway. He slid his hands down the front of his pants, relieved to find out that he had not wet Uncle Will's bed.

After watching a dozen cat videos, Tom returned to his own bed, and spent the next three hours waiting to fall back asleep. Across the room, Nick gently snored with his book still propped open, blissfully unaware that evil might be lurking close by, ready to take advantage of those who weren't smart enough to stay alert. Like when Kaa, the conniving python, wrapped Mowgli into his warm, comforting coils, hypnotizing the unsuspecting boy into sleep.

Tom knew *The Jungle Book* was just an old movie, that the real jungle was not nearly as nice or joyful. But he had known and loved Mowgli for as long as he could remember. On weekends, while Mom slept in, he and Dad would settle into the living room, eat blueberry pancakes and watch Mowgli run away from mankind, into a world of adventure and fun. Then, if Mom was still sleeping, they'd rewatch their favourite songs on YouTube (Tom's was the "The Bare Necessities," while Dad liked "I Wanna Be Like You"), first in English, then Spanish, Arabic, German and Dutch. They were like jokes that only got better the more often they were told.

But now, he knew that Baloo the bear had gotten it all wrong. Eating ants was disgusting; Tom had tried it. And some worries cannot be left behind. They sneak up when you're unaware, in the middle of the night, or when you're looking for controllers, but find your dad's ashes instead.

Tom got up to turn off Nick's light and tiptoed to the window overlooking the street. The parked cars had turned into gigantic marshmallows, the trees into magical animals with fluffy limbs. Illuminated by a lone streetlight, a woman walked by, kicking up thick plumes of snow. Christmas would be white this year, not that Tom cared.

Last year had started well enough. Mom made the most delicious cookies ever, decorated the house, wrapped a gazillion presents but then Dad sneezed so hard, he threw out his back. Bent over in pain, he had refused to drive up to the cottage. "It's for the better," he said when Mom complained. "Tom should be allowed to wake up in his own bed on Christmas morning, with his own tree, in his own living room, with his own family."

At first, Tom had been delighted. He loved his new toys (especially Brawl), but even before he had fully unwrapped his skates, Mom and Dad had gotten into a fight. The more Mom talked, the quieter Dad got. And then the humming had started. Instead of eating, Dad had hummed. Instead of pretending to like his new brown slippers, he had hummed. And then, instead of watching *It's A Wonderful Life*, he had gone out for a drink. "It's okay," Mom kept repeating. "It's okay."

Tom was woken late that night by a scream. His mother's. He bolted out of his bed and ran over to his parents' bedroom. "Mom," he said through the closed door. "Are you okay?" "Of course," she said, without coming out to give him a hug. "Go to bed now, please."

The next morning, they packed up their stuff and drove up north, even though a blizzard had hit hard overnight, clogging the ditches with dented cars. Mom kept avoiding Tom's eyes, wearing a scarf even though it was super hot in the car.

"If we'd gone up with everybody else," Mom finally said, "we'd be sitting in front of the fire right now."

"Oh shut up," said Dad, his eyes blinking in unison with the click-clock of the wipers struggling to push the snow off the windshield. "Just shut it, okay?"

"Playing Monopoly. Having a drink."

"If you don't shut up right now," Dad said so softly Tom felt sick to his stomach, "you'll have to walk."

The rest of the ride passed in silence. Dad's fists clutching the steering wheel, Mom staring out into nowhere. Aside from a quick stop for gas, donuts and tea, they pushed on without a word. Stuck together in the car, unable to escape.

By the time they arrived at the cottage, even the leftover turkey soup was gone. They rewatched *It's a Wonderful Life*, which made Aunt Sonya cry, even though she had seen the movie a billion times. Aunt Rose kept going on about how sexist the movie was and what a ridiculous attempt at glorifying the American small town that never really was. When Dad told her to shut it, surprisingly, she did. Uncle Will left to chop more wood. Mom just kept watching, not saying a word, the scarf still wrapped tightly around her neck.

Still, the next day had started the way every other holiday morning had started for as long as Tom could remember: Dad made pancakes, Mom slept in. Aunt Sonya decided to sort out the attic, and Uncle Alex tried to beat Nick at chess. After breakfast, Tom set off to build an igloo the way he had seen on the Internet. With a shovel, he cut up blocks of snow, hauling them to the site on an old wooden sled he had found in the shed. Soon Nick, having let Uncle Alex win, joined Tom outside.

After lunch, which was breakfast for Mom, Tom watched his parents walk away on the frozen lake, two diminishing figures in a vastness of white. No more than a step apart, yet separated as if each had settled on different sides of the moon. Tom considered running after them, abandoning Nick and their half-finished igloo, squeezing himself between his parents, closing the gap and slipping his hands into theirs. Maybe he could make them laugh by telling a joke, or challenge Dad to a race back to the house. But something made Tom stay, something made him watch, something made him believe that nothing needed to be done, that everything was fine.

For the next hour, the two cousins worked without exchanging a word. As the igloo grew, they lugged snow in from further afield, eventually having to go up all the way to the driveway. Tom's toes got wet and his fingers felt brittle, like twigs of a dead tree. Just as he and Nick were about to finish the roof, Mom and Dad returned. Not from the lake, but from the driveway. Dad walked by without so much as a glance, and all Mom had to say was, "Pack your bag—now."

"This is it," Dad said, as he turned their car out onto the country road that was covered in black ice. "I'm done with this shit. Will's a jackass, Sonya's a cow and Alex's a jerk who can't keep his eyes off Rose. Her tits are fine, granted, but she's his sister-in-law, for Christ's sake."

"You've been checking out Rose's tits?"

Dad's fist hit the dashboard so hard, it left a dent. Mom started to cry, but that only made Dad scream louder. Tom shrunk back into his seat, singing *Jingle Bells* in his mind fifteen times in a row. When they still weren't done fighting, he started to count. Three times to a 100. Forward and back. Again and again and again and again.

By the time they arrived in the city, Mom agreed with Dad. There would be no more Christmases up at the cottage. As it turned out, she was right.

When Tom woke up the next morning, Nick had already left and Aunt Rose was on the phone downstairs. He slipped into his hoodie and looked in on Uncle Will. The bruise on his uncle's forehead had turned puke-yellow, his greasy hair mushroomed into a mad crown above his unshaven face and drool leaked from his slack mouth onto the sheets. But he was getting better. Already Uncle Will was able to sit up by himself and his casts would be removed the week before Christmas. Still, Aunt Rose had ruled out a trip to the cottage. "Too much hassle," she'd said. "And anyway, it's time for new traditions."

Tom continued on to the bathroom to brush his teeth. As much as he hated that stupid school with all its stupid kids who had no clue about how stupid life really was, sitting at his desk had become routine. Something reliable in an unreliable world.

Aunt Rose appeared at the bathroom door. "Nick will bring you to Ms. Colter's after school," she said. "But then, he's got hockey in the park, so you'll go along to that, okay?"

Ever since Uncle Will's accident, Aunt Rose had walked Tom to school, making pickup arrangements for the days she had to work late. Sometimes she paid Deirdre, a geeky biology student who used to babysit Nick; other times, she asked Jeff's mom who had to pick up her son anyway and lived nearby. Nick was by far Tom's least favourite option. "Don't think for a minute that I enjoy dragging you around," his cousin had said, "So don't make it worse by being a dope. And stop biting those nails. It's gross."

"It'll be fun," Aunt Rose said. "But put on your long johns and don't forget your mitts. It's going down to minus five, and I don't want you to get sick."

Amazing how adults don't know even the most basic things, Tom thought. Getting a cold had nothing to do with being cold, and hanging out with Nick's friends did not sound like fun at all.

Tom had grown to love his sessions with Claire. Her office was like a lifeboat in a rough sea: safe, with a warm sofa to snuggle into when the going got rough. Her directions were clear and often cushioned by a smile. She asked him to play with different toys, brought in drums, a xylophone and once even a tuba, and asked him to draw pictures of what he felt, of what he imagined, and of his mom as he'd last seen her. Tom was ashamed that he could no longer remember the lilt of his mother's laugh, but he knew exactly how she had been laying on the floor covered in blood, the angle of her twisted leg, the texture of her blood-caked hair.

"Interesting," said Claire as she considered the drawing, turning it around in her hands as if it wasn't obvious which way was up. "Do you want to keep it?" she finally asked.

Tom shook his head, knowing he would never ever forget the last time he'd seen his mom.

"Thank you," said Claire and put the drawing into her desk. Then she shut the door with a bang. "One day," she added without looking up, "one day you might just do the same. Put those memories away in a safe place to keep, knowing where they are when you need them, but just far enough so that they no longer hold you back."

When Nick and Tom arrived at Trinity Bellwood Park, Tom could hear the clamour of a dozen boys circling the skating rink, still hundreds of meters away. "Let's move it," said Nick and raced ahead. "Thanks to you, I'm so totally late."

Nick sat down to untie his boots. A string of girls huddled at the far end of the bench, pretending not to care about the antics on the ice. A boy with pink shorts pulled over purple long johns slid to a perfect stop, shaving ice like a pro. "We start at four, man. If you can't make it on time, Julian's happy to take your spot."

"There was shit I couldn't get out of, so piss off, Nuwan."

Sitting next to Nick on the bench, Tom folded into himself, ready for a barrage of insults, but Nuwan simply laughed and skated off. Tom was amazed. Was that how you get rid of a bully?

"Stop that!" said Nick, swatting Tom's hand away from his

196

mouth. "I told you, biting's gross."

"You're such a dick," said a girl whose head was shaved down to her scalp. Then she looked Tom straight in the eye and asked, "You okay?"

Tom glanced behind him, but there was nobody. She was talking to him. With a smile as crooked as her teeth, she was different from the other girls. She seemed fearless. Alive.

"Don't encourage him, Carmen," Nick said. "Unless you're ready to mop up the mess."

Tom closed his eyes and started to count: 8, 16, 24, 32, 40 ...

"What's wrong with him?" she asked.

"He's been through stuff."

56, 64, 72 ...

"Like what?"

9, 18, 27, 36 ...

"Like stuff stuff."

"Gee, you sure got a way with words." Then, turning directly to Tom, Carmen added, "So what's your name?"

Tom bit his tongue, fighting hard not to run away.

"Just leave him alone," Nick said. "He hasn't spoken in months and he's not going to start just like that, here in the park, with you."

54, 54, 54. The number kept ringing out in Tom's head, like a bell stuck on repeat. Why could people not just leave him alone? Mind their own stupid business? Especially people like Carmen, who had a way of looking that made Tom feel all exposed.

"He probably needs help," said a different girl, her voice squeaky like a little bird. "Like a shrink or something."

Tom opened his eyes, finding a circle of teens staring at him like he was an animal in a zoo. Like he was a different species. Like he couldn't hear. Or see.

"Is he for real?" asked a girl in a pink parka. Tom slid his fists into his coat pockets, relieved to find Will's harmonica.

"Are we here to play hockey or what?" Nick asked, standing up.

But no one else moved. Hoping to will them all away, Tom closed his eyes.

"Wow," said Nuwan. "He really doesn't talk. Cool."

"I tried that once," said one of the girls, "but I got bored after a few hours."

"My mom's best friend's sister's kid didn't speak for three months," said the girl with the squeaky voice, "after they moved to B.C."

There were others who refused to talk? Tom opened his eyes, waiting for more.

"Then her mother bought her a dog, and all of a sudden, she talked just fine."

"Maybe there's something wrong with his brain," said Nuwan, suddenly all scientific-like. "I saw this show about this guy who had no idea who he was. It took them like five years to figure out where he had come from."

"I'm sure it was someplace awful. Like Tajikistan."

"Like you even know where Tajikistan is."

"Of course I know. Don't you?"

How long until they stopped babbling and went back to their game?

Nuwen turned to Nick: "So he's staying with you guys for how long?"

"I don't know," said Nick, sounding tired. "Forever, I guess."

Tom pulled out the harmonica and brought it up to his lips.

"Does that mean you've got to share your room?" asked Nuwen.

"Yup."

"Oh shit, that sucks."

Tell me about it, thought Tom. Then, taking the deepest breath ever, he blew into the harmonica, producing a most violent shriek. Instantly, all talk stopped, replaced by nervous giggles, and then embarrassed frowns. Still, Tom kept blowing and blowing and blowing and then blowing some more, stopping only when the boys had retreated to the ice and the girls back to the far end of the bench. Mission accomplished.

For the next hour, Tom watched the boys play. The silly girl in pink and her equally silly friends left, but Carmen stuck around, fiddling on her phone. By the time Nick scored the winning goal, Tom's feet felt like ice cubes.

"How about a quickie?" asked Dillon, a boy with droopy eyes and matchstick legs. Instantly, Nick's face turned red.

"You guys knock yourselves out," said Carmen and grabbed her backpack. "Later."

Something was up. As soon as Carmen was around, Nick couldn't leave his hair alone. He talked too much and laughed at stuff that wasn't even funny. And as much as Carmen pretended to love playing on her phone despite the cold, every time Nick had touched the puck, she somehow knew to look up.

"Get your mind out of the gutter, you weirdos," said Dillon, pulling an oddly shaped cigarette out of his bag. "That's not what I meant."

Carmen laughed, and put her backpack down on the bench.

Shielded by the northern wall of the community centre and behind a thick row of bushes, Dillon took a ginormous inhale of the most crooked cigarette Tom had ever seen. His inhale was deeper than Aunt Rose when she was really pissed off, and longer than Uncle Alex before finally diving into the lake. Nick, after an equally long drag, slid down to sit the snow, his head coming to rest against the brick wall, his outstretched foot almost, but not quite, touching Carmen's. Then, she dissolved into giggles and after one more drag, Dillon closed his eyes, the still-glowing butt resting in his fingers. Gone somewhere far away, somewhere relaxing and peaceful and fun.

Tom leaned forward to tug the joint away from Dillon. The soggy paper felt gross on his lips, but he inhaled anyway. Only there was no peace, no happy smile. Instead, the smoke burnt into his lungs, forcing him to cough and gag. Carmen popped open her eyes:

"That's sooooo fucked up," she said, sounding concerned, but still not moving. "He's wayyyyy too young for that shit. Way, way, way too young."

"What the fuck!" said Nick, grabbing the stub and throwing it away, as if that could undo what already had been done. "If Mom finds out, I'm dead." Looking at Tom, he stopped himself. "Shit, I'm sorry, I don't meant to bring that up…"

But Tom didn't care about what Nick had to say. Coughing hard, tears flowed down his cheeks and his lungs felt like they might implode. He kept coughing until the pain melted away, until his breathing levelled out and the tears stopped. Then, as he lay on the ground, the weight that had threatened to smother him ever since that night he found his mother dying, lifted. He rolled onto his side, surprised to suddenly feel free. The snow cooled his hot, throbbing face, and he closed his eyes, hearing—from far far away—Dillon saying something about racing for the swings. Instead, Tom began to count, but the numbers no longer made sense: 83, he thought, to be followed by 73. Or was it 38? How about 84 or 804? 888 he decided, because who's to say what comes first, second or last?

★

"So you just couldn't keep your hands off the one guy you couldn't have!" said Sonya, dropping the watch onto Rose's desk. "Is that it?"

"Let me explain," started Rose, not that she could. Wrapped in a huge forest green parka, Sonya towered above the desk, her face distorted by anger. Rose looked around but thankfully Martha had gone home early, and the library was empty, save for a homeless man asleep by the window.

"I'd rather you not 'explain,'" Sonya said. "I'd rather you get out of my life and go to hell. And take your sick bullshit with you. How could you even think about fucking Alex? Are you insane? Idiotic? Heartless? What is it?"

"What do you want me to say, Sonya? It just happened one day and then—"

"And then you couldn't help it? Then it was just too much fun to pass up?"

"I don't know, Sonya. I couldn't stop it. Not in time, anyway."

"You're an asshole."

Rose grabbed a pencil and started to doodle on the acquisitions report she'd been proofreading when her sister first stormed into the library. Dark circles slowly but surely blotted out numbers and facts. Maybe she could wait this one out, Rose thought. Let this blow over without talking back. Somehow hold on and survive.

"It's always been like this with you, Rose. You're incapable of considering other people, of looking beyond your own stupid nose. You're self-centred and mean. A thirty-five-year-old with the emotional maturity of a teenager. Just as needy and selfish, except with none of the potential or charm."

"That's not fair. I—," but Rose stopped. What was there to say? She had fucked her sister's husband. She had done it more than once. She knew it was wrong. And then she had done it again.

"You're pathetic, Rose. You really are."

"I am not."

"You are so!"

"No I'm not!!!"

"Do you hear yourself? By arguing like that, you've just proven my point. You're revolting, you really are."

"Actually," Rose began, standing up as if being at eye level with her sister might somehow even out the playing field. "I know what I did was wrong and I am sorry, I really am. But back then, right after Mona was gone, everything was so totally fucked up, and…" Rose took a deep breath before continuing: "and being with Alex, as fucked up as that is, was the only thing that made me feel anything."

"And so a girl's got to do what a girl's got to do?"

"Kind of, Sonya. Yes."

Sonya gathered her enormous coat, holding herself tightly, hoping maybe to feel comfort by embracing herself, by standing tall. Taking a good moment, she finally spoke:

"Just so you know, Alex has had affairs before."

"Are you saying you knew?"

"No, of course not. How pathetic do you think I am? Do you honestly think I would've cleaned up your dump if I had a clue that you were fucking my husband?"

"No."

"Exactly. And just to be clear," Sonya lowered her voice, making her sound even more menacing, "I will never forgive you. Ever. He was not yours to take."

Then, she turned and walked away. With no hesitation, no good-bye, no last turn by the door.

Rose picked up Alex's watch and weighed it in her hand. Heavy, with multiple dials and a chunky silver band. Why hadn't she returned it? Hidden it better? Thrown it away? But also, why hadn't Alex returned to retrieve it? Was the idea of seeing her alone one last time really too much to bear? Or had he left it as a memento for her to keep? A reminder of the solace they had found in each other in those desperate weeks after Mona's death, when everything felt hollow, when there was no comfort except for the comfort they found in each other.

Rose grabbed the watch and flung it across the room. She knew that she had gone back long after the first crazed state of grief had passed, even after it became clear that she and Alex had little in common but sex. She had returned to that hotel week after week, unable to make the right choice. Unable, like Mona, to get out, before it was too late.

The watch, having ricocheted off the wall onto a stack of grey boxes and then past a pile of Korean books, had come to a rest on the stained library floor. Lying there unscathed, taunting Rose with its gleaming perfection.

She walked over, and stomped down hard. Her shame and anger now at war with Swiss engineering. She jumped up and down until sweat dripped off her forehead and stung her eyes. Her anger was ferocious, but for once, the target was real. Available. Assailable. Finally, the glass shattered, exposing the watch's innards, useless now, irreparable, crushed. Just like her.

*

That bitch. Slut. Skank. "Cunt." Did she really just say that last word out loud? Sonya glanced over her shoulder, as if somebody—her mother—might pop up in the back seat of her car, deriding her for giving into vulgarity. But Sonya was still alone.

"You cunt," repeated Sonya, and even though she only whispered the word, it left behind a taste as sharp as rancid milk. Only now instead of shame, she felt relief. "Cunt," she said a little louder, a little less unsure. There was something liberating in speaking the unspeakable, something cleansing and true. "Cunt. Cunt. Cunt. Cunt. CUNT!"

Sonya pulled down the rear-view mirror. Her mascara had smeared down to her lips, but her green eyes were on fire. If she were a sorceress, she would turn Rose into a turd. If she could redo her life, she'd un-marry Alex, run off to Bora Bora and never see anybody she'd ever known again. Gladly. With zero regrets.

"Cunt!" she said, again. And again. Repeating it like a mantra. Holding on for dear life to the word that used to make her feel dirty and crude, but suddenly set her free. As Sonya's rage transformed, clarity blossomed inside her, engulfing her in a sudden lightness that was blinding after so many years of living a lie. She had returned to Toronto under false pretences. Married an unworthy man. Allowed her sister to die and then, worst of all, put her own needs above those of Tom.

"What a fucking cunt *you* are," she said to herself. "What a cunt, indeed."

*

When Tom came to, the world was bright and bitterly cold. He moved his head, relieved to find it still attached. One by one, he wiggled each of his fingers awake, then his toes, his arms and legs. As blood flowed back into his extremities, thoughts slowly returned. Where am I? he wondered just as a ravenous craving for Mom's brownies took hold of him, startling after months of not wanting to eat at all.

Tom shifted onto his side and opened his eyes. Slanted as he was, the world looked askew. Trees grew sideways, a dog peed upward against the playground fence. The snow turned yellow and steam billowed off to the side. The natural order of things had been switched by the tilt of the head. What would it be like to walk on walls and lean against floors? Skate upward and sit facing down?

Tom twisted his head to watch a barrel-chested dog race after a Frisbee. The red saucer spun against a world covered in a blanket of white. Was this the Frisbee he had lost last summer with Dad? Had that dog run all the way downtown? Could a dog actually run all the way downtown? Hoping not to lose sight of the Frisbee again, Tom twisted his head farther. His cheek brushed against the snow, its coldness jolting him upright. Bracing himself against the wall of the community centre, he found it warm from the sun.

Tom closed his eyes and smelled Sonya's lemon cake, almost touching the chocolate scones his mom used to bake, but his Baccio ice cream melted away before he could taste it. Torn between disappointment and anger, Tom opened his eyes. Thirsty now, he licked his lips, but all he could taste was salt from his tears.

Somewhere toward his left, cars pushed through the slush, a church bell rang out and voices from a snowball fight echoed through the frigid air. "Duke, come here!" a man yelled over by the playground. "Duke! Come here NOW!"

Heavy, wet, guttural panting drowned out the man's voice. Turning his head forward, Tom saw the dog charging toward him, no longer interested in Frisbees or what his master had to say. Its solid legs pounded the earth, snow spraying off in all directions, the distance between the dog and Tom was disappearing in a flash. He opened his mouth to scream, but instead, laughter escaped. Ebullient. Fresh. Clear.

The dog stopped inches away, his sweat turning into steam in the freezing late afternoon air, drool dripping from his huffing snout, his breath smelling rank. Unable to focus any longer, Tom closed his eyes, and the world dissolved. The panting turned into waves, the waves into laughter and laughter into tears.

When Tom woke next, the dog was gone. The sun, too. Hidden now behind a large cloud. Tom struggled to sit up, each muscle scrambling to remember its function. When finally, he steadied himself in an upright position, nothing looked familiar. He had come here with Nick, but what had happened next remained a riddle. How was he supposed to find his way home? Tom knew that Rose's house was somewhere close by, but where?

He pushed himself up and followed the wall of the community centre toward a small residential street that ran alongside the park. The houses here were bigger than those on Claremont, some of them detached, with more expansive front yards and no fences. Inside one of the homes, a mother rocked her infant child. Tom was tempted to ring her doorbell and ask for help, but then he didn't. What was there to say?

Instead, Tom turned north until he hit a busy street, divided in two by streetcar tracks, lined with crooked, low-rise houses and a few shabby stores. A car passed by inches from the curb, covering Tom in slush.

Looking left and then looking right, Tom had no clue where to turn. Where was Claremont? Home. Left or right? Right or left?

★

"Have you seen Tom?" asked Nick, as he burst into Will's room, his hair matted with sweat, his jacket unzipped. Will paused the show he'd been watching on his laptop.

"You're asking me? Aren't you supposed to be babysitting?"

"Yeah, well, but you know … well … like … whatever," Nick said, sputtering to a stop like a car running out of gas.

Will looked at the discombobulated teen in front of him, missing the fun kid Nick used to be. A kid who had started eating olives at age two, used words like "hypocrite" correctly by five and smiled and said "Sure!" to whatever cockamamie idea Will might come up with. Like scouring Chinatown for the most ugly T-shirt ever (not an easy choice) or hanging out on some seedy terrace in Kensington Market, playing cribbage all afternoon. Once, Will got stuck with Nick 24/3. Rose went to a librarian convention three days, leaving him alone in charge, which they had spent watching TV and eating ice cream with chips.

But sometime around Nick's last birthday, he turned into a teen straight out of a sitcom, minus the laughs. Now, standing in the doorway with bloodshot eyes and twitching limbs, Nick looked desperate. Will pulled out a triple-chocolate cookie from his stash, and predictably, Nick stepped forward immediately.

"See," Will said, as he popped the cookie into his own mouth, "it's not nice if you don't share. I'm stuck in this bed here, itching and aching and bored out of my mind, and you think it's okay to waltz in here all happy-like."

"I'm not all happy-like."

"Nick, I'm old, but I'm not an idiot. Next time you get your grubby little fingers on some dope, share it. We're family. You need to help me out."

"I've got to go, Will, I really do. I ... we ... anyway, I've got to go."

Will looked at his nephew, suddenly concerned. "What's going on, Nick? Where's Tom?"

"Well, you see, Mom, she said ... well, I thought—"

"Yes?"

"Okay, so here's the thing. Tom came with me to the park and at first everything was fine but ... but then we went to the swings and—"

"You got Tom to go on the swings? That's impressive."

"Well, no, actually ... Carmen and I, we went to the swings for like a few minutes, like five max, but when we came back, Tom was gone."

"Gone?"

"Yes, gone."

"Are fucking joking? Please tell me you're joking."

But he was not.

Panicked Nick returned to the park to keep searching for Tom. Will called Rose, but her voicemail picked up at once. He considered reaching out to Sonya, but what would that do? She'd tell him how irresponsible he was, how clueless, how immature. And anyway, by the time Sonya got over to Claremont, hours would pass. Hours in which Tom could freeze to death.

Will picked up the phone and pressed 9 and then 1, but hung up before he could make himself dial the final 1. Maybe Tom was already on his way home. Maybe Nick would find Tom and everything would work out just fine. Calling others for help was for people too weak to take care of life's challenges on their own, a lesson their father never tired of giving. Having grown up in a country run by strongmen and crooks, Tato insisted that real men didn't need to ask others to sort out their affairs.

All that made sense—up to now. Now, Will was stuck in this warm bed, at home, safe, while Tom was out there somewhere alone in the freezing cold. What if he'd been hit by a car and was dying in some hospital? What if he had fallen and was suffocating underneath a snowdrift, or been picked up by an Eastern European porn ring? Even if Tom's silence was voluntary and he could start speaking at any moment, how would that help now? Did he even know their address? The name of their street? Any of their cell numbers?

And that's when Will knew that Tato's reasoning was insane. Tom was lost, and they needed help. The way he had needed help, when he laid sprawled at the bottom of the stairs, or Marissa when she almost drowned, and Mona, facing Russell's rage. There was no shame in asking for help when help was needed. It was wrong not to.

"Please," said the policeman, when he finally arrived. "Please be assured that no matter what the media makes you believe, ninety-nine percent of all kids who're reported missing are found safe and sound. Now let's start at the beginning. Where're the boy's parents?"

Will answered each question, as best—and as quickly—as he could. For he was scared. More scared even than that time when they were kids and Mona had locked him in the trunk of the car. "Let's see how long it takes for Tato to notice," she had said with that mischievous smile. If it took more than an hour, Will would win Mona's desserts for the next three weeks. "It'll be hilarious to see Tato's face," Mona said and slammed the trunk shut. But, instead of coming home, their father went to watch a baseball game and then Mona ran into her friend Mary, forgetting all about Will.

Trapped in the dark, musty trunk of their old Ford Escort, Will realized he was truly alone. Convinced that he would suffocate and die, Will composed imaginary good-bye letters to his parents, Sonya and Rose, but not Mona, who he hoped would feel nothing but anguish and guilt. His last words were for Mrs. Petrovsky, the best teacher of all time: *"Dear Mrs. Petrovsky, Due to unforeseen circumstances, I am not able to return to school. This has nothing to do with me shirking responsibilities. I have finished my assignment, "The Origins of the World," and you can find it in the orange folder on my desk. Yours truly and forever, Wilfred"*

In the end, it was Rose who had noticed that Will was gone.

It was her who got Mona to talk and who pulled Will out of the trunk. She had worried about him, and acted on that worry.

By now darkness had set over the frozen city, Nick wasn't answering his phone and Tom might just be that one percent who was never found.

"Please," said Will to the policeman. "Do whatever it takes. We need to find Tom. He needs to come home."

★

Alone in the library long after Sonya had stormed off, Rose was surprised to feel relief. There would be no more small talk, no more pretending, and no more lying when all she felt was shame. The truth was finally out.

Rose grabbed her handbag from under her desk. In the trash, she glimpsed the remnants of Alex's watch. Tangible proof of just how cruel she had been, how reckless. She had eased her own pain by being selfish, assuaged her own suffering by inflicting pain on others. Just like Russell.

Like a dam giving out after holding back the flood for too long, tears filled Rose's eyes and uncontrollable sobs escaped her lips. Sliding down onto the floor, she wept like she hadn't in years, not since finding her dead mother after coming home from school early. Bawling then just like now, as if the hurt would never end, endless tears smudging her make-up, stinging her eyes.

When she was finally done, Rose wiped her face and straightened her shirt. Then she turned off the library lights, surrounded by row upon row of books, written by men and women who had needed to tell their stories, to share whatever lessons they'd learned along the way, to explain how they'd survived. But today Rose needed something more than escape. Today, she would not lose herself in the stories of others. She closed the library doors and ran down to Bloor. She had no idea what lay ahead, but what she needed right now was to be home, to be with Nick and Will and Tom. Time to cherish those she loved and forget all that she had failed to accomplish. She would order pizza, and they'd pick a movie to watch, something light and fun, to enjoy together like the family they were supposed to be. Like the family they were.

★

While Sonya zigzagged aimlessly through downtown, her mind regurgitated the events of the past few months. It had been her who suggested Alex drive Rose home after the wake. Was that when all this started? What about those two empty glasses in Alex's office? He had looked guilty when she had taken a swig. Why? And then there was Rose's unwillingness to visit while Tom was still living with her. Alex stopped playing hockey. Why? And who else knew? Did Will? Tom!

Sonya's mind turned to revenge. She could take a young lover, right in their marital bed, and make sure Alex came home in time to witness her supreme sexual satisfaction. She could write a tell-all book about her deceitful sister and snake of a husband. She could burn down their house and disappear, starting a new life in Vancouver or Honolulu or maybe Berlin. But even in the midst of her fury, Sonya knew that with her bulging body it'd be unlikely that she would have the energy to lure a hot young gigolo into her bed. No one, not even her, would read such a sorry tale and what would be the point of living in a place as unfamiliar as Berlin?

And then, just like that, she was spent. Feeling like a limp balloon, she relished the simple pleasures of making predictable movements, of holding onto the wheel, setting the turning signal, pressing the brakes. Sonya could have gone on driving in circles forever—but she ran out of gas.

She took out her cell phone, about to look for the nearest gas station, when she felt a jolt in her womb. For a few days now, she had noticed these strange movements within her. Pangs of pain. Sudden spasms. Small but undeniable. Terrified that she might be heading for yet another miscarriage, she had made an appointment with Dr. Blumenthal, scouring the Internet for information in the meantime. From what she had read, this was most likely just her baby working hard toward completion. Her child, who was only the size of a banana, but who was already able to swallow, poop and hear.

Sonya slid her hand under her thick woollen cardigan and massaged her growing bump. She'd been surprised that neither Will nor Rose had noticed it, but then they were both better at looking in than out, and even at work nobody had said a word. Like she was a ghost, invisible.

Sonya was just about to google the Canadian Automobile Association when her phone rang. She instantly recognized the hospital's number. Please, no more devastating news today, she thought. Please. Please. Please.

"Everything is fine," said the nurse in her dark, raspy voice. "No chromosomal condition has been found." She went on, but Sonya could no longer follow her.

"Really, you're sure?" Sonya kept asking. "A hundred percent?"

And so it was, as this most dreadful day turned into night, as she sat in her car with an endless stream of traffic racing by, that Sonya finally believed that her baby, her daughter, was here to stay. Lily.

★

"You scared the hell out of us," said a voice that startled Tom awake. Still lying on the bench, he opened his eyes and saw a teenage girl staring down at him. Her face was covered in freckles, her skin almost translucent. Her shaved head looked familiar. Was she one of Nick's friends? Coco? Candice? Carmen? Thoughts slowly trickled back into Tom's still-numb brain. Yes, that was it: Carmen. The girl Nick liked—the one he kept trying to impress.

"We were gone for, like, ten minutes," she said and pulled out her phone. She talked on, while her thumbs flew across the screen. "Tops. Where did you go? We friggin' looked all over for you. Anyway, Nick's in so much trouble. I feel sorry for him already. Move over, why don't you?" she added, now that she was done with her phone. "I need to sit down after all this running."

Tom sat up and looked around. Oh, right, he was in the streetcar shelter, just in front of a large stone church. Wanting to escape the snow that had started falling, he had sat down on the bench, trying to figure out what to do next. But then he must have nodded off, because now it was dark.

Tom moved over to let Carmen sit down. Her flushed cheeks were beaded with sweat. Still huffing and puffing, she pulled off her parka, exposing her bare arm for a moment, before she could pull the shirtsleeve back down. "Oops," she said with an uncertain laugh, "not sure about stripping in a bus shelter."

But Tom was not listening. Carmen's arm was lined with a zigzag of scars. Some of the cuts looked thin and timid, like the ones he used to make when he first started out. Others were deeper, dark and angry, like the ones he was working on now.

"I've been doing it since I was 11," said Carmen. "If you wanna judge me, go ahead, but I'll think that's plain ignorant and not very evolved."

Tom hesitated, but then pulled up his sleeve. Lesions ran along his arm all the way up to his shoulder, some of them faint and almost invisible now, except for the one almost in his armpit, the one that looked like a barbed wired tattoo.

"Shit," said Carmen, gently touching his tender skin, careful not to press too hard. "That's fucking intense."

Tom pulled down his sleeve. This was dumb. He was dumb. This was his secret, not to be shared, least of all with some random girl.

"We're not the only ones who do it, you know," said Carmen, as if she had read his thoughts. "There're tons of people like us on the Internet. Doing what it takes to survive. Cutting to feel alive. I don't know about you, but the part I like best is watching them heal. It makes you feel like things might get better one day. So screw those shrinks with their know-it-all talk. I will not give up cutting. No way."

Tom looked straight into Carmen's unblinking eyes, surprised to learn that others used pain to silence their brains. He watched a young woman crossing the street, unconcerned by honking cars, and wondered if she, too, had figured out how to keep the world at bay with the stroke of a cut.

When they got back to Claremont, Tom slipped inside, and Carmen took off without saying good-bye. Racing upstairs towards his room, Tom was stopped by a police officer coming out of the washroom: "Look what the cat dragged in," he said with a deep, booming voice. "Didn't I just know you'd show up all by yourself?"

"You're back!" Uncle Will exclaimed, sounding angry, but looking relieved. "Where the hell were you?"

Embarrassed at being caught, Tom focused on a crack in the ceiling.

"Your uncle's been worried like hell," said the officer. "There're cruisers looking for you all over the city. Tax dollars wasted, just because of your little prank. But actions have consequences, you surely are old enough to know that, so tell me, what happened?"

Tom slipped his hand into his pocket, clutching onto the harmonica.

"Hello," the officer said, almost shouting now, "did you hear me? What happened?"

"He hears just fine," said Uncle Will. "I told you, it's the talking he doesn't do."

"Yeah, well I'll need that information for my report."

"He's not going to start talking, just because it's convenient for you. From what I understand..." but Tom was done. Quickly, he brought the harmonica up to his lips, blowing hard.

"Fine, Tom. You win," said Uncle Will. "Now scram!"

Tom slammed the door to his room, shaking with rage. He had not run away, this was not his fault. He had been abandoned in the cold. Left alone for no reason at all. He pulled his suitcase out of the closet and snapped it open. Ironhide's windshield wipers were gone, Bumblebee's head was stuck on backward and Powerglide's limbs were cracked. Pathetic, his army of Transformers. Just like him.

Tom tossed Powerglide across the room, followed by Brawl, Ratchet, and Jazz. Megatron bounced into the trash, followed by Optimus Prime, the Maple Leafs sweater and books Tom had long outgrown. He hesitated over the Bart Simpson snow globe, but the memory of Old Orchard Beach, of tasting salt-water taffy and hearing his mother's laugh, made him want to throw up. Instead, he grabbed the globe and smashed it into the wall. Another unwanted memory gone.

Finally, there was only one item left: Mom's blue album. Like so many times before, Tom opened the book, hoping to find comfort as he had in the past. In the first photo, he was less than one hour old, his fists covered in white gloves, his forehead wrinkled like an old man. "Tell me about the day I was born," he would ask his mother again and again, yearning for stories about the times he couldn't remember, and details he feared to forget.

"I had eaten a wild-mushroom omelette," Mom began. "So when my stomach started acting up, I thought it might be food poisoning."

"But then you peed in your pants," interrupted Tom, this being his favourite part of the story.

"Well, Pumpkin, kind of. Yes," Mom admitted with a smile.

"And that's when Dad freaked out?"

"At first he got all excited and he did his dance, you know, the one when he goes down to his knees and spins until he falls? Anyway, it was when he couldn't find the keys to the car that he got mad."

"Real mad?"

"No, not real mad. Anyway, we jumped into a cab and—"

"And what did the nurse say when you told her I was about to come out?"

"She said: 'No way! It'll be hours.' And then she went out for a smoke."

That's when Mom would take him into her arms, as if he were still a baby in need of coddling. "But you were then just like you are now: impatient and fast. You were born less than one hour later."

Flipping through the album now, Tom looked at the photo of himself as a baby taking a bath in the kitchen sink. *June 2009: My Son the Fish*, read Tom in Mom's tiny script. Next, he found Dad pushing the stroller while reading a book, labelled: *March 2010: Double-tasking*. Then another of himself, covered in stings, *Aug. 2015*, he read, *Invasion of the Killer Bees*. And finally, his ninth birthday party: *January 8th, 2018: Tom Blows Out the Candles. Nine!* He looked at his own smiling face, so excited and young and clueless and dumb.

The first rip was onerous, but as fragments of Mom joined disconnected bits of Dad, as the past turned into a jigsaw puzzle nobody would ever be able to solve, all Tom felt was a huge sense of relief.

"What the hell?" Nick yelled out when he entered the room twenty minutes later, leaping across the room to pin Tom down. Like a beached turtle, Tom let go without a fight. "This is fucked up," said Nick and recoiled.

Tom didn't move, so Nick got up. "I told you to wait. Why didn't you wait? Why must you always make everything so complicated? You're such a turd."

"Fuck off."

Wait. Had he really just said that? Tom was sure that Mom would be disappointed in him for being rude. But then Mom could not scold him. Mom was gone. And he, he was still here. Faced with stupid Nick and his idiotic lies.

"Wow. After all this time, that's the first thing you say?" asked Nick. "Cool."

"Leave me alone," said Tom, his voice forceful despite the long rest. He grabbed what was left of the tattered album and looked at a still-intact photo of himself and his dad, labeled *Canadian National Exhibition*. They'd gone there last year to ride the rollercoasters and say hello to the sheep. They'd eaten corn dogs until their stomachs hurt and brought a big candy heart home to Mom.

Three rips later, that memory was gone.

"Stop it. Enough," Nick said, grabbing the album, but Tom refused to let it go, done with giving up or giving in. And so the two boys found themselves in a standoff, each clinging onto one side of the book, each determined to get his way.

"What's going on here?" demanded Aunt Rose, stepping into the room just as the album ripped in two. "What's wrong with you, Nick?"

"You're asking me? He just told me to fuck off."

"Language, Nick."

"Exactly."

★

By the time Nick cleared out, Tom had retreated into the far corner of the bed, burying his head between his knees. Uncertain about what to do next, Rose started tidying up. She dumped the dismembered Transformers back into the suitcase, swept up the broken pieces of glass, the shredded photos, and what was left of Mona's album. In one fragment, she recognized Tom's chocolate-covered face, beaming next to a half-eaten cake. Neither Nick nor she had been invited to his last birthday, and Rose now was ashamed that she had never wondered why. How easy it was to lose sight of those who wanted to slip away.

"You need to stop this," said Rose finally.

"Why?"

"What's that?" Rose stepped back in surprise. So Nick was right, Tom had started to talk.

"Why do I need to stop this?" repeated Tom, speaking calmly, as if the last six months' silence was nothing but a dip in a landscape of perfect communication. As if he could simply pick up where he had left off. Exactly as Ms. Colter had predicted.

Rose sat down on the bed. Close, but not so close as to actually touch. "You need to stop this," she whispered, trying not to scare Tom back into his shell, "because the only one you're hurting is yourself."

"That's not even true," replied Tom, now looking straight into Rose's eyes. Gone was all hesitation and fear, replaced by near impossible sadness.

"What happened to you ...," Rose began, but then she hesitated. What if Tom could see right through her? What if he already figured out that she was a fraud? That she held no magic key, had no deep wisdom to impart, and knew nothing of what lay ahead.

"What happened to you," she finally said, knowing that the only thing she had to offer was her own, tainted truth, "was the most awful thing imaginable. Your parents died in the most horrible way and that is a burden you will have to learn to live with. We all do. But as impossible as that might seem right this moment, we will. Together."

And then Tom leaned forward, right into her arms, like a baby wanting to be held. Relieved beyond all measure, Rose pulled Tom tight, vowing to never let go.

★

Sonya sat at her kitchen table without bothering to turn on a light. She felt tiny in this huge, empty house. Alone. From down the hallway, Sonya heard a creak. Thankfully, it wasn't Alex. She still needed time to figure out what to say to the prick. Torn between wanting to dump her cheat of a husband and feeling the obligation to provide a father, a family, and a home for Lily, she felt stranded on an island of indecision. As soon as she decided to stick it out for Lily's sake, her resolve flipped. What would that teach her child? That lying cheats can get away with fucking their sisters-in-law and still get to live happily ever after?

"I guess it's my turn to make dinner?" Alex asked, his voice jolting Sonya out of her thoughts. "How about pizza?"

Sonya looked up to see her husband standing in the doorway, smiling like it was just another day. Like life could just go on. How long had he been standing there, Sonya wondered. Sneaking around unnoticed, doing stuff right under her nose? Unafraid that she'd ever find out?

Alex switched on the light. "Do you want Capri, or Spinotta or—"

"What I want is for you not to have screwed my sister."

"What?"

"Don't make things worse by playing me for a fool."

"Sonya, it's not what you—"

But before he could finish his sentence, Sonya stood up and walked out of the kitchen. At the door, she turned to take another look her husband, but the man she had once loved was barely detectable now. Somewhere along the way, Alex's youthful vigour had given way to indifference, contentment had turned to complacency, and then he had betrayed their solemn promises of love until death do us part.

Sonya went into the living room to visit with Mona. She still smiled, but the flowers beside her photo had long since shrivelled into brittle dust catchers. Next to her urn sat Rose's candle. Sonya read *Hope* and snorted out loud. What a joke, coming from her bitch of a sister. *Hope* you don't find out, Sonya? *Hope* you're as stupid as you look? *Hope* you don't actually care?

Sonya considered throwing it out, along with the other candles embossed *Trust, Love,* and *Faith*, but she changed her mind. It might be pathetic, but guidance was what she needed now. Even more than revenge. For how does one become unstuck, when even the smallest change hurts?

And then Sonya had an idea. Lining up *Hope, Trust, Love* and *Faith* on the coffee table, she lit each of the candles, one by one. Then she lifted Mona's urn up to her cheek, its soothing marble touching her skin. The urn felt heavy—reassuring, even. Sonya closed her eyes and heard her sister laugh, smelled her lemony scent, watched her jump off the dock into the lake. Mona, her sister, Tom's mother, a cherished human reduced now to ashes weighing less than four pounds, no more than a sack of flour, a wrought iron pan, a miniature dog.

Sonya pulled up her shirt, grabbed *Trust* and rolled Mona's urn back and forth across her pregnant belly, hoping that the light and the pressure might waken the baby.

"Hey Lily, meet Mona. She's my baby sister and—"

"Shit, Sonya. What's going on here?" Alex asked, as he came into the living room.

Startled, Sonya let the urn slip from her arms.

"Boy, you're weird today," said Alex, catching the urn just before it crashed onto the floor. "Give me that."

"Leave us alone," Sonya said and pulled away.

"Are you okay, Sonya? Do you want me to make you a tea?"

"Actually, what I want is for you to be gone."

As soon as those words left her mouth, Sonya knew they were true. They had not been there for one another when it mattered most so now she and Alex would not get to grow old together. They would not be laughing at jokes nobody else found funny, recount to bright-eyed grandchildren the story of how they met and fell in love or sit on park benches, holding wrinkly hands. A door was closing, and Sonya no longer had any interest in keeping it ajar.

"I know what I did was wrong," said Alex, "but after all these years, I deserve a second chance."

"After fucking my sister?" Sonya replied. "I don't think so."

Even more surprising than her sudden certainty was her over-whelming sense of relief. Betrayal of trust could not be undone, and innocence could not be regained. If Mona's death taught her anything, it was to stop living a pretend life and to accept reality for what it was.

"Nothing good can come out of living a lie," Sonya said, her resolve as crisp as air on a bright winter day. "We're done, Alex. Leave."

Not wanting to watch Alex pack, Sonya retreated to her sewing room. She pulled out brightly coloured pieces of fabric—yellow, green, red and pink. Then, she began working. She measured and cut and stitched, letting the cloth slide through her machine. The lines she produced were straight and true, reassuring in a world in which everything else had gone awry. Finally, she cut the threads and held up her handiwork: a string of thirteen triangles that would form a garland over Lily's bed. She would embroider a letter onto each to spell HAPPY BIRTHDAY. A yearly reminder, not only of Lily's passage through life, but also of the time before her arrival, the time when Sonya was pregnant and alone, when there was no one else to love.

Sonya recognized that she had failed. She should not have returned from Montreal under false pretences. Shied away from a life she had loved, just because it was hard. Married an unworthy man to fill a hole in her heart. She should have been there for Mona, even if Mona had not wanted her to interfere, and she should have been there for Tom, even if she had not known how.

Sonya pulled out her phone and dialled Ray. After everything that had happened, she was done with pretending that things were one way, when clearly they were another.

"I'm sorry to disturb you this late," she said, "but we need to discuss Tom. I'm his legal guardian. That's what Mona wanted. So please, help me bring him back."

★

"Fine," said Rose, without sitting down, even though Ray had already settled into the old recliner. "Nick's a pea-brained twerp, and he made a mistake, a colossal mistake, I am the first to admit that. Totally. But he's also really, truly, deeply sorry. All teens have these weird lapses of judgement. The other day, we watched this show on how the frontal part of a teen's brain isn't fully formed yet. That's why sometimes they make completely irrational choices, when other times—"

"Rose. No need to enlighten me about teenaged idiocy," Ray said. "I'm a social worker. Now, please, have a seat."

"It was one mistake, Ray. Let's not be holier than thou. We all make mistakes. And anyway, Tom's back home safe now—oh, and I have some great news to tell you—"

"Rose," Ray interrupted, "I give you that all's fine now. But that's not how everybody will look at this situation. Fact is, your pot-smoking son got Tom high and then abandoned the boy in the park. Your brother stole your money, took Tom gambling, and then got into an altercation that led to serious injury. You must be aware that these days parents get into trouble for letting their kids walk to the playground alone."

"Well, that's ridiculous."

"I agree, but these are the times we live in. Anyway, that's actually not what I came here to talk about."

"It isn't?"

"Why don't you have a seat?"

Rose knew that only the worst news was delivered when sitting down, so she did not comply.

"Your sister came to see my supervisor this morning. She asserted that you're incapable of providing adequately for Tom and then reinstated her claim to exercise her guardianship."

Rose could not believe what she just heard. She had imagined Sonya going home to cry, to maybe kick Alex in the butt, but this? This was low even for her. "Oh, come on Ray, clearly that's nothing but retaliation. You can't take that seriously."

"Retaliation for what?"

"For me being an idiot. Anyway, Sonya couldn't handle Tom when she had the chance. Why would she be able to handle him now?"

"Bruce agrees, so he's decided to—"

"Who's Bruce?"

"My supervisor, Bruce Colburn. He has decided that since neither you nor your sister seem to be capable of providing suitable care for Tom at this point in time, he will be transferred to a foster home, until a full psychiatric assessment can be made and a long-term solution can been found."

"Are you kidding?" Rose asked and sat down, no longer able to stand on her shaking legs. "You're kidding, right?"

Tom's meagre belongings were packed in no time at all. A few clothes, some books, a couple of Transformers that had survived his fury, and a bag of chips for the road. The foster home where Tom would stay "until a more permanent solution could be found" was just north of the city, but it felt to Rose like the end of the world.

Rose closed the suitcase and looked around. Tom had lived with them for half a year, but there was no evidence at all that he had ever shared their lives. No drawings, no craft projects, not even a line on the door to measure his height. Once the inflatable mattress was returned to the basement, this room would snap right back into a fourteen-year-old boy's sanctuary, all traces of Tom gone.

Rose went downstairs, finding Tom already waiting with his coat zipped up. Eager, she feared, to leave.

"We'll get you back before Christmas," she said.

"We'll try, Rose," said Ray, "But best not to make promises."

"How about saying good-bye to Will?" Rose suggested, struggling hard to hold back her tears. She'd known that having sex with her brother-in-law was despicable, but it had never even occurred to her that Tom would be hurt by her reckless behaviour. "Go on, now," she added, when Tom refused to move. "He's already upset, let's not make it worse."

Just then, Nick came down the stairs, thrusting a heavy plastic bag toward Tom. "For you," he said.

"Really?" Tom asked. "All six volumes?"

"Yup. All six volumes," Nick said to Tom. "But don't mess them up."

"Of course not," said Tom. "They're collector's items."

"Exactly."

"Wow, so he really speaks just fine," said Ray. "Amazing."

"Contrary to popular belief," said Rose, "I'm not actually the lying type."

★

"Calling the cops was stupid," said Will as soon as Tom entered his room. "I'm sorry. I really am."

Tom shrugged, and Will could not blame him. Saying sorry was easy, changing what had happened impossible. It was his fault that Tom was losing his home for the third time this year, hauled away to some godforsaken shithole, his fate now in the hands of the Family Court. If only he hadn't panicked, they'd be watching *Storm Chasers* right now, eating ice cream and chips.

"I'll come and visit," said Will, instantly ashamed at this empty promise. Even though his casts would come off in four days, how would he get all the way to North York and what would he do once there? Sit in a stranger's home, make conversation with a boy who was barely speaking, pretend that this was somehow all for the best?

Tom turned to leave.

"And keep practicing that harmonica, so that when you come home, you can play me a song."

"Thanks," said Tom.

"Seriously? You don't speak for six months and then the first

225

word you say to me is 'Thanks'?"

"Oh please," said Tom with a smile. "That's not the first word I said, and you know it."

Then he pulled out the harmonica, took a deep breath, and produced a sound so mournful and true, it brought tears to Will's eyes. So much sadness had been trapped inside that little boy, and only now had he found a way to let some of it out.

★

Sonya stretched, savouring owning the bed. All of it, not just a thin sliver of real estate off to the left. Sleep was no longer cut short by drunken snoring, 3 a.m. toilet runs, or incomprehensible mumblings. The worst were Alex's reoccurring nightmares about being trapped in a tent during a storm. Sonya had no clue why he kept having that particular dream, or why he couldn't simply unzip the flap and step out, but the idea of being trapped in a wet orange tent had haunted Alex for years. Sometimes he was caught in blizzards and at other times in torrential rains. Then there were snakes, bears, or murderous bikers. Once a nymphomaniac appeared, though Alex had refused to divulge any details about her.

But there would also be no more breakfasts in bed. No more midnight sex. Nobody to snuggle up to, no more buffer between her and her fears. Last night, Sonya had awakened in a cold sweat, her thoughts gyrating in ever tightening coils. Who would warm up the car? Assemble the crib? Would she ever get to sleep once Lily arrived? What if she got postpartum depression? Also, now going back to work was a given. Would Lily be okay at daycare? How would Tom be with Lily? And Lily with Tom?

It was her fault that Tom was now housed with the children of drug addicts, criminals and other fuckups. That was not the scenario Sonya had in mind when she called Children's Aid. She could not allow this to play out. Already, she had written dozens of emails, joined a support group for parents with difficult children and retained a lawyer. Today, she would go on a pilgrimage downtown, armed with a cheesecake.

"I'm sorry," said Bruce Colburn, Ray's supervisor at Children's Aid. "But there's simply nothing to be done until Family Court reconvenes. Mid-January at the earliest, though given the current case backlog, February is not out of the question. But please, rest assured, the Ivansons are a fantastic couple. Very experienced and kind. They currently have only three other kids, so Tom will get plenty of attention and care."

"But how could they possibly be more qualified to take care of Tom than I am?" asked Sonya. "I'm his legal guardian. I'm his family. Mona, my sister, his mother, wanted him with me. Why can't I just take him home?" Then she pushed the cheese cake across the desk. "Here, I thought you might like a treat."

Bruce barely looked at the cake, before shaking his head: "The best I can do is to arrange a visit. Would next Wednesday work?"

After a week of fretting about what she should do or what he would say, Sonya went to the mall and bought a remote-control truck, three books, and a shirt. She arrived an hour early at the offices of Children's Aid, waiting in a room furnished with a vinyl sofa, a desk, and three chairs. Finally, Tom was brought in. He was no longer wearing his hoodie and Sonya was surprised at just how tiny he looked. How lost. Still, he refused to open the presents, never mind look at her, or speak. Instead, he pulled out Will's harmonica and played "Silent Night." Over and over and over again. Beginning anew every time he got stuck on a note. A relentless, joyless, disheartening loop that made Sonya feel so helpless, she was out the door before her hour was up.

★

When Tom first arrived at Meadow Lane, the Ivansons let him be. Charlene, an excruciatingly friendly woman with hair just as bouncy as her step, cooked breakfast, lunch and dinner with the radio blasting, while chatting to her friends on the phone and checking eBay for deals. Trent, her husband, was almost as wide as he was tall, and he reminded Tom of Baloo, the fun-loving bear from the Jungle Book. Except that Trent's head was so shiny, Tom suspected that Charlene might wax it, maybe even before they climbed out of their enormous bed. Just across the hall, Tom had to share a room with two other boys. Kevin, whose mother was hospitalized after fear of food poisoning made her stop eating, and Blake, whose mom had run away three years ago, but who kept writing postcards with pictures of palm trees, beaches, and monkeys dressed as old women, promising to return home soon.

After three days of letting him settle in, all special allowances were now off. "Your hoodie's a disgrace," Charlene said, when Tom showed up for breakfast in the same outfit again. "It's ripped and dirty and it needs a wash."

Before Tom could protest, she unzipped the sweatshirt and slipped it off, along with the T-shirt beneath. "Trent," she said, when she found a fresh cut on Tom's arm. "I need your help."

After disinfecting the wound, Trent wrapped half of Tom's arm in gauze. "Are there other spots that need taking care of?" he asked, a relieved smile on his face when Tom shook his head.

"We're here to help," Charlene said, "so when you're ready to talk this out, you know where to find us."

But Tom was not into talking things out, and thankfully the Ivansons let him be—except he was no longer allowed any time alone, even having to brush his teeth with the bathroom door open.

Still, Tom managed to settle into his new routine. Breakfast at 7:30, bus at 8:15, school until 3:45, supper at 6, shower every other night, bedtime at 8, lights off at 8:15. Snowstorms came and went, then Christmas with strangers, more unopened presents, New Year's, a polar vortex, but Tom wasn't bothered. His life was over and he didn't care.

January

There are many shades of numb, and Rose hated them all. In the morning, she felt too numb to get up and go to work. Sedated by numbness, she had all but stopped eating. She hadn't washed her hair in two weeks, had given up on makeup. All her life, she'd been adamant about limiting the hours wasted in front of the TV. Not any longer. Ensconced on the sofa, she let her brain be lulled by fake sit-com laughter, commercials for cars she'd never buy, and tips on how to upgrade a wardrobe she'd never own.

"Sunnyside up or scrambled?" asked Nick one evening. All Rose could manage was a shake of her head.

"Scrambled it is," he said and slid the plate of eggs onto Rose's lap. "Eat, Mom."

Her appetite stirred by the delicious aroma, Rose ate a slice of bacon and then another, allowing the smoky meat to satisfy a deep, previously unknown desire. That's the thing about kids, she thought, they pay attention—especially when you think they don't.

"It's a bit late for breakfast, no?" Rose asked.

"It's what I know how to cook," Nick answered. "Plus breakfast at night is perfect, when you want to pretend that this stupid day never happened."

"Why? What's wrong now?"

"Nothing."

Nick picked up the remote. Evidently, there was only so much of *Tidying Up with Marie Kondo* a teenage boy could endure. "How about a game of cribbage?" he asked, turning off the TV. "I might even let you win."

When Rose woke up the following morning, she found Nick curled up next to her on the couch. Still a kid, despite a fresh outbreak of acne on his chin. How hard these last few months must have been on him, she realized. How lonely. After years of being the undisputed centre of her universe, Mona's death had upended the only order Nick had ever known. Quietly, too quietly, he had slipped away, hanging around with friends she no longer knew, retreating into his own, separate world, poking into hers ever more rarely.

Rose got up and walked up to the boys' room. Now that Tom was gone, Nick's clothes were once again strewn all over the floor, his desk overflowing with crap. Rose sat down on the unmade bed, taking in the faded posters, the worn-out picture books, long abandoned toys that had once made her son jump with joy. Next to the waste bin, Rose noticed a multi-coloured piece of plastic. She picked up Brawl's severed arm, machine gun still attached.

What was it about boys and their guns? Rose remembered how Nick, he was maybe five years old, used to aim his toy gun at her, saying with a laugh: "I shoot you," meaning, "I'll love you forever." A game she had loathed, making it all the more fun for Nick. Now, this toy gun was all that was left behind from Tom's life in this room. A reminder of just how neglectful, irresponsible, and short-sighted she'd been.

"Enough," Rose said aloud. She should never have lost sight of Nick. She should have held onto her son, told him she loved him even if it made the boy blush and run. Just another of her many mistakes. Like trusting that Mona could fend for herself, or fucking Alex, and worst of all, allowing Ray to take Tom away.

Rose dropped Brawl's arm into the pocket of her robe and stood up. If Tom was to have a chance, if they were to have a chance, they needed to learn that there was more to family than betrayal and grief.

Rose brushed a layer of fine beige powder onto her cheeks, forehead and neck. For lipstick, she chose Politely Pink, the least flashy in her collection. Then, she straightened herself out in front of the mirror and assessed the situation. She needed a haircut, a dye job and possibly a little Botox to soften the furrows that had grown between her eyes. But, she concluded, in low light, with the right angle, and a smile, she still looked fine.

"Look who's back."

Rose spun around to find Will standing in the bathroom doorway. It was still unsettling to have her brother pop up unexpectedly all over the house.

"Isn't it a bit early to get dolled up for a date?"

"I'm done dating."

"Whatever, Rose. It's not like you'd gussy yourself up just to go to work."

"You should apply to the secret police, Will, put your investigative skills to monetary use."

"Oh, I got it—you're trying to get Mr. Olivier to pass Nick in French."

"Wrong," Rose turned to leave.

"Oh come on, this isn't a quiz show, just tell me what's up."

"Fine," said Rose, "If you must know: I'm finally doing what I should've done already. I'm going to bring Tom home."

"Oh really? Just like that?"

"Doing something's better than doing nothing, Will. The least I can do is try."

"Wow, Rose the activist, never thought I'd get to see the day."

"I failed Mona by staying out of it," Rose replied, unwilling to get knocked off course by Will's sarcasm. "Actually, we all failed her. We stood back, instead of leaning in. We let her slip way, instead of pulling her closer. We should've interfered, taken her and Tom away from that house, no matter how much she might've kicked and screamed."

Rose took one last look at herself in the mirror, and then she was off: "I won't make that mistake again."

★

Mornings were hard, and this morning was no exception. Unwilling to open his eyes just yet, Tom pulled the blanket tightly around his body, unconcerned that it was wet again. Let it stink, Tom thought, let me rot, see if I care. Downstairs, the Ivansons' three-legged cocker spaniel barked for food, somebody was taking a shower, and as always the radio was blaring in the kitchen.

Tom pulled out *Scott Pilgrim Gets It Together*, number four in the series of graphic novels Nick had given him. Tom wasn't sure why he kept re-reading this tangled tale of finding love. It only made him miss people more. People he was not allowed to live with, and Claremont, a place that was now as inaccessible as the moon. By the end of the books, Scott learns he can't run away from his mistakes, that he has to face what he's done. But Tom knew that was ridiculous. In real life, people made the same mistakes over and over again. And then they died.

Tom's door opened, and Trent entered. "Rise and shine," he said, his voice even more cheerful than usual, causing Tom to slide deeper under his duvet, determined to wait this one out.

"Seeing that this is your special day," continued Trent undeterred, "I've got a treat for you, Tom—breakfast in bed!"

Was it possible that he had forgotten his own birthday? Tom peeked out from under the covers, just as Trent put a tray on the floor next to his bed. On it sat a cup of steaming hot chocolate and a bright blue cupcake with a candle lit. "I could sing," said Trent, "but believe me, you'd probably prefer that I don't."

My first birthday alone, Tom realized with a start. Trent's mouth kept flapping, but Tom was no longer listening. The edges of the room disappeared. His heart beat quickened, his guts leaped and churned. Tom grabbed his pillow and brought it close to his face. Closing his eyes, he struggled to push the bile back down his throat.

"I've told you," Trent said, as he pulled the pillow away, "that this kind of behaviour will not do around here. Sit up and eat."

Tom jerked his head over the side of the bed, clinging onto its frame as if holding onto the railing of a sinking ship. Below him sat the tray with the cupcake and above him towered Trent, who now called out for Charlene. Then Tom's stomach turned one last time, and he let go, covering the cupcake with puke. Charlene appeared, a wet towel at the ready, followed by Kevin and Blake, both gagging yet unwilling to miss out on the action.

When Tom was finally done, the entire household stood agape. But Tom couldn't care less. He had found a way forward. He wiped away bits of vomit clinging to his cheek and sat up. To rinse away the bitter taste in his mouth, he picked up the hot chocolate that had miraculously been spared.

For he knew, that from now on, the story of how he blew out a candle with puke would be the story that was told on his birthday. Nobody would know about the piñata he hadn't been able to crack, or Mom's triple chocolate cake, or their yearly trip to the mall for a new outfit. From now on, Tom would get to write his own story. Away from the past, away from what happened to him, to Mom, and even to Dad.

★

Two more weeks and they would be safe, thought Sonya, as she gently caressed her now undeniable belly. At twenty-five weeks, Lily already had accomplished most of the more intricate work in building her brain. Her biggest task now was to develop her lungs, get the nose ready for her first breath, and gain weight—half a pound every week for the rest of the term.

Sonya sat up, suddenly unsure when she'd last felt her daughter move. Was Lily already too big for somersaults? Sonya pressed her hand into her belly, yet still Lily did not react. Worried now, she slid her hand toward her pelvis and pushed hard.

Still no response.

Panicked, Sonya typed *How to make my foetus move* into her phone. She tried shining a flashlight against her belly, ate a banana, and drank a litre of cold orange juice, but still Lily did not stir. Sonya cupped her belly with her hands, intuiting movements where there were none. The kettle began to scream, and bread popped out of the toaster, but Sonya was frozen in place. Petrified that once again the ultrasound would confirm her worst fears, that the baby was dead and she'd have to call Alex, listen to his tears, holding back her own until she was alone.

Then, a bump underneath her right hand. A kick.

Sonya closed her eyes, able now to breathe fully, to let go of the tension that had gripped her body. Lily, she thought, stop messing with me.

Vowing to comment on each of the Internet links that had offered up help, Sonya returned to her computer, nearly stumbling over the LEGO bulldozer she had bought for Tom's birthday. With 1,384 pieces, it was, or so the lady in the store reassured her, what all ten-year-old boys craved. This time, though, she would present the gift unwrapped and bring earplugs in case Tom's obsession with the harmonica had not yet waned.

The doorbell rang just as Sonya stashed the LEGO away. Who, she wondered, who would come to her house unannounced?

"Wow," Ray said, instead of a hello, when she opened the door. "You're pregnant."

"Gee, I hadn't noticed. What do you want?"

"Could I come in please? Have a talk?"

"You're the jerk who got Tom locked up. What more is there to talk about?"

"I've got an idea."

Without moving the door one inch, Sonya said: "Okay. Let's hear it."

"Please Sonya, let me come in. It's cold out here, and it will take me a few minutes to explain."

Ray settled down on Sonya's sofa and laid out his plan: "Joint custody," he said. "It's an unusual setup, but this case is unusual, so it might just work."

"What, like in a divorce?"

"Sort of. As you're well aware, Tom needs all the love and care he can get, and probably more. This is more than one person could possibly handle, so by setting up joint custody, Tom would get the best of both worlds. Living with Rose, Nick and Will, but getting a more traditional family experience with you and your husband. And as it turns out, your child."

"But I'm Tom's guardian, not Rose. His stay with Rose was supposed to be temporary, until I got a few things sorted out. Now that I've done that, he needs to return here, to where he belongs. To me."

"The thing is, Tom wants to live with Rose."

"How do you know that?"

"He told me."

"He actually said that?"

"Sonya, helping Tom to heal, to grow, is a task for the whole family, it's a task you and Rose can share, *should* share."

Along with my husband, Sonya thought.

"Why do you even care so much about Tom?" she said instead. "Don't you have two hundred other kids you should be worrying about?"

"The thing is …, " Ray said, taking a sip of tea before continuing. "The thing is, I like Tom. I recognize myself in him. You see, my own mother, she was killed when I was six. Hit by a car as she was crossing Broadview. For years, I wondered what would have happened if I had stayed home from school that day. I could've stopped her from going to work, made her look left instead of right, and then, she wouldn't have died."

Sonya put down her cup and looked at Ray. Like her riddled with guilt.

"I offered God my spider collection," Ray continued, "I promised to wash the dishes for a year, anything for Mom to return so she could read *How the Grinch Stole Christmas* to me once more, and this time I would smile and say thanks."

Sonya cupped her hand around her belly, suddenly overwhelmed with just how fragile life was. And yet Ray, so marked by loss, had somehow turned that sadness around, dedicating his life to helping others.

"Fine," Sonya finally said. "What needs to be done?"

★

Are You the Ambitious Type? FANTASTIC!! CLICK HERE, Will read. An online ad that sounded only slightly less phoney than *Earn Cash Filling Surveys. Paid daily. Seeking 80 Candidates*. A restaurant downtown was looking for a pastry apprentice, but they wanted someone young and enthusiastic. There were ads for chefs, sous-chefs, and chefs de partie, but without proper training or professional experience, nobody would take a chance on him. *Retail Manager, Nanny, Piercing Artist,* Will read before clicking 'next'. Sonya had been right. He should've stayed in school, got a teaching degree or learned some other skill he'd be able to sell.

Looking for a place to live was just as much fun. A one-bedroom apartment on Queen Street, right above the Bovine Sex Club, cost $2,300. For $1,800 you could rent a 300-square-foot loft downtown in a "boutique building," which was realtor-speak for overpriced and cramped. There was a self-contained bachelor pad for $800, but how would he get to Brampton without a car?

Staying at Claremont, however, was no longer an option. With Tom gone, Rose's moods oscillated between toxic and morose, and Will had yet to determine which one was worse. Toxic could be amusing, even if sometimes he was the target of Rose's scorn. Morose was considerably less hurtful, but seeing your deflated sister watch TV for days on end, uninterested and sad, was no fun at all.

"Where's Mom?" asked Nick, standing in the doorway to Will's room, clad in his pyjamas, sucking on a rogue strand of hair. Despite the soft stubble that had started to grow on his pimply chin, he was still a boy, deflated since the day he had lost Tom in the park. Guilty, Will realized, just like him.

Will tossed the fennel seeds into the hot cast iron pan to let them toast. Crushed in the mortar with a good helping of salt, they smelled of grass, of wide-open fields. Freedom. They would marry beautifully with the tomatoes, which were reducing into a scrumptious sauce on the back burner.

"So you have no idea where Mom went?" Nick asked.

"Women move in mysterious ways, Nick. Best to get used to it. It'll save you disappointment later."

"Mom's not mysterious. She's messed up."

239

CLAREMONT

"True. Now, make yourself useful and set the table."

Will finished the sauce with a handful of freshly chopped coriander and a touch of sea salt. Placing the lamb balls onto the couscous, he slid the plate over to Nick.

"Here, that'll cheer you up."

"Carmen's mom has a small restaurant out on Roncesvalles. Sort of Middle Eastern and super yummy."

"So?"

"She's nice."

"Who? Carmen?"

"Yes, sure. But no, I mean her mom. She needs more time off. You're really good at her type of food, so maybe you could work at her place once in a while."

"Where's Carmen's dad?"

Nick shrugged. "Can I have seconds?"

"Are you doing the dishes?"

"Sure."

"And you'll tell Rose that I made you lunch?"

"Okay."

"And—" A knock at the front door put an end to their negotiations. "You expecting somebody?"

"Nope."

Will opened the door to find Sonya standing on the stoop. "You," he said, but then he looked down, noticing her belly sticking out from her coat. "Shit, what happened?"

"Not sure if you've heard," Sonya replied, "about the birds and the bees ... "

Will reached for his sister's belly, and she did not step away. This bump was for real, even through a thick layer of clothes. Had Sonya been pregnant when she came over last? Had that really escaped his attention?

240

"This is… awesome, Sonya. When are you due?"

"April 16th."

"That soon?"

"Not soon enough. I need to speak with Rose. Is she in?"

"I thought you guys were done talking."

"Do you mind if we wait inside?"

It was only now that Will noticed Ray, who was hanging back a few paces on the ice-covered sidewalk.

"What's he doing here?"

"Will, please. I'll tell you in a moment, but right now I need to get off my feet."

"So how's Alex holding up with … you know, all that," Will asked, trying hard not to stare at Sonya's bulging belly. Then he took a sip of his Tension Tamer tea, not that it did much to tame his tension. He knew that when Rose got home, he'd be stuck in the eye of the storm.

"He's gone," said Sonya, sitting on the sofa with Ray.

"Gone where?"

"Gone gone."

"Alex is dead?" Ray asked, a look of shock on his face.

"To me he is. But no, he moved into a condo at Spadina and King."

"Good," said Will. "because I'm not sure what it is with my sisters, but you guys really suck at picking men."

"Okay, so let me get this straight," said Ray. "You split up with your husband just weeks before giving birth. Why?"

"Because—," Sonya and Will said as one. They stopped, looked at each other and burst into laughter. A laugh the likes of which they had not shared in years. When they finally wiped away the tears, Sonya spoke: "It's for the best," she said, and all Will could do was nod in agreement.

241

"But Sonya, why didn't you tell me right way," Ray said. "This might change things."

"Trust me," Sonya replied. "It'll be easier without him."

"She's right, Ray. That man's a prick."

"Sonya, you really think that the court's going to grant you custody of Tom, while being a single mom with a newborn?" Ray shook his head. "You'll be sleep deprived, overwhelmed, flustered and anxious for months. A baby's a lot to take on, never mind alone."

"Maybe I could move in for a while," said Will, surprised at the words that had just dropped out of his mouth. But they felt right, so he continued: "I'm happy to look after Tom and could help out with the baby, once she arrives."

"I thought you hated babies," said Sonya.

"Think about it. I could cook for you, provide male guidance for Tom and the baby, and you, in return, would put a roof over my head."

"Male guidance? From you?" Sonya chuckled, even as tears of gratitude filled her eyes.

★

By the time Rose reached Wellesley Station, her bravado was tainted by doubt. Why would anybody listen to her, an incompetent mother, a lying cheat? Maybe the jerks at Children's Aid were right: maybe getting away from this family, from her, was exactly what Tom needed to heal.

But still she kept moving forward, walking up the slushy stairs of the subway, out into the bright and bitterly cold January sunshine. Heading north on Yonge, Rose passed cafeteria-style Thai restaurants, Money Marts and overlit shops peddling outdated electronic devices, sex toys and shoes. Despite the gentrification that had sanitized most of downtown, refreshingly little had changed in this part of the city.

Outside the Children's Aid Society, Rose paused. Her plan, which had felt so inevitable in the safety of her own home, seemed idiotic now. They would never let Tom return to her home. She didn't have a leg to stand on. It was her fault that Tom had been abandoned in the park, stoned and freezing. Exposed. Rose would never forget the look on the cop's face. She was pathetic. He was right.

But then she thought of Tom turning ten years old today without a mother or father or any family around him. She climbed up a short flight of stairs to the revolving door at the top. Halfway through, another wave of doubt swept over her, urging her to make a 360-degree turn, to forget about fighting a fight she was unlikely to win, to retrace her steps home, to go back to bed. But then she remembered Tom, who despite everything, had finally found his voice. If he was strong enough to push through to the other side, why couldn't she?

"Obviously, what happened in the park was a terrible mistake," said Rose, when she finally got to sit down with Ray's supervisor Bruce. "But Nick's a kid and kids make mistakes. That's how they learn, and trust me, Nick will never ever let anything happen to Tom again."

Bruce tried to interject, but Rose nudged up her volume, drowning him out: "I know that our household might look a bit odd. I'm a single mother, yes, and working, too. Clearly, I should've been a more thoughtful guardian, and a less cruel sister. And Will, he's not the most together person ever, granted, so maybe you think we can't handle it, but you're wrong. We, my family—and by 'family' I mean all of us, Tom, of course, but also Nick and Will, Sonya and even my father—we've all gone through hell this past year. I know this might sound terribly old-fashioned, and awkward and dumb, but Tom is our flesh and blood. We love Tom unconditionally and forever, and therefore he needs to return home."

"What Tom needs," said Bruce, leaning forward in his large purple chair, "is a stable and supportive environment. Not a place where nobody notices that he's been cutting himself for months."

"What are you saying?"

"You didn't know?"

Rose shook her head but suddenly, Tom's unwillingness to wear anything but hoodies made sense. As did his refusal to go for a swim. Sickened by the thought of Tom hurting himself while she had stood by unknowingly made Rose want to scream. Instead, tears filled her eyes. "And here we thought giving the boy space to heal was the right thing to do. How stupid is that?"

"Cutters tend to be experts at hiding what they're doing," said Bruce, his voice much more consolatory now. "Also, it's not your fault that Tom started to cut. What a traumatized person does cannot be controlled by anyone but themselves. Still, this needs addressing, and thankfully the Ivansons are used to dealing with this. However, leaving Tom with a teenager who thinks it's okay to abandon the boy in the freezing cold, that's another story."

"I already told you, Nick screwed up. Nobody's disputing that. And on the bright side, it's that very incident that got Tom to finally talk."

"Really, you're going to go down that road?"

"No."

"Good."

"But Tom is speaking again, and so we should listen. He wants to be with us, his family."

"Except being with family," Bruce crossed his arms over his paunch and leaned back, "does not necessarily protect anybody from anything. You of all people should know that."

If he had a moustache, Rose thought, he'd be twirling it now.

To level the playing field, she conjured up an assortment of imaginary flaws. A porn addiction? A mother dumped in an old folk's home, a childhood friend left in the lurch? There was a skeleton in everybody's closet. A wrong committed by even the kindest soul. A cruelty imagined that could not be unthought.

"Fine," Bruce conceded, as if he could read Rose's mind. "Give me one solid reason why Tom should stay with you."

Rose stood up and walked to the window. On the sidewalk below, a girl no more than six years old ran circles around her laughing mother, pigtails bobbing, hope illuminating her innocent face. Was it possible to regain trust in the goodness of people, in the future, in yourself, after discovering at such a young age that cruelty might lurk just beneath the surface, that those you love most may turn on you, that life as you know it can be destroyed in a blink?

"We lost our way," Rose finally said. "I lost my way. And now, there's a huge mess that needs cleaning up. But we need to do it together, as a family. Because otherwise...." Rose paused before going on. "If we let our family be torn apart, Russell will win and I cannot allow that to happen."

Rose turned back toward Bruce, and she instantly knew that she had been wrong yet again. Confronted with heartbreaking stories day after day, the sorrow on Bruce's face told her that this was a man trying to be fair.

"Everything I've ever believed in," Rose said as she sat back down, "was thrown into question when Mona died. But if I've learned anything, it's that the only chance we have to heal is to do it together. As a family. And that's why Tom needs to come home."

By the time Rose stepped off the streetcar, the freezing rain was coming down hard. The dreary chapter of winter had arrived: boots that were stained with squiggly lines of salt, snow banks streaked with dog urine, faces ashen from months of sun deprivation.

When Rose finally got to Claremont, she was pleased to find the walkway shovelled. Will was looking for brownie points, but this would no longer work. He had to move on. Sonya was right: as long as Rose kept picking up after her brother, as long as she kept mothering him, allowing him to stay with few responsibilities, he would never grow up.

In the front hall, she was greeted by two pairs of boots, neatly lined up next to her own pile of shoes. One pair a man's, the other pair a woman's, both somehow familiar. Fighting her instinct to run, Rose stepped into the living room, where she found Sonya sitting on her sofa, drinking tea, with her belly protruding like a balloon.

"What happened to you?"

"Surely, Rose, you of all people have heard about the birds and the—."

"She's already twenty-five weeks in," interrupted Will, speaking fast. "So she's due April 16th. Isn't that great?"

Rose sat down. The math here was confusing.

"Why didn't you tell me, Sonya? If I'd known ..."

"Really? If you'd known, you wouldn't have fucked Alex?"

"Who fucked who?" asked Ray, who just then stepped into the living room.

"I'd suggest staying out of that one," said Will, slipping away into the kitchen, and Ray, smartly, followed closely behind.

"I'm sorry," said Rose when the two sisters found themselves alone. "I really am."

Sonya did not respond. Something had happened to her older

sister, Rose noted, something had shifted ever so slightly, like tectonic plates that had moved by a hair but were now perfectly realigned. There was a feeling of stillness about her, a sense of calm.

Rose remembered her final weeks being pregnant. Swollen feet, constant heartburn, and nights spent dreading her upcoming pain, worrying that Eugene would faint (which he did). But she had not been alone. Sonya and Mona had kept a vigil with her, making tea, and watching silly movies that made all three of them cry.

Rose looked at her sister, gently rubbing her belly. Ashamed now beyond all measure. "I really don't know what came over me," she started. "It was irrational and stupid and callous and cruel. I should never have—"

"Shut up, already," Sonya said, as she tried to heave herself up from the sofa. "Whatever you say is not going to erase what you did. And anyway, I need to piss, so give me a hand."

March

As if pulled by magical strings, the harmonica slid effortlessly up and down Tom's lips, producing deeply satisfying notes that settled upon him like a warm duvet on a long winter's night. Then, after a last, sustained breath, he ended his song with a sigh.

Tom now shared the room with just Blake, because last week, Kevin got to go home to his mom. The night he was leaving, Kevin promised to return for a visit, but Tom knew that was a lie. There was no coming back here. No turning back the clock. Not even for people you like.

Blake, encouraged by Kevin's sudden escape, packed his bag too, even though he hadn't heard from his mother since last summer, when she'd sent him a postcard from somewhere in Spain. Every night Blake prayed for her return, kneeling on the floor with his hands clasped, like the little boy in the painting that hung in Grandpapa's room at the cottage.

Trent entered without knocking, as always. Tom hadn't cut himself in weeks, but he still wasn't allowed to close doors, no matter whether he was sleeping or taking a crap. But that had not stopped Tom from hiding what needed to be hid. The morning he left, Kevin had given Tom his pocket-knife. Twice Tom had tried to use it, in the middle of the night, under covers, but oddly the sharp blade against his skin now felt scary, rather than kind.

"You better get dressed," said Trent. "Someone's here with some pretty outstanding news."

Tom walked into the living room, surprised to find Aunt Rose. "Let's get you home," she said. Then, a gigantic smile appeared on her face, and Tom disappeared into her outstretched arms.

"I'll visit for sure," Tom told Blake less than an hour later. "And at least now you'll have the room all to yourself."

"As if," said Blake, who slouched sad-eyed on his bed. "I bet they'll pick up some other retard soon. But whatever," he continued with faked conviction. "Ma's coming any moment now, and then we'll travel the world. If I have time, I might even send you a postcard."

Then he picked up one of the *Captain Underpants* books, even though he hated reading.

Watching Blake, Tom suddenly understood why Kevin had lied. A Get-Out-Of-Jail card was great, but having to leave a friend behind, not so much.

"Here," said Tom, pulling the knife out of his bag. "A loan— until our first visit."

★

"Just remember to have fun," said Will, tossing roasted cauliflower with arugula, spices and oil. "And don't worry about cleaning up; I'll do that after work."

Sonya wrapped the last melon slice in prosciutto, suddenly unsure why she was bothering with this baby shower. It was not like she had seen much of her old friends over the past months. Penelope was still stuck on an assignment in St. John's, Newfoundland, and Sonya had not felt like reaching out to anyone else. But Will had insisted, "Once Lily's born, you'll be totally preoccupied," he said. "Might as well celebrate now."

To Sonya's unending surprise, she enjoyed having her brother around. Turned out Rose had trained Will well. He shovelled the driveway, got rid of racoons that had invaded the garage, and then there was his cooking. No wonder he'd gotten a job at that Middle Eastern restaurant on Roncesvalles. What a shame that it had taken Will so long to find his calling.

"Open it," said Rose, seconds after arriving, shoving a box awkwardly wrapped in brown paper into Sonya's hands. "I promise, this one's unique."

"Later," said Sonya. "Let's serve the potato torta first."

As soon as Rose left the kitchen, Sonya dropped the gift into the trash. It was one thing to allow her cheat of a sister back into her life, but it was quite another to forgive her.

"This one's already empty," Kiara announced, as she stumbled into the kitchen waving a bottle of bubbly like it were a magic wand. "Where's your stash?"

Sonya had not wanted to invite her boss. But then, with Alex gone, she had no choice but to return to work as soon as her maternity leave ran out, so best to keep on Kiara's good side. The timer beeped, and Sonya opened the oven to the reassuring fragrance of citrus. Mama's lemon loaf was done.

"Oh, wow," said Kiara, still struggling to uncork another bottle of champagne. "I love your stove. Is that a La Cornue?"

"If you're interested, I'm selling it ... along with the house."

"Oh, no, what happened? Did Alex lose his job?"

"I'm downsizing. *We* are downsizing," Sonya said, cupping her hands under her belly, as if including Lily would make that statement less of a lie. "I'm thinking of moving somewhere closer to downtown. Spend less time commuting and more time with Lily."

"Are you serious? Are you planning to raise her in a box? My boys would kill each other if I couldn't send them out into the backyard to burn off steam."

Sonya felt anger blossom within her, poisonous like oleander. "Rumour has it," she said, "that perfectly functional humans have been raised in apartments."

Never mind needing to build bridges, she was done backing off.

Sonya grabbed the tray of stuffed piquillo peppers and left Kiara behind. Who gave a crap where she and Lily lived? As long as there was love, all would be fine.

It was well after nine when Sonya closed the door behind her last guest. Then she went to the shrine to say goodnight to Mona. Lightly, as if not wanting to wake her, she touched the photo of her sister's still smiling face. It seemed impossible now to imagine that Mona had not known that something was terribly wrong with her marriage. Yet she had chosen to keep up a happy façade, to paint over the cracks that must have run deeper and wider with time. Tears welled up in Sonya's eyes, but just as she was about to give into her grief, a kick in her belly set her straight. Lily was right. She was who mattered now. Time had come to leave the past behind. There was nothing heroic about turning the other cheek, about enduring violence. Sonya would teach her child to stand up for herself, to trust her gut, and to walk away before getting trapped.

In a sudden frenzy, Sonya cleaned away the cards, the candles, and even Mona's portrait. Her sister's smile was as sweet as ever. Her face would never wrinkle, her hair would not turn grey. What a privilege it was to grow old, what a waste to complain. For a moment, Sonya considered preserving the flowers, but even that seemed obscene. She would never stop missing Mona, and not a day would pass without thinking of her, without wishing she had stepped up, but now time had come to think about the future.

As the flowers tumbled into the kitchen garbage, Sonya noticed Rose's gift.

Today, her remaining sister had come through. She had served food, replenished glasses, offered coffee and even called a cab for Kiara, who had wound up too drunk to drive. Sonya pulled the present out of the garbage and opened the card decorated with a baby monkey on a swing. It was signed by Rose, Will, Nick and Tom. *Can't wait to meet you, Lily!* it said. *Thank you,* Rose had added, as if forgiveness had already been granted.

The present itself was taped up like bondage gone awry. When Sonya finally succeeded in cutting the bubble wrap off, she found a brown ceramic mug, almost identical to the one Tom had smashed so long ago. *Families,* it read in Mona's uncertain script, *are like fudge—mostly sweet with a few nuts.*

★

Tom woke to creaking stairs, clanking radiators, and Aunt Rose yelling at Nick to hurry up. Bliss. With Uncle Will living with Aunt Sonya, Tom had moved back into the little yellow room. His room, Aunt Rose promised, from now on and forever more. Tom checked his sheets, but they were dry. It had been two weeks since he last wet his bed, and before that, it had been more than a month. He pulled on his hoodie and followed the smell of burnt toast downstairs.

"Why do people keep messing with my toaster," complained Aunt Rose, as she dumped the charred bread into the garbage. "Yesterday, it was working just fine. Here," she added, as she pressed a glass of milk into Tom's hands. "What's it going to be? Cereal? Oatmeal? Huevos rancheros?"

"I'm not really into breakfast," Tom answered.

"You're not?"

253

"Nope. Never was. Never will be."

"Aren't you a little young for 'never'?" asked Aunt Rose with a smile.

"I—" but before Tom could answer, the doorbell rang out. After months of complaining, Uncle Will had finally gotten that fixed.

"What now," said Aunt Rose and walked toward the door.

"Let's do it," said Aunt Sonya, even before the front door was fully open. In her hands, she cradled the urn. "We should've done this ages ago, and you know it."

"Now?" asked Aunt Rose, "I haven't even had breakfast yet."

"No time like the present."

"But what about Tom?"

"What about me?"

Both aunts swivelled around, looking like they'd been caught.

"Oh hi, Tom," was all Aunt Sonya could come up with. "How are you?"

Looking at the urn in his aunt's arms, Tom asked: "What're you doing with Mom?"

"Oh, never mind her, Tom," said Aunt Rose before turning back, "And Sonya, please, I can't believe you would spring this on us just like that."

"It's not right for your mom to sit in my living room," Aunt Sonya said to Tom, ignoring her sister. "When really she deserves rest. So let's go up to the cottage and get it done."

"But why now?" Aunt Rose interjected, "Why not wait 'til Tato's back in May?"

"Just because Tato chooses to spend his time down south, does not mean that we shouldn't do what's right. And anyway, I need to do it now—before Lily arrives."

"Which by the looks of you, might be tomorrow."

"Well, the sooner we leave, the sooner we'll be back."

"Let's do it," said Tom, shutting up both of his aunts. "But let me get my mitts first."

Tom looked out the window as the countryside flew by, a study of grey, white and muted shades of brown. The stubble of last year's grains stood rigid despite the freezing cold wind, trees were reduced to spindly trunks, twisted and gnarled. Desolate, just like Tom, who was not looking forward to what was lying ahead.

Outside, wet, splotchy snow started coming down hard, covering the windshield, despite the wipers' relentless efforts to push off the slush.

"Are you okay, Will?" asked Aunt Sonya, looking at her brother, who was driving. On her lap sat Mom's pink urn, clutched closely to her belly. "Or should we stop for tea?"

"We'll have tea at the cottage," said Uncle Will without taking his eyes off the road. "I'd rather get this over with."

Squeezed in between Aunt Rose and Nick on the backseat, Tom was not enjoying another first on his ever-growing list. Christmas, New Years and then his birthday alone, and now, going up to the cottage without Mom wanting to stop for tea.

"Seriously, this is insane," said Aunt Rose. "Let's just go home."

"Don't YOU talk to me about being insane," said Aunt Sonya. "And anyway, there's no point turning back now."

★

When finally they arrived, the cottage was bone-chillingly cold.

"Will, be a darling and build me a fire," said Sonya, placing the urn on the coffee table before plopping onto the sofa and pulling a wool blanket up to her face, still dressed in her boots, coat, hat and mitts. "Tom, why don't you come here and keep me company until this place warms up?"

"Last one to the dock does the dishes!" hollered Rose from the kitchen and sped out the door, down the steep path that led to the lake. Will dropped the fireplace poker to chase after Rose.

"What's going on?" asked Tom. "It's way too cold for a swim."

"It's a thing they do," said Nick as he settled into the creaking rocking chair and pulled out his phone. "It's weird, don't ask."

"How's that even fair?" yelled Sonya after her disappearing siblings. "You guys know I can't run, so I'm not doing the dishes. No way."

Still, she heaved herself up from the sofa. "Nick," she said, confiscating his phone. "Be my hero and give me a hand."

By the time Tom made his way down to the dock, his two aunts, uncle and cousin all stood by the edge of the lake, watching sheets of ice reluctantly giving way to the oncoming spring. Around them, the air was filled with the sound of melting snow, above them circled a lone turkey vulture.

Sonya, alerted by Tom's steps in the snow, turned. "Really, honey?" she asked, noticing the urn under his arm. "You want to do that now? I thought we'd wait until after lunch."

"No time like the present," said Tom.

Careful not to drop his precious cargo, he approached the edge of the dock, coming to a stop right between Sonya and Rose. For a moment, they all stood in silence, united at the edge of the frozen lake, in the midst of a frozen country, needing to move forward, but wanting to step back, surrounded by nothing but the sound of their breath.

"Mona will stay with us no matter what," Sonya finally said, taking the urn from Tom, "but today is the day we set her free."

Then she opened the urn, taking out her portion of the ashes and letting them escape into the lake. Most of them drifted away, but some clung onto the melting ice, staining grey what had once been white, stubbornly refusing to disappear. With a sigh, Sonya returned the urn to Tom. Even if she had ceded her rights to being his legal guardian, Sonya vowed that she would never give up on the boy again. She would be there on all the days that mattered, big and small. The day he graduated from high school, when he failed his driver's test for misusing the clutch, when he got hit by a crane and had to stay in the hospital for five weeks, when he got married to Imogen, a lovely blonde with an endless smile, when Mona, their first child, was born.

Sonya put her arm around Tom's shoulders, relieved when he did not move away.

"We would sit on this dock for hours," said Rose, taking her sister's urn, holding onto it like it was a buoy in a sea of loss. "We would dream about what the future would hold. The countries we would travel to, the men we would meet, the fun we would have. We had no idea how quickly things can change, how fragile we are in the grand scheme of things."

Rose spread her share of the ashes, determined to never again let sorrow cloud her judgement. They were here today, as a family, in spite of what she had done, and for that she was grateful beyond all measure. Unlike Mona, she had been given a second chance. To honour her sister, Rose would do whatever it took to create a home for all of them to thrive in, one without violence though not without hurt, one without rage though not without disagreements, one with laughter, compassion and love.

When Rose was done, she put her arm around Tom, finding Sonya's arm already there, unwilling to move, to concede her place in Tom's life, but able now to share. Two sisters united, however furtively, through their common love for Tom.

"I can't imagine the shit you've been going through, Tom," said Nick after dispensing his share of the ashes, his eyes now misty with tears. "I totally should've been less of an ass. Next time I'm mean, just kick me, okay?"

"Sure," said Tom. "No problem at all."

Tom turned to pass the urn to Will, but his uncle had retreated to the far edge of the dock.

"Get over here and do your bit," said Rose. "It's cold, and Sonya ought to get off her feet."

"I have no right to be here," said Will, inching even further toward the path that led back up to the cottage. His face twisted, his voice impossibly sad. "Russell was my friend. I brought him into the house. Without that, without me, Mona would still be alive."

"Bullshit," said Sonya. "What happened was not your fault."

"Totally," agreed Rose, her hand now firmly attached to Sonya.

"I knew things were bad," Will said, "and I did nothing to intervene. I could've spoken to him, I should've spoken to her, but instead, I did nothing, and then she died."

"Don't you think we all feel that we failed?" said Rose, her voice almost a whisper. "And in fact, we all did."

Looking at Tom, standing there with his mother's ashes in his arms, Will decided to join the rest of the family. "Actually, that's bullshit. Tom did not fail anybody. He's been incredibly brave and strong and should he work hard, he might even turn out to be an okay harmonica player."

Will took the urn to spread his share of his sister's ashes. Evil comes in many disguises, some of them charming and endearing and fun. From now on, he vowed, he would look beyond the friendly facade, speak up when things started to feel off, chose carefully those he could trust and turn away from those he could not.

When Will was done, he passed the urn back to Tom. "You survived to live your own life, Tom, now just don't mess it up."

"I'll try," said Tom, even though he was certain at times he would. Then he turned the urn upside down, and the last of his mother's ashes fell into the lake.

"Not that I care a whole lot," said Sonya just as Tom replaced the lid on the empty urn, "but whatever happened to Russell's ashes?"

"Nothing," said Tom and Will in unison.

"Nothing," Tom added, "that matters at all."

Acknowledgements

This novel is an act of defiance. Like all books, like any work of art. The obstacles to creation are enormous. Doubt looms, inertia rules, success is fleeting, failure a given. And yet, this story of defiance, of survival, is finally ready to go out into the world. This would not have been possible without the community I am so grateful to be a part of. My family and friends in Germany, in Toronto and of course Montreal, who listened for years about the progress, or lack there of, on 'my goddamn novel'. There are too many to list here, but know that there is no way I could have continued without you.

And then there are friends who also became readers. Like Natsu Hattori whose first edit convinced me that this manuscript could indeed one day become a book. Edeet Ravel, whose insights and encouragement pushed me to keep going when the going was tough. My writing group pal Lisa Pasold, who would never let a bad Skype connection get in the way of her sharp mind. Elise Moser, Jocelyn Brown, and Mary Asbil, who read drafts, providing much appreciated feedback. Claire McCrea whose edit whipped the manuscript into good enough shape so that it could finally be sent out into the world. And last, but certainly not least, Saskia de Boer, whose keen insights and incredible dedication made this manuscript so much better than I could have ever hoped for. I am forever grateful.

Coming from cinema, the world of literature was terra incognita for me. Again, I was blessed by the help of so many. Edeet Ravel, first and foremost, but also Michael Crummey, Meg Wolitzer along with the many wonderful writers I met at the Banff Centre, Aislinn Hunter, Anna Leventhal, Laurie Petrou, Kyo Maclear, Linda Schubert and many more along the way. Receiving Linda Leith's email about wanting to publish this book is a moment I will never forget. Many thanks to her for taking the leap, to Kodi Sheer for being such a discerning and kind editor, and to everybody at Linda Leith Publishing for making my dream of being a published author a reality.

Finally, my deepest gratitude goes to the love of my life, Patrick Olivier. Having read this manuscript too many times to count, he never gave up on it, or on me. This book is for you. My Tom, my Will, my everything.